Siren Song

by Erik Boman

Published November 2014

This book uses some actual locations and family names, however all events are fictionalized and all persons appearing in this work are fictitious. Any resemblance to real people, living, dead or lost in Hell, is entirely coincidental.

Proofread by Pauline Nolet, Editors' Association of Canada

Cover image montage by Wandering Mind

www.wanderingmind.net

STORIES BY ERIK BOMAN

The Detective Lena Franke series

Siren Song
Book 1

Summer Nights
Book 2

Into the Woods
Book 3

Other books

Southbound
A dystopian thriller set in Sweden and the UK

Short Cuts
Collected short stories

Short Cuts 2: Stories from the Brink of Dusk
Collected short stories

SIREN SONG

Erik Boman

PRELUDE

Stockholm, western suburbs

January

Friday evening

First John hears the scream.

He's standing next to his car, plastic shopping bags in one hand, car keys in the other. Snowflakes land on his face while he frowns at Molly's window, three storeys up in the block of flats. It was definitely Molly who screamed. Her voice was muted and distant, but it touched him in a way no other sound could.

Then comes the bang. A small crack of thunder from inside her flat. The two windows flash white, shudder, and grow still.

He runs towards the front door. The air is already cold enough to freeze spit in minutes, but a worse chill reaches inside his clothes and in under his skin. People around him stop and stare as he skids on the ice-coated pavement.

He ignores them. All that matters is reaching the flat and making sure he is wrong.

Friday, afternoon, almost dark. The mundane tail end of a routine week. Snow on the windowsills, cars crawling along white roads, purple-blue sky. Trees covered in frost and icicles waiting to drop. Everything in order. Until now. A shout, a bang, and a burst of light. It could be an accident, a TV, maybe fireworks. Never a gun. That was impossible. Not here, at this time.

He is less than twenty metres from the door when it bangs open. A man stumbles out and runs in the other direction. Dark hair, dark shoes, blue track pants, a backpack in faded red. The man's rapid footsteps creak in the snow as he disappears around a corner. The door swings shut.

John is still moving. Five metres left.

Panting hard, he reaches the door. His hands shake violently while he fumbles with the keys. He should let go of the shopping bags, but he holds on, as if their triviality were a lifeline to safety, a ward against this brutal intrusion.

He gets the key in, turns it and shoves the door open. Stumbling, he runs up the stairs, past thick doormats and wet orange plastic sleds, past rows of boots and pots of wilted flowers. By the time he reaches the third floor, he is wheezing. A cramp stabs at his left side.

Molly's front door is wide open. Two more steps and he is inside, shouting her name. He turns to the bedroom and stops.

Molly lies on her back across the bed. Her head hangs off the mattress, but while she is facing him, she is not looking at him or something behind him: her eyes are flat like porcelain and perfectly still. Blood runs freely from her ruined neck.

Minutes pass while John stands still and watches the blood spread out from the bedroom and into the hall. Silence fills him, muting cars and distant voices. His pulse is a remote drum in his head. With rapid and shallow breaths, he pulls the reek of gunpowder into his lungs.

Lying around him are the contents of his dropped shopping bags, bloodied and inert. A bottle of red wine *(same as last weekend and a bit expensive, but she loves it)*, a box of organic milk chocolate *(breaking off uneven pieces and watching them disappear between her lips)*, his toothbrush *(hoping he will be able to leave it at her place again)*.

His eyes sweep around the apartment and drift from detail to detail. A dress flung over a wardrobe door. Mismatched china on the table. Two wine glasses backlit by a candle and waiting to be filled. A slow drip from the tap in the kitchen. Molly's blue slippers outside the bathroom. Neon-lit dust swirling in the living room. His attention keeps sliding off the bed in search of a crack, an opening back to normality, an escape to life ten minutes earlier.

"What a mess," says a woman behind John.

*

John freezes in place as if bound by chains. It's Molly's voice. Although it can't be, because she's dead, gunned down, irreversibly slain. Her torn body rests on the bed, right in front of him.

The woman behind John steps around him and moves into full view. She walks casually, even languorously, as if dancing to an unheard tune. It is indeed Molly. Unharmed and unblemished, perfect down to the last freckle and wrinkle. Yet it is not.

This woman's a lie, a small vanishing part of his mind warns. *A vile mirage, a toxic smokescreen. Your Molly is no more. The warm, whimsical, eccentric woman you gave your heart to is gone.*

Yet he can't stop staring. This creature who wears Molly's face has his undivided attention. It may be a hallucination, but it's all that remains of the woman he loves. The moment he looks away or stops listening, he'll be completely alone.

"And such a shame, too," continues the woman. "Look at that wound and all the blood. My poor flesh in tatters. I didn't deserve this."

"What's happening?" John's voice sounds distant to his own ears.

"I was murdered." She makes a pained face. "While I was waiting for you."

"Am I dreaming?"

She shakes her head. "This is real, I'm afraid. You lost me. This moment will be brief. I'm lingering, but only for a while."

"But you can't be dead," John rasps. "You were – everything. It's wrong. It isn't fair."

"That's right." She moves closer. "It isn't. But you can make it fair."

"I can have you back?" John is aware of how absurd his question is, but hope lurches in his mind.

The woman shakes her head again.

"That's against the rules," she says. "Gone is gone, and must stay gone. Otherwise, the streets out there would be a perfect mess." She steps closer. "But you can settle the score, John. You can get even. Get back at the man who hurt me. Tooth for tooth, eye for eye."

"I don't–"

"It hurt so much, John. The moment when the bullet ripped through me lasted an eternity. Every second was torture. Whatever they may tell you later, my death wasn't quick."

Deep inside John, something cracks.

Far beneath shock and incoherent thoughts, a fissure opens and lets in a voice. It's reassuring but commanding, wordless but brimming with promise, pulling him nearer as if he were trapped in a maelstrom. The voice whispers of the chance to right wrongs and reset balances. Ways to give his overwhelming rage a physical target, one that can feel pain and deserves to do so.

It is the sweet, magnetic siren song of revenge.

"The one who did this," John rasps.

"Yes?"

"I want him to – to feel this. I want him–"

"Go on."

"Dead," John whispers. "Gone. Erased. I want to – murder him."

"Again."

"I want to kill him." The words taste of iron in John's mouth. "I want him *dead*."

The woman smiles. Her face glows with glee and hunger. Seeing joy on Molly's face has always made John feel lighter and more complete, but if he were able to move, this woman's expression would make him back away.

Yet because of the treacherous nature of the heart, John's resolve keeps withering. None of his principles stand a chance against this near-perfect impersonation of Molly. It can ask him anything, call for any action, and he will leap to the task.

"I thought so," the woman says. "Now that, I can help you with."

"What are you?" John asks.

"I'm not one, but many. We open secret doors and shine a light on banned paths. And, as you'll see, we are fond of games. You flung the door open and invited us in, which is rare, but always welcome. Now tell me again," she demands. "Do you want Molly's killer to pay?"

John nods weakly. "What must I do?"

"Just let go. Stop clinging to this lump of flesh."

"I-I don't understand."

"You don't have to. All you need to do is yield."

There's a sharp tug at the essence of John's being, as if hooks were driven into his mind and pull him away from the room in which he's standing. He senses behind him a gaping emptiness, vast and icy, like an immense chasm filled by an arctic storm.

He tries to turn away, but he's losing the grip on his own body. Little by little, he slips out of its warmth, away from his own limbs, back from daylight and into dusk. The sensation fills him with a savage, numbing dread.

"What are you doing to me?" John screams.

"Isn't that obvious?" The woman's smile is sardonic. "We're evicting you."

"*Why?*"

"To turn your body loose. All that pent-up rage will help us trap someone else. We don't need your conscience, your morals or any of those other confused principles that rattle around in your skull."

She takes a step closer.

"There's a particular woman out there," she continues. "Someone who should've been ours long ago, but who refuses to make the leap. She's on her way here as we speak. You'll be the bait that leads her to where she belongs. You'll leave a bloody trail that will push her over the edge. Then, at last, she'll be our plaything. We have an entire carnival of sensations prepared for her stubborn soul."

John tries to wrench himself away from the horrifying woman, but he can no longer move, not even speak. The phantom makes no sense, although her words are enough to make him panic. Slowly but irreversibly, he's dragged backwards into a chilling darkness, closer to the abyss that waits behind him.

"Are you wondering what place I'm talking about?" The woman's smile widens to a feral grin. "It's the final destination for people like you, John. A prison for all who deserve it, and for some who don't, but who still manage to condemn themselves out of accident or stupidity. We don't judge. All we do is tend to the interns. With teeth, tools, and creativity."

"No." John searches for a way to stop drifting away, but his hands move through the furniture around him like smoke.

"All it takes to descend," the woman says, "is one tiny little slip. And believe us, Lena Franke has done much more than just slip."

"*No!*" John cries.

He doesn't know who Lena Franke is, or what is happening to him. All his senses scream in protest against losing a battle he doesn't even understand how to fight. His body is still in Molly's flat, but the rest of him is already a world away, tethering on a precipice. At the periphery of his consciousness is the wail of approaching sirens. The police, rushing closer quickly, but far too late.

The woman who has stolen his murdered girlfriend's appearance flicks her finger in front of John's face. He flinches and recoils from her touch.

Then vertigo clutches him, and he is falling.

*

John's world fades like a postcard sinking in tar.

Darkness wraps itself around him like a web while his thoughts dissolve. Before long, he is only an ember floating down a chasm, the last light of the world lost far above. Oblivion winds itself tighter around him until, at last, he is entirely gone from this world, his soul swallowed by a horror he could not endure.

Or so he would have thought.

*

But part of John stays behind.

A shell of a person, filled with purpose and fuelled by hate, remains in the flat. His pulse slows down. The throbbing in his ears ebbs away. After a moment, he turns to the bed and meets Molly's unmoving eyes. This time he does not blink. A single ambition lodges itself in his mind. Alternatives and possibilities fall into place, cementing his route.

Careful not to touch the blood, he leans down and unties his shoes. The sirens outside grow sharper, more eager, but he does not rush. One action needs to follow another. In his mind is only a chain of events that stretches into the future all the way to the conclusion. A single mistake can break it.

He steps out of his shoes, away from the blood, and into the small white-tiled bathroom. The contents of Molly's bathroom cabinets are raked into a plastic bag: razors and lotions, toothpaste, two old toothbrushes, deodorant, tweezers, nail cutters, perfumed tissue.

Next, he goes to the bedroom and switches on the light. After stepping over the blood, he opens the narrow, built-in wardrobe and takes out a black canvas bag. Inside are a towel and a thick yoga mat covered with stiff rubber spikes.

John shoves the half-filled plastic bag into the larger black bag, followed by a woollen blanket, a scarf and a compact sleeping bag. He unclips from his belt two rings, each the diameter of a finger and holding dozens of keys, and tucks them deep into the black bag.

There is just enough space left in the bag for a two-litre plastic bottle that he fills from the kitchen tap. In the fridge are a box of milk, jars filled with olives, salad, carrots and mustard. Three tubs of hummus, a large bowl of nuts. A steel bowl with soy steaks in marinade. A near-empty bottle of vinegar. Enough food to last him a few days, but too cumbersome to carry.

He closes the fridge and looks out through the kitchen window. The sun has almost set. Past the curtain of snow are sidewalks lined with cars, many parked so close to each other their bumpers almost touch. Most of the windows in the three-storey block of flats across the street are dark. Two children are building a snowman while their mother waits nearby, rocking her pram and stamping her feet to keep warm.

Below the window, a man in a wheelchair negotiates the entrance of the corner shop. John studies the shop's entrance and registers details that never before have mattered. Another part is added to his plan.

Police sirens fill the air. Children turn and point down the street; the vehicles are almost here. Blue flashing lights are reflected in the windows outside. He hefts the bag and walks out of the kitchen, pausing in the doorway to take a set of knives from a rack next to the stove. He slips the knives into the bag, zips the bag shut, steps over the blood, and looks out through the open door into the stairwell.

Faint echoes of dropped cutlery, the mumble of news shows, someone coughing. A power box in the ceiling hums and clicks. The stairwell is dark; no one has pressed the timed light switch in the last five minutes. No curious neighbours yet; most will need time to admit to themselves that the bang may, in fact, have been a gunshot.

He waits until his eyes adapt to the gloom and walks down the stairs. Wearing only socks on his feet, his footsteps are almost soundless as he pads down the cool steps. He reaches the front door, a thick pane of glass framed in pale wood, and peers out.

A police car accelerates down the street through the snow. The driver blasts the horn while other cars struggle to swerve out of the way. Blue lights flood the street and brush the façades of nearby buildings. People stop and stare, mesmerised by the spectacle, but no one is looking at him.

He opens the door, steps out into the whirling snow, and runs south.

The hunt has begun.

*

CHAPTER 1

Lena

"I haven't got many notes," Agnes says to Lena, "but I can give you a summary. Do you want to hear it now or wait until I've sorted the notes?" she asks. "I'm afraid they're a mess."

Staring out the kitchen window at the crime scene, Lena Franke does not hear the younger officer's question. She checks the small clock on the wall. Half past three. Fifty minutes since the first police car arrived on the scene. Outside, the slow sunset is bleeding into dark grey. Soon the sky will deepen into the black of winter nights.

She has been on the scene less than twenty minutes, but it feels like hours. The deep bass from a nearby party rumbles in the building like a subterranean thunder. Tiredness makes her eyes water. She wants to lean against a kitchen wall, but the forensic team in the bedroom would tell her off; as far as they are concerned, the officers' presence is bad enough. The sidewalk outside is closed off, although as usual, the blue-and-white plastic tape is a magnet to bystanders trying to look diffident while they hope for a fragment of drama.

A metallic clatter sounds from the bedroom, where the forensic team hovers over the body. In the kitchen, the stench of gunpowder is giving in to the fragrance of incense, spices and tea leaves. The room and its decorations look disconnected, unrelated to the dead woman in the adjacent room. She never gets used to the contrast. Cutlery and teacups, the metal sieve, the bottle of soy sauce and the kitchen towels. All in suspense, ready to be used, but destined to remain untouched.

Half an hour ago, she was in her car, cursing the snow along with thousands of other drivers while heading towards the city headquarters to wrap up a long week. She pictured a weekend of silence and serenity. Hours in the calmness of the basement gym, uninterrupted lines of thought. Perhaps, if she was lucky, even some solid sleep. Then the reports of a shot came over the radio.

Without thinking twice, she had flicked the siren on, cut through the traffic, and raced to the suburb. Sleep would have to wait: she was in the area and on duty. For some reason, this particular alert had jolted her badly. She had even been looking at the radio when it beeped, as if expecting the call. It was odd, but not enough to distract her from the task at hand.

On her way, she called to make sure no trains would stop at the nearby underground station, and roped in three local patrols to search for suspects. They need all the luck they can find: the western suburb is peppered with dark parks and alleys, and hundreds of people have passed the streets outside the victim's home since the shot was fired. This search will be a nightmare. Her hope for a good lead rests with the forensic team and the patrols.

Lena glances at Agnes Petersen, who stands next to her with a thick notepad in her hands. She has known the younger woman just over two months. A fresh cadet, keen and analytic. Perfect superintendent material. Physically, they are almost diametrically opposite, as if they had been paired to balance each other. Agnes is slim and lithe; Lena a head taller and heavier, much because of her weightlifting regime.

While Agnes keeps her blond hair tied back, Lena's dark curls escape every attempt to keep them out of her face. Their faces mark the greatest difference: Agnes is pale and freckled, with eyes so deep blue they border on indigo. Lena is brown-eyed and darker, an echo from her distant Bulgarian lineage.

"Detective Franke?" Agnes asks. "Are you all right?"

Lena blinks and straightens up. By this point, Agnes and she have moved past the use of surnames, but the younger officer sometimes slips back into the habit. Especially when she's concerned.

"Right." Lena shakes her head to clear her thoughts. "Sorry. I'm listening. Go ahead."

"Of course." Agnes leafs through the papers. "The flat owner's driver's license matches the victim, so for now, the forensics believe she's the owner of the flat. They'll know for certain soon."

"What else?" Lena asks.

"The victim's name is Molly Marianne Berglund. Born in Uppsala in 1978. She moved to Stockholm seventeen years ago. Both parents deceased, unmarried, no siblings or children. She worked at Brunnen Natural Health. No criminal record, debts, or signs of abuse or other illegal activities. That we've seen, I mean," she adds.

Lena nods absently. Over the past three days, she's had eight hours of rest altogether. Far too little, especially given the dream that waits in the alleyways of her mind, ready to pounce on her as soon as she drifts away. Always the same vision, her bespoke nightmare, recurring over and over, varying only in length and intensity.

She uses her empty polystyrene coffee cup to cover a yawn. *You're a senior officer,* she tells herself. *Act like one.*

"Another bad night's sleep?" Agnes asks.

"I'm fine," Lena lies. "It's obvious how the woman died, but we need more details. Have the forensics come up with a statement yet?"

Agnes nods hurriedly and sifts through her papers. "A single gunshot to the jugular," she reads. "They're still trying to get the bullet out of the wall. They think it's heavy calibre. It hit the arterial vein on the right side of the victim's neck, ricocheted off a bedpost, and struck her bedside clock."

Lena studies Agnes while she talks. The other officer is uncomfortable, and she knows why: they should not be here yet, in the way of the forensics. But Lena needs to form an idea of what happened, and for that she needs context. She has to see the backdrop.

"It bounced off a bedpost?" Lena asks.

"The bed's made of cast iron." Agnes pauses. "What do you make of the shoes?" she asks. "His feet must be frozen solid by now."

Lena glances at the shoes surrounded by blood in the middle of the hall. Men's size, neatly arranged.

"He must've been afraid he'd leave tracks in the snow." Lena nods at the window and the streets below. "A bad idea in many ways. Being shoeless in this weather might draw attention and make him easier to track. He's given us plenty of DNA samples, too. I want the coroner's full report as soon as it's ready. Not that it'll change much at this point." She pauses. "What's your own preliminary?"

Agnes pauses and clears her throat. "Jealousy," she says. "Her boyfriend caught her in bed with someone else, and he snapped. Maybe the shot was meant for the other man. Or woman, of course. As far as we can tell, only one shot was fired, but there might have been a fight before that happened."

"Maybe," Lena agrees.

When Lena arrived at the flat, she took a long look at the body before escaping to the kitchen. Her thoughts turn back to the dead woman. Sprawled on the bed, on her back, thrown halfway down onto the floor by the impact of the bullet, her pallid face framed by blond hair. Lena glimpsed purple lingerie under the woman's black bathrobe. Not expensive, but pretty. Not the kind you wear for work.

She turns to the burning candle on the table. The flame dances in a slow draft from the window. She reaches out to snuff it, then pauses and pulls her hand back. The candle had probably been lit by the victim. A tiny, transient legacy. Better left alone, for as long as it'll be allowed to burn.

"Detective?" calls a voice from the bedroom.

"What?" Lena says, still looking at the candle.

One of the forensics, a young man with freckles and a large silver ring in his ear, stands in the kitchen door.

"We have secured two sets of fingerprints," he says. "One by a woman, another by a man. The woman's prints are everywhere, so we reckon they belong to the victim. Those left by the man are in many places, too. They're definitely by someone who comes here often."

"Any other prints?" Lena asks.

"Only a few, and they're old."

"Signs of the weapon?" Agnes wonders.

The forensic shakes his head. "We haven't had time to search the flat thoroughly, but I wouldn't be surprised if the shooter still has it. There aren't that many places in here where it can be hidden. At least not quickly."

"Anything else that's out of place?" Lena asks.

"Not that we've noticed," the technician says. "Although it'll take time to produce a full report. Do you think we've missed something?"

Lena studies the hallway. A perfectly mundane space, in an ordinary building, deep in a typical suburb. Jackets and coats, rows of shoes, an old mirror, IKEA furniture. The walls are solid and the floor intact. Nothing seems amiss except for the blood.

And still, just as she crossed the doorstep, that quick brush of coldness, gentle as a feather. As if a window just had been closed. Or a door.

"Thanks," Lena says. "That's all for now. Keep me posted."

The forensic leaves for the bedroom while Lena glances at her phone. No missed calls. No messages. Before the night grows much older, that will change: a handful of officers at the central police headquarters are already putting together details and circumstances for the coordination brief later. She loathes those meetings. Everyone available, including her, should be on the scene or the streets, looking, thinking, asking questions.

"Tell me about the suspect," Lena says to Agnes. "I know even less than the patrols."

"Absolutely." Agnes slips out a paper from the back of the pile. "This is a statement by Ola Larsson, a neighbour. His door's opposite the one to this flat. He saw a man standing in the hall a few minutes after he heard the shot. He was looking in the peephole, but moved away when he saw someone there."

"Sounds like a sensible man," Lena murmurs. "So the front door to this flat was open all the time?"

"According to the witness, yes," Agnes says.

"Did Ola see the man's face?"

Agnes browses the handwritten statement and shakes her head. "I'm afraid not."

"So how does Ola know it was a man?"

"He remembers the jacket. Dark blue with white print on the back. He didn't know what the print reads or the man's name, but he said a man wearing this jacket has been seeing Molly since a few months back."

Lena nods. "Go on."

"Ola also said he'd met the same man several times in the stairwell. One morning, he helped the man in question get the snow off his car."

"Imagine that," Lena says. She pokes with her pen at a pile of Post-it notes and postcards on the windowsill. The forensic team would scream if they saw her, but clues like to hide everywhere. Especially in the open.

Agnes frowns at Lena. "Imagine getting snow off a car?"

"I meant imagine that we're lucky," Lena replies. "At least someone has seen the man and can give us a good description. But Ola didn't see the man's face tonight, right?" she asks. "Only the jacket?"

The officer nods. "I'm afraid so. However, he's sure it is the same person."

"What does the man look like?"

"According to Ola, he's in his late thirties, maybe early forties. Short dark hair. A bit chubby, no glasses, usually has a stubble. Not shabby, he said, but a little worn. About five foot six. Friendly. Smiles a lot, apparently."

Lena nods, lost in thought. Chatting with the neighbours rather than skulking around. That makes the man her boyfriend. "Did Ola mention other men coming here?"

"He hasn't seen any. I asked."

"I thought as much. Although if Molly were cheating, her lover would've kept a low profile." Lena pauses. "Did Molly own a car?"

14

"She had a license, but there's no car registered in her name."

Lena pushes a crumpled sheet from the pile of papers over to Agnes, who looks at it and back at Lena.

"A car mechanic receipt?" Agnes asks.

"Two weeks old," Lena says. "It's got license plate details. Given that Molly didn't have a car, I bet it belongs to the man we're looking for." She takes the note and walks towards the front door. "Call in and check the number plates."

"Where are you going?"

"Down to the street. His car might still be here."

*

CHAPTER 2

The other John

John runs down the road, pausing to ask people walking in the other direction if they have seen the man John follows. He keeps his description brief: male, dark hair, dark shoes, blue pants, red backpack.

Most people he asks hesitate, shake their heads, and frown at John's socks. John says the man he is looking for is mentally ill but harmless. The man has stolen John's shoes. This makes a few nod, in doubt or concern. A woman points down the street, towards the underground trains. John thanks her and runs on.

A minute later John sprints down a flight of stairs overshadowed by sixteen storeys of glass and concrete. When he enters Brommaplan's open-air bus terminal, he stops and looks around.

Commuters mill around the area, moving between the underground station, crowded grocery shops, fast-food franchises, a liquor store, and dozens of bus shelters. Some hurry towards the shops that encircle the nearby large roundabout. The weather mutes all sounds, but the hum of cars carries through the air like a murmur. Falling snow obscures everything outside the plaza.

In front of John, red local buses crawl along the streets as they make their way around trees bent by layers of snow. An underground train rattles past on a viaduct and slows down as it nears the station platform. People march past John without looking up, their faces turned to the ground to ward off the biting wind.

John walks towards the entrance of the underground station and stops outside the glass doors. Inside the hall, people fill the escalator that leads up to the platform. Everyone who enters the underground train passes through the manned ticket control or one of the turnstiles. Two security guards lounge near the ticket controller, chatting idly while their hands rest on their batons.

After a moment, John turns away and looks around the bus terminal. Facing the station is a hamburger franchise with an empty outdoor serving area. On warmer days, vendors in thick clothes offer vegetables and flowers from heated stalls right outside the station. Today the stalls are closed, snow piling up against the shutters.

Past the closed stalls, three men on a bench are laughing and gesturing. One of the men holds a wine bottle. They seem oblivious to the cold.

John walks over to the men and looks down at them. Their faces glow red in the snowfall. Grimy clothes, sluggish movements, broken blood vessels riddling their cheeks. A sour cloud of alcohol and lament.

"Evening," one of the men says and looks up at John. He is severely underweight and sports a thin beard that reaches halfway down his worn alpine jacket. Suddenly aware of John's presence, the other two men turn to John. Suspicion glazes their eyes.

"I'm looking for a man," John says and describes how Molly's murderer was dressed. "Have you seen him? He went too far, if you know what I mean. Took too many. I'm really worried; if he passes out, he'll freeze to death." The mental illness card won't work with these men, John suspects, but perhaps another addict will spark some sympathy.

The men on the bench look at each other. One of them loses interest and turns back to nursing the bottle in his scarred hands. Another man shrugs and shakes his head, but the bearded man nods. "Yeah, I've seen him. He was here a minute ago. He's your friend?"

"Sure," John says and nods keenly.

The man shakes his head. "He should give the drink a break. Looks like a walking skeleton, you know? He'll be dead inside a month." He spits in the snow between his boots. "Seen it happen before."

"Where are your shoes?" The man who had gone back to drinking is pointing at John's feet. "Hey, I've got socks just like those. Aren't you cold? You could lose your toes, you know."

"You're right," John says, "but I need to find my friend quickly. Do you know where he went?"

The bearded man points to the underground station. "He took a train. About twenty minutes ago, something like that. Looked like he was in a hurry."

John looks at the station. Rush hour. Trains in two directions every three minutes, security guards, cameras on the trains. He knows the man's clothes but not his face. Finding the killer there will be difficult, if not impossible.

In the distance are sirens, coming closer.

John turns back to the men. "Have you seen him here at Brommaplan before?"

"Yeah, he's a regular," the bearded man says and shrugs. "I think he scores from—"

One of his friends, an obese man with a skin condition, elbows the man, who catches the hint and falls silent.

John does not need to hear the rest of the sentence. "Who does he score from, did you say?"

The men exchange uneasy glances, shake their heads and mumble that they have no idea. Inside the station hall, the guards are looking John's way.

John runs again, this time north, away from the underground station. He jogs past banks, kiosks, and a post office. Cars swerve and drivers curse as he rushes across a large roundabout. He crosses the knee-high, untouched snow in its centre, runs over the lanes on the other side, and walks into the parking lot of a gas station. Behind rows of gas pumps is a small shop.

John walks in and inspects the shelves. Racks packed with magazines, oil cans, batteries, takeaway meals and soft drinks. Stacks of shovels, packs of ice scrapers, semi-obscured pornography and bundles of expensive firewood. Near the counter, glistening sausages roll on a grill under bright fluorescent lights. In a far corner is an open cardboard box brimming with discounted summer-season wares.

John walks over to the discount box. Cheap badminton rackets, inflatable bath toys, plastic jugs, sunglasses and water guns. And, underneath the bric-a-brac, cheap unbranded shoes.

He takes a pair of black canvas shoes and walks to the checkout, leaves the shoes on the counter, and goes back to the discount box for a pair of binoculars and three pairs of grey fleece socks. He returns to the counter and places the socks and the binoculars on top of the shoes, then adds a box of twenty chocolate bars and a disposable cigarette lighter.

The young woman behind the counter looks wide-eyed at John. She holds a pen close to her side.

"Is there a problem?" John asks.

"No," the woman says quickly. "Of course not." She flashes a smile and clears her throat. "It's just, you know, we're close to the liquor store. Sometimes we get strange people. And, well, you have no shoes."

"I'm not one of those people." John smiles. "My shoes fell apart. Ripped them open on the gas pedal. One of those freak accidents."

"I'm sorry, I didn't mean to stare. I'm just skittish. Ten minutes left on a long shift. But hey, then it's the weekend." Her fingers tremble as she punches the buttons on the till.

"I hope you enjoy it." John swipes his card in the credit card reader.

"Right," she replies and swallows. "You too." She stuffs the wares into a plastic bag, gives it to John, and snatches her hand back.

John thanks her and leaves.

He pauses outside the door to put on the socks and the shoes. The rest of his purchases are tucked down into the black bag.

Once again he runs, towards the station, past the shops and the men on the bench and the station. His feet hurt, but they will have to carry him. When he spots a cash machine between a chemist and a bank, he slows down, walks past the queue, and inserts his card.

"Hey." A man in a black leather jacket lowers his mobile phone and taps John's shoulder. "I'm talking to you. There's a line, you know? Your place is at the back."

"I'm in a hurry." John enters his code and waits for the machine to respond.

"Who isn't?" the man asks. "Will you move, or do I have to move you?"

John turns to face the man while the cash machine processes the withdrawal. Behind the man are five other people, all of them looking everywhere except at John and the man in front of him.

"Do you want me to break your teeth?" the man asks, his face growing red.

John studies the man's eyes and says nothing.

"Come on, do your worst. I dare you." The man balls his fists at his sides and breathes hard, but doesn't move. Behind John, the cash machine churns and clicks. A child starts to cry at the back of the queue.

"Are you going to do something," John asks, still holding the man's eyes, "or will you stand down?"

"I – oh, fuck this. Whatever." The man walks away, pausing to look over his shoulder as if to make sure John is not following him.

John turns back to the cash machine, pockets the ejected notes, and leaves. After turning a corner, he runs under the viaduct, past the tower block and back up the hill, cutting across unfenced backyards and keeping away from sidewalks.

He has to go back to where it began. A few more stops and he will know the face of his enemy. Then, the true hunt will start.

*

CHAPTER 3

Lena

Lena scans the street through the clouds of steam from her breath. Behind her, a police officer makes sure only residents enter the block. Those who leave are pressed for statements.

Two officers have joined Agnes in the flat along with the forensic team. Three police cars and one ambulance are parked in clumsy angles between the vehicles along the sidewalks, slowing down traffic to a zigzag crawl. Their lights turn the area into a spinning inferno of blues and reds.

The snowfall makes it impossible to see car number plates more than a dozen metres away, so she zips up her jacket and walks down the street, peering at the cars while whispering the license plate number she found on the receipt in the flat. Six damned characters and she struggles to remember them. Her short-term memory has always been bad, and lack of sleep does not help. The car probably will not be here, but staying in the flat was unbearable. This is a good excuse to get out.

The phone in her pocket buzzes. She stops, digs it out, and shields the screen from the snow with her hand. Her superintendent calling from the headquarters in the city. She takes the call.

"Franke," Lena says and continues down the sidewalk. Three more cars, then she will cross the street and double back.

"This is Gren," her commander says. "Are you preparing the briefing?"

"I'm still at the scene."

She checks the next number plate while she waits for Gren to respond. There is a long pause, and she knows why: Gren wants her to set up the meeting, but he knows she wants to scour the area first. In the background is the mumble of the office. She pictures

Gren sitting straight-backed behind his desk, wearing his crisp shirt and his permanent, slightly pained grimace. He's by-the-book and overprotective, but to his credit, he trusts and listens to his people.

"All right," Gren says eventually. "What do you have so far?"

"A lot of statements," Lena says. "One of them is pretty extensive," she says. "Lots of details. Agnes did a good job."

"Are you two still working well together?"

"She's an asset," Lena says. "No complaints from me."

She doesn't add that Agnes is more than a benefit to the police force. Even though they haven't exchanged many details about their private lives, the officer is quickly becoming a close friend, on a peculiar and unfamiliar level. Being around Agnes is like standing in shadow on an unbearably hot day. A watchful, concerned shadow, constantly on lookout. For what, Lena has no idea.

"A neighbour gave a clear description of the suspect," Lena continues. "He didn't see the man's face tonight, but he's convinced that the suspect is – I mean, was – Molly's boyfriend. The neighbour has met him before. And we've got a car registration number that we're looking up."

"Any fingerprints?" Gren asks. "Something that ties our suspect to the shooting? Are the forensics done?"

"Nothing definite yet. I'm looking for the car as we speak. We found the numbers on a receipt in the flat." She watches snowflakes arc down through the glow of the street lights. A long, peaceful flight, a moment in the light, and it is over. No such luck for the woman in the flat.

"Have you talked to the prosecutor?" Gren asks.

Lena shakes her head and sighs. Sometimes she wonders if her boss is paid on the basis of how many questions he asks per day.

"I'll call him." She stops and turns to cross the street. "Eight officers are searching for the suspect at the moment. Like I said, we have a close description. He might still be armed."

"Thanks. Anything else?"

"He's in his socks."

"Come again?"

"The suspect took off his shoes before he fled the scene. They were bloodied, so I think he was afraid he'd leave tracks."

"I see," Gren says. "That's a pretty calculating thing to do after shooting someone."

"And stupid," Lena agrees, although that idea no longer sits right with her. A panicked idiot would not have made it far in this weather, but so far, he is eluding the police.

"I have to go," Gren says. "I'm already getting phone calls from above. I'll call back soon."

"Right." Lena ends the call, pockets her phone, and slows down near a white car. It is parked outside the entrance of a small convenience store, not far from the flat. She looks at the plates and runs through the numbers in her mind. They match.

The car is a white Opel delivery van. Apart from a few scratches, it looks almost new. A large logotype on the van's side reads *Argenti Advertising* in blue letters. She circles the van and glances through its windows to make sure the vehicle is empty. At least the front seats; one or more people could easily fit inside the windowless loading compartment.

She keeps her eyes on the van and calls Agnes.

Agnes answers almost immediately. "Have you found anything?"

"His van's right outside," Lena says.

"I'm on my way."

Thirty seconds later, Agnes trudges through the snow and stops next to Lena. "Is this the one?" she asks, nodding at the white Opel.

Lena nods. "Did you tell the forensics?"

"They'll be here in a few minutes." Agnes studies the van in silence. "Do you think he panicked?"

"The killer?" Lena crosses her arms across her chest and rubs her arms. "Probably," she says. "That would explain why he left his shoes behind. But unless he's back indoors, he'll soon freeze his feet off."

Several witnesses have pointed down the street towards the underground station, so she sent four officers that way. She has also alerted the underground management to make sure no trains stop at Brommaplan. Another escape route cut off.

Buses leave the terminal near the underground station in all directions, but the gridlock means most buses drive at less than walking speed. A warning has been issued over radio to all drivers. The shooter will not get away by public transport.

"Do you reckon he'll come back here?" Agnes asks.

"There's no telling what's going through his mind," Lena says. "But yes, he might come back. At any rate, he'll break down as soon as his pain outgrows his panic. He might even turn himself in."

Statistically, it was almost certain that the boyfriend was the murderer, and this had all the hallmarks of a jealousy crime. But a stubborn edge of unease tells her that the scenario is more fractured. She needs to shake the kaleidoscope to get a better picture.

Lena's phone beeps: a text message. She checks it and then touches Agnes's arm to get her attention. "They've matched the number plates."

Lena and Agnes jog to Agnes's car and sit down in the front seats. Agnes presses a button, and details flash onto the screen of the car's communication unit.

"The suspect's name is John Peter Andersson," Lena says, repeating the information to herself as she reads. "Forty-two years old, lives in Grimsta. Works for Argenti Advertising. Lone occupant at the address. A few previous addresses, all of them west of the city. No criminal history."

The photo from John's driver's licence is attached to the file. Unkempt and thinning dark hair, slightly overweight, two-day stubble. His bright blue eyes are unfocused, as if his thoughts are elsewhere.

"Grimsta isn't far," Agnes says. "Five stops from here with the underground train, then a fifteen-minute walk. Or ten minutes by car if we cut through the suburbs. Make that twenty in this weather."

Lena nods. She has been there before. A sprawling group of three-storey houses below Vällingby, a refurbished fifties-era shopping centre with a small bus terminal and an underground station. The district's major hub.

A quiet place, she recalls. The impression had been reinforced by the nearby nature reserve, a dense carpet of old pine trees, rocky ground and winding paths.

"We'll go by car." Lena reaches for her radio. "Franke calling patrol Caesar Twelve," she says.

The radio hisses and spits static for a few seconds before the reply comes. "Caesar Twelve here."

"The suspect's address is Bjurvagen 12 in Grimsta. His photo and file are online. It's the victim's boyfriend," she adds. "It's unlikely that he's there, but we're going to have a look."

"Understood."

"Any sign of the suspect where you are?" Lena asks.

"Nothing yet, but a lot of people think they've seen him around the shops outside the Brommaplan underground station. We've got a lot of confused statements."

"All right. Over and out."

Lena releases the button and slips her radio into her pocket. Provided that a prosecutor is available, they can fast-track a search warrant while they drive to Grimsta. She turns to Agnes, who is peering through the windows of the car.

"We'll leave the car to the forensics," Lena says. "I don't want John to hole up at home. Do you know the way?"

Agnes nods. "It's been a while since I was there, but I remember. It's along the underground, the left."

"I'll follow your car." As Lena turns to open the car door, she glances at the corner shop near Molly's flat.

A man behind the counter inside the shop is looking at Lena through the yellow-tinted window. Middle Eastern, lean and wiry, in his fifties, sporting a thick beard and a black beanie.

Less than five seconds pass before he looks away, but Lena has seen enough: there had been more than curiosity on his face. *Sadness*, she thinks. *Caution. Perhaps guilt.*

Or fear.

"Wait here," Lena says. "I'll be right back." She steps out of the car, squinting at the corner shop.

"Where are you going?" Agnes calls after Lena.

"I'm having a quick word with the shopkeeper."

*

CHAPTER 4

Lena

A bell jingles as Lena opens the door, then again as the door swings shut behind her.

The shop is not much bigger than her flat, which in turn is the size of most of her friends' kitchens. Two strip lights in the ceiling illuminate half a dozen shelves loaded with wares essential for the desperate or absent-minded: White bread, discount DVDs, canned beans, fruit-scented shampoos and microwave meals. Dirty snow streaks the linoleum floor. A whiff of incense hangs in the humid air. She is the only customer in the shop.

She walks over to the counter, faces the man whose eyes she met through the window, and waits for him to speak.

"Can I help?" he says. His voice is deeper than Lena expects.

Lena reaches for her inner pocket. "I'm Detective Lena Franke," she says. "I'd like to ask you a few questions."

He nods to the window. "I saw you come. I heard the shot."

Lena studies the man. He doesn't ask if someone has fired a gun; he already knows.

She shows him her badge and puts it away.

"What's your name?" she asks.

"Abbaas," he replies. "Abbaas Kouri. What has happened to Molly?"

Lena hesitates. "I can't give you that information right now."

The man's face falls, and he mutters what Lena suspects is a curse in what might be Arabic. Somehow, he knows what has taken place, or at least that Molly was hurt.

"Have you recently seen a man in a blue jacket?" Lena asks. "About my height, dark hair. In his early forties. No shoes. Possibly carrying a large dark bag."

Abbaas starts to nod halfway through Lena's question. In one of his hands is a wad of large notes, but the till is closed.

"I know who you're looking for. I saw him not long ago. Ten minutes, maybe. He's wearing shoes now."

Lena tenses at the unexpected load of information. "Where did you see him?" she asks.

"Here."

"What?" Lena looks around the shop in disbelief. Perhaps John came back to watch the scene, or maybe he left something behind. At least he might still be in the neighbourhood.

"Do you know where he went?" Lena asks.

"I am sorry." Abbaas shakes his head. "I would tell you if I knew, but I have no idea."

Lena runs to the door and flings it open.

"He's nearby," she shouts to Agnes. "Get on the radio and call the patrols closer. He was here not long ago."

She leaves the door open and stalks back to the man behind the counter.

"Tell me exactly what the man said," she demands. "What he bought, everything he did. Think hard."

"John is in trouble, isn't he?" Abbaas asks.

"Please answer the question. Did the man say anything out of the ordinary?"

Abbaas takes a deep breath. "Yes." He sighs. "You could say that."

"Go on." Lena takes out her notepad. Whatever John has done here will be a valuable lead. She gets the man's name and phone number.

"What did the man do in your shop?" she asks.

"He bought my computer. Paid in cash. I got a good price."

Frowning, Lena looks up from her notepad. "Why?" she asks. "Did he seem irrational or shocked?"

"No," Abbaas replies quietly. "Not irrational." He glances at the ceiling, towards Molly's flat. "I heard what happened to her. A neighbour came in and told me. You know that John and she were together?"

"How do you know?"

"He talked about her. John came to visit her often, and he used to buy her chocolate. Flowers too, when I have them."

"I see." Lena stares at her notepad. One day John is courting her, the next he arrives as a vengeful killer. It happens more often than she likes to consider.

"Molly was a regular too," Abbaas continues. "She came many times every week. We talked about the weather, local gossip, things like that. Beautiful woman. Shy." He searches for a word. "Frail."

"Why did he buy your computer?" Lena asks, noting that Abbaas uses past tense when he speaks about Molly. The shop is hot and the incense pricks her eyes, but she needs to stay and make sure she learns everything the man knows.

"Look." Abbaas's voice is hushed. "John loved Molly very much. I could see it. Every time he came here, he was happy." He shrugs. "We men don't often show when we're happy in that way, but with John, it was written on his face."

"Sure," Lena says. Then Molly had cheated on John, and John had cracked like an old vase. A scenario as tragic as it was common. "But the computer?" she pressed. "Why did the man want it?"

"I cannot say for sure."

A realisation dawns on Lena, and she stops with her pen hovering above the notepad. Returning to a crime scene to gloat is one thing; coming back to buy a computer is a different matter. Add to that statements that describe John in a myriad of ways.

There have been two different men in Molly's flat.

Once the thought comes to her, she is certain. John has been there, or at least near it, but so has someone else. And only one of the men is the shooter.

"One last question," Lena says. "Did you ever see this Molly with other men?"

"Never." Abbaas shakes his head. "Just John."

"Right." Lena takes a card from her wallet and leaves it on the counter. "Here's my number and my email address. If you think of anything else that might help us find him, contact me. Another

29

officer will come by later for a full statement." She turns away and walks towards the exit, longing for the frigid air outside.

"I think John bought it for the footage," the man calls after Lena.

Lena stops just inside the door. "What footage?" she asks and turns back. "On the computer?"

"Yes."

"Footage of what, exactly?"

Abbaas grimaces. "I have a camera outside," he says. "I don't have a permit to use one, but I am often alone in the shop."

"Go on," Lena says.

"John came in and asked if the camera was real. Some shops have fake ones, but mine works. So I said yes."

"And then?"

"He asked if it had recorded the last hour. When I said it had, he wanted to buy the footage. It was on my computer. A laptop."

Lena nods. John wanted to cover his tracks, so he needed the recording in case it shows him leaving the flat. He took a great risk going back to get the film, but she has seen worse. Desperation is the mother of many moronic ideas.

This particular idea had compromised her work in a bad way. The film could have been useful, maybe critical for finding John, and now it was gone.

"You saw us arrive," Lena says, "and you know the footage could be used as evidence. And you sold it, just like that?" Lena asks.

"No." Abbaas pauses. "Not 'just like that'."

"Did John threaten you?"

Abbaas shakes his head slowly. "He was very polite. Always calm, like always. The reason I sold the computer to John is that he would have taken it anyway."

"What's that supposed to mean?" Lena demands. "You said a moment ago that he didn't threaten you?"

Abbaas looks up and meets Lena's eyes. "I came to Sweden in nineteen eighty-two." He holds up a hand when Lena begins to interrupt him. "Please listen," he says. "It's important."

After a moment, Lena nods.

"I was in a war for about a year," Abbaas says. "Iran, then Iraq. First in Mehran, after that in the Zagros Mountains. I can see that you do not recognize the names. That doesn't matter. But this does.

"I met many men who had lost everything. Women, too. Some eventually fled, just like I did. Others broke down and sat on the ground while they waited to die. A few stayed and struggled to survive. But some lost their minds, or maybe I should say their souls. They became very good soldiers. Fearless, efficient, merciless. We called them walking corpses, but never to their faces."

"John is probably in shock," Lena says, "and possibly violent, but he's not suffering from a war trauma."

"Shock, trauma, madness." Abbaas shakes his head. "Those are only empty words. Different dresses for the same thing. The people who became good soldiers were once good fathers and loving men, but the war turned them into stone. I'm telling you this because I want to help John. I liked him. He was an honest man."

"Why the past tense?" Lena asks. "He's not dead." She had almost added *in difference to his girlfriend.*

"That," Abbaas says, "depends on your point of view. Perhaps there is still time. Please, hurry to find him."

"I hope to." Lena points at her card on the counter. "Contact me if you can think of anything else, or if John comes back again." She leaves the shop and finds Agnes waiting for her outside with a question on her face.

"Did he know anything?" Agnes asks.

"John was here," Lena says. "He bought a computer."

"In the corner shop?"

"I'll tell you why on the way to his flat," Lena says. "There's more. I'm beginning to think that John isn't our man. Or rather that he's one of them."

Agnes looks up from her notepad. "They were a group?"

Lena shakes her head. "One man shot Molly and ran, and John set off after him. Now both of them are gone."

"Are you sure?"

31

"Of course not. But I will be, once we've pinned John down and brought him in."

"But if John isn't–"

"We want both of them. Gren will want to turn all resources to finding the presumed killer, but we have to get John too. Trust me."

"I do. You know that."

"Good." Lena nods in approval but wishes Agnes was not so unquestioning. That blind faith will come back to haunt Agnes if Lena loses control of the case. Or of herself.

"No word from the patrols yet?" Lena asks.

"Nothing new, but they've tightened the search. I told them to concentrate on people leaving the area. And I've requested backup. Two cars will meet us at the flat as soon as they can."

Lena turns to Agnes. "Call the forensics and tell them to make sure they cover every spot of the flat when they look for prints. Including the front door and the walls just outside it."

"I'll call them straight away."

Lena nods absently. In her mind, she goes over what the shop owner has told her. Flowers and smiles, chocolate and frailty. Caring people reduced by atrocities to callous machines.

Some of those women and men would have been hanging by a thread before they fell. Maybe a few had managed to claw their way back from the slide into callousness and returned to daylight, healing themselves by helping others, one compassionate act after another.

Perhaps she could, too.

"Then let's go," Lena says. "The storm's getting worse. Or at least colder."

*

CHAPTER 5

John Andersson

The part of John that was torn away in Molly's flat awakes.

He's naked, lying flat on his stomach, while strong winds tug and tear at his hair. His body is coated by a powdering of snow so cold it burns like hot ash. Patches of frost have bolted his cheek to the ground.

Around him is only a whirling whiteness. More snow, whipping past his face, whirling around him and lashing his skin. A storm, but not the one that rages in Stockholm. He is no longer there.

A single stubborn thought pierces the mayhem, like a beacon on a distant shore. He clings to it and pulls his thoughts together, strand by disjointed strand.

I was deceived.

Slowly, he raises his head and looks around.

*

CHAPTER 6

The other John

John walks down a series of stone stairs running through a patch of forest on a crest between Brommaplan and Abrahamsberg.

Around him are clusters of low blocks, most of them hidden by hedges and pine trees. He walks carefully while the wind rips between the trees at his sides. Every step is slippery and obscured under layers of snow. His bag is slung over his shoulder. The folded laptop computer is held tightly under his arm.

On his left, a train rumbles past. Its wheels screech and hiss as it nears Abrahamsberg's station, but the train is still going fast. He turns away as shafts of light from the train's windows sweep over him; the chance that anyone on the train will notice him is minimal, but he cannot take any risks.

While he walked, he watched the trains continue past Brommaplan without stopping. The police had ordered the trains to isolate the station. This surprises him, but it is not a major obstacle. He can find another way to reach his destination. Perhaps the trains will pick up passengers here, one stop away from Brommaplan.

Halfway down the stairs, John pauses to shove the computer deep into his bag; the snow might damage the hardware, and he needs it to work.

"You have to be careful," says a voice behind him.

John pushes the bag behind him and turns around.

A short, plump woman almost twice his age leans on the railing a few steps away. She is breathing laboriously. A raincoat hangs draped over her brown coat.

She peers at John from under the brim of her hat. "I'm sorry if I startled you," she says. "It's the snow. One can't hear a thing. Not cars, not people, nothing. Everything's so quiet."

"You're quite right," John says and smiles at her.

The woman squints and looks at John as he turns back to his bag and pulls the zip halfway shut. When the woman does not move, John slips one hand into the bag and finds one of the knives.

A teenage boy with a large dog on a lead appear at the top of the stairs. The boy descends the stairs, hooting with laughter as the golden retriever bounces down before him, eyes wild and tongue lolling. The boy and his dog flash between John and the woman and disappear in the darkness at the foot of the stairs.

The woman shakes herself. "You take care now," she says. "These stairs are treacherous. It's very easy to fall down." She turns away and continues her climb, one cumbersome step at a time.

"I'll make sure to look after myself." John takes his hand out of the bag and zips it shut. "You have a good evening, now."

When the elderly woman is out of sight, John walks down to the street. In the distance, the light from Abrahamsberg's underground station spills out on the snow. The train that passed John earlier slows down, stops, and opens its doors. Abrahamsberg's station is not shut down.

John runs again, past yellow brick façades, green metal bins and rows of shrubs visible only as carpets of twigs above the snow. The rail crosses Abrahamsberg's central street on a low viaduct. On the other side of the underground rail is one of Stockholm's arterial roads, running parallel with the rails. Hundreds of cars clog the four lanes.

He pauses near a closed shoe shop and studies the station on the other side of the street. Inside the station are three turnstiles: two automatic and one manned. Two guards flank the gates and peer closely at those who pass through. Abrahamsberg is a small suburb; even though it is rush hour, the guards have time to inspect everyone that enters the station.

John scans the area. A fence topped with barbed wire separates the pathway from the rails. A woman's voice from the platform's PA speakers reminds passengers that no trains stop at Brommaplan. The station is the main source of light, but the whirling snow outside is a grey veil that renders people and buildings into dark shapes.

On John's right is a fenced-off building site, distinguishable only as a hazy framework of reinforcement bars and cranes. Between the site and the train platform are trees and bushes. Running between them is a pathway, unlit and covered by deep snow.

John crosses the street to the pathway and continues until he is sure that the shadows hide him. Two chimes from the speakers on the platform announce the imminent arrival of a westbound train. A minute later, the train arrives, drops off a handful of commuters, and continues deeper into the suburbs. People trickle out of the station, all of them shielding their eyes while looking down at their mobile phones. No one walks down the pathway or looks at John.

John finds a stretch where the barbed wire has been cut apart, possibly by some graffiti artist. He waits and listens for the whisper of electricity that precedes the arrival of a train. A few people stand on the other side of the platform. Everyone is looking in the other direction. A camera is mounted to the ceiling over the platform, but it is positioned to cover passengers, not the fence.

John scrambles over the fence, slips just as he balances on its top, and crashes down on the other side. He lies still and makes sure he has not injured himself. No alarms have gone off. The people on the platform are still looking the other way. An arm's length away is the live rail; one touch means instant and ozone-reeking death.

The rail gives off a metallic *ping*. A train is coming.

Crouching, John steps over the live rail, walks up a metal staircase, and enters the platform. Inside the doors where stairs lead down to the ticket control, an old man on a bench frowns at him and turns back to his magazine.

A train arrives thirty seconds later. When the train's doors open, John walks in, finds a seat, and waits for the next stage of the hunt. Soon he will have what he needs. In the meantime, he will rest and regain some of his strength. He must last a little longer.

Slowly, John's eyes close.

Soon his head is rolling with the movement of the train. The car shudders, and his jacket shifts to reveal the notes tucked down his inner pocket.

In the seat next to where John is seated, three young men look at each other. They all wear plain black or green jackets, blue jeans, and trainers.

One of the men, ginger, freckled and wiry, points to his own chest. He mouths *pocket* and glances at John.

His friends, a heavyset man with Mediterranean looks, and a slimmer and taller man with close-cropped black hair, follow the first man's gaze. The three men look at each other and smile. No words are said. None are needed. The plan is already agreed and in motion.

"Next stop," the ginger man whispers. His friends nod in agreement.

In the pale man's pocket, a knife is snapped loose from its sheath.

*

CHAPTER 7

Lena

Lena negotiates the icy road while she fiddles with the stereo to silence a current affairs debate. In the bad reception, the frenzied voices sound like mad wasps trapped in a can.

She turns the radio off, waits a few seconds, turns it on again, and stabs at a button in search of a decent channel. After several tries, a slow growling beat fills the car. A woman's whisper emerges over the deep bass tones. A Friday night dance mix, blissfully free from talking.

She sits back and puts both hands on the steering wheel. Agnes's car is just ahead. Passing through the web of smaller streets alongside the main road is hazardous; many of them are not ploughed. Getting stuck is easy. But in difference to the thousands of cars queuing on the bigger roads, she is still moving. This is a good time to summarize certainties, guesses, and loose ends.

A woman is dead. No immediate witnesses of her death. Her boyfriend, killer or not, is on the run and has bought footage of another man. Someone was present at the scene and disappeared. One body, two missing suspects, and no weapon.

The idea that John is not the offender feels more and more likely, but it is crucial to keep her mind open to new evidence and sudden leads. Latching on to one particular theory too early is risky. It is one of the many reasons why the murder of Sweden's prime minister twenty years earlier never had been solved, or so many claimed.

But she needs to know what is on that film.

Her phone buzzes as she clears a small roundabout. She turns down the music and looks at the screen. It is the prosecutor.

"Lena Franke here."

"This is Lars Rosenberg," the prosecutor says. "You have requested a search warrant?"

Lena goes over the details for the warrant while she watches the tail lights of Agnes's car. After a few minutes, they pass under a viaduct where the underground train crosses the road and starts its climb up to Vällingby. Far away are two hulking office buildings, almost all windows dark. Across the road is a small lake surrounded by thin copses of trees.

She had been here many years ago, at a competition on a shooting range beyond the lake, tucked away behind the sprawling yard of a marina. It had gone well; lack of concentration and technique had been offset by her good eyesight and some luck.

That day had been full of small rushes: the smell of hot cartridges, the gun slamming in her hands, the tight cluster of holes in the paper targets. Press the trigger, open a hole, claim the prize and walk away. Organized and focussed. At a firing range, every shot is neat and clean, small loud textbook procedures.

The real world, she had found later, is anything but tidy.

She runs a hand over her eyes and forces her attention back to her conversation with the prosecutor. "I think that's it," she says.

"Anything else?" Lars asks.

"Not for the moment. I'm – I have to hang up."

Lena ends the call, flings the phone in the passenger seat, and breathes out. The firing range is not close, but she imagines its smells reaching her: oil, fire, friction and attention. Unmoving targets, fluttering and shuddering.

She blinks slowly and stares at the lights ahead. *Eyes on the road. Keep driving. Think of John Andersson. And Molly.*

Focus, damn it.

Farther up the road, Agnes stops at a red light at a new roundabout. On Lena's left are lines of low flats, most windows lit by kitchen lamps, TVs or the azure glow of computer screens. Neon signs point to pizzerias, barbers and flower shops. At the top is the bright red logotype of a local pub. John's home is a few corners away.

Lena and Agnes drive onto a parking lot framed by three interconnected buildings. Four other cars are parked nearby, all of them covered in snow. No sign of recent arrivals. Lena checks the address she has scribbled down on a note.

"Number nine," she says to herself and looks up. "First floor."

She spots the entrance in the corner. Going by the look of the block, there are two flats on each floor, each with two windows facing the parking lot. The two windows on the left on the first floor are dark, and the blinds are pulled down. The windows on the right are lit. She can make out people inside: two adults and two or more children, all with Asian complexions.

John's flat has to be the dark one. On foot, he has not had time to get here, and the snow looks undisturbed. She reaches for her radio.

"This is Franke," she calls. "Petersen and I are outside the home of John Andersson, wanted for questioning in regards to a shooting earlier tonight." When her report is acknowledged, she stuffs her radio in her pocket, braces herself for the wind, and leaves the car.

Shielding her face, Agnes walks up to Lena. "I've called the locksmith," she says. "He should be here any minute. His office is up in Vällingby."

They wait with their shoulders hunched and hands shoved deep in their pockets. The wind builds up strength on the flat meadows around Grimsta and is channelled by the buildings into frosty streams, rocking traffic lights and shaking trees.

At least the air is crisp, all dust and fumes wiped away by the storm. Lena inhales until the cold burns her lungs. Maybe it will help her to concentrate.

"I heard the forecast," Agnes says. Her voice is muffled; only her eyes and nose are visible over her scarf. "There's more snow on the way. Stronger winds, too." She rubs her gloves together and looks at Lena. "Can I tell you something?"

Lena's throat tightens. They have worked together far too long for tentative questions like this. Besides, Agnes usually handles conversations the same way pointer dogs treat quarry. Straight to the core or the crux, without pause or reluctance. This hesitation is a bad sign. Then again, it was a matter of time before Agnes heard the stories.

"I'm listening." Lena forces her voice to stay steady. "It's a personal question, I suppose?"

"Not really a question, as such." A smile flashes on Agnes's face. "It's something I've been wanting to say for some time."

"Uh-oh." Lena manages a bravado smile while she prepares her usual explanation.

"I'm glad they teamed us up."

"What?" Lena breathes out and looks at Agnes in surprise. That was not what she expected.

"I've learned so much from you during these months," Agnes continues. "And I'm still learning. You're a good mentor. I was nervous when I came to the force, because I know what some officers think of being burdened with a graduate. But you don't look down on me. You're professional and kind."

"I'm – of course I don't look down on you."

Lena stares at the parked cars and wonders what to say. The compliments shot straight past her guard. In truth, Agnes is the one who is professional, while Lena is a paranoid, absent-minded wreck in the making.

"As far as I'm concerned," Lena says at last, "you're as good as anyone else." She winces. "I meant that as a compliment. I'm no good at praising. It's one of the many reasons people say I'm prickly."

"They said that about me too," Agnes says.

"You can't be serious."

"I had a nickname back at the police college."

"Really?"

"Little Miss Tetchy."

Lena scoffs. "Not very original." She blinks as a snowflake finds its way into her eye.

"I argued with a lecturer once. That's all it took. He started using the name, and it stuck."

"That's ridiculous." Lena takes a deep breath. "You must've heard some of the monikers they have for me."

"A few," Agnes admits. "But I don't listen to what they say. People talk. In any case, what I've heard doesn't matter."

"Tell me what you've heard," she says. "I don't care much, but it's good to stamp out lies."

"As I said, rumours don't matter." Agnes looks away. "Not at all. Your private life is no one else's business."

Lena pauses. She expected Agnes to look wary or at least guarded, but she seems concerned, her eyes intent, searching and wondering.

"What exactly is it that doesn't matter?" Lena asks slowly.

"Whom you live with."

"Come again?" Lena asks. "I'm hopelessly single. That's no secret."

"I mean whom you'd prefer to live with if you weren't single."

"How could—" Lena stops and chuckles. This is new, but not entirely unexpected. "Oh, I see. They say I'm gay?"

"Some do," Agnes confirms. "As you'd expect, usually the nervous ones. Those who have problems with your methods or your hobby."

Lena sighs. Her workouts are a way to hone and regroup her thoughts. Only during a hard session, coasting on the adrenaline surge and her hands tight around the iron bar, can she shed her everyday ghosts and think freely. It seems eighteen months in her basement lifting weights to get some peace of mind has turned her into a threat. And she is working with people who are supposed to shine at guesswork.

"As far as I can tell," Lena says. "I'm straight as a ruler. Or at least an old measuring tape. I'd be lying if I said that I know exactly how I tick. But I haven't been seeing anyone lately. There hasn't been time."

Although time has little to do with her solitude. In the wake of her career is a series of brief and collapsed relationships. More than two years have gone by since her most recent affair. She would love to think that she is not the problem; however the power of self-deception is only so mighty. All her partners had signalled their looming departures with variations on *I know your work is important to you* followed by *but*.

And that had been before she had taken up the weightlifting to keep her sane. Before the sleepless nights, and the memories that came back to her at the worst of times.

"Right." Agnes looks away and smiles into the blizzard. "I understand. I'm sorry."

Lena can tell that Agnes does not believe her; the officer's smile is strained. For some reason, it is also strangely secretive.

"And," Lena adds, "just like you said, it's totally irrelevant. Each to her own. Look, our man is here."

A red van with a large yellow key on its roof drives onto the parking lot. Lena waves, and the car parks close to where they stand. A young man in a red company jacket and a yellow cap steps out and slams the door shut. In his hand is a large toolbox. Young and tired, eager to get home.

Together they trudge through the snow to the block's front door. Lena scans her note, punches in the code, shoves the door open and pauses on the doorstep in surprise. Stairwells usually smell of disinfectants, damp and cold stone; this one is warm and thick with the scent of flowers. She switches on the light and blinks in surprise.

Flowerpots in a multitude of colours stand on every step in the curving stairs. On the first landing are two large plants with large lush green leaves. Lena touches a radiator inside the door and snatches her hand back. It is scorching hot.

Agnes takes off her gloves and looks around. "It's a greenhouse in here."

"Sure is." The locksmith nods and scratches his neck. "Where to?"

"First floor," Lena says.

On the first landing are two doors. One reads *Wau-Pong*, the other *Andersson*. As Lena suspected, it is the flat with the dark windows. No peephole, decorations or special features on the door. Only a sticker reading *No Junk Mail Please*. Agnes rings the doorbell, and a stifled buzz sounds from inside the flat.

Lena flexes her fingers and tries to imagine the inside of the flat. Despite having done dozens of similar searches before, the sense of brutal intrusion is the same every time: they are about to trespass into someone else's territory.

John should not have been able to get here yet, and it would be an idiotic decision to run home, but there is always the possibility that she is wrong. Perhaps he has his gun trained on the door right now, waiting for it to be opened. The locksmith is experienced; he stands away from the door, out of the likely line of fire.

No one opens the door. Agnes rings again while Lena quickly peers through the thin mailbox. No light or movement. She lowers her mouth to the mailbox. "Police," she calls. "Open up."

Still no reaction from inside. She nods to the locksmith, who puts down his toolbox, opens the lid, and takes out an electric lock pick, a black, slim instrument that looks to Lena like a reciprocating saw.

The locksmith gestures at the door. "It's a standard lock. Shouldn't take long to crack."

"Okay," Lena replies, then spins around as the door opposite John's flat opens.

A man in his late thirties leans out. Asian complexion, shaved head, black jeans and football shirt. A boy in diapers clings to one of his legs. Toys are strewn around on the floor behind them. The smell of spicy meat and ginger blends with the scents of the flowers in the stairwell.

"Excuse me," the man says. "Looking for John?" The boy looks up at his father, who ruffles his son's hair.

"We'd like to talk to him," Lena said. "Have you seen him recently?"

The man nods. "This morning."

"Do you know where he went?"

When the man hesitates, Agnes produces her identity card. He looks at it, frowns, then turns to the boy and says something in a language Lena does not understand. When the boy has walked back to the kitchen, he turns back to Lena.

"Is he in trouble?" he asks.

"Please answer the question," Lena says.

The man sighs. "I don't know where he is. He's seeing someone, but I have no idea where she lives. I've met her a few times. Blonde woman, his age. She said hello to me once."

"Do you know John well?"

"Fairly well, yes." The man shrugs. "He keeps to himself, but he's been over for coffee a few times. He's picked up my children from the childcare centre when I've been stuck in queues."

"I see." Lena unzips her jacket; the humid stairwell is making her sweat. "Is there anything you could tell us to help us find John?"

The man looks pained. "Is it about the radiators?"

Lena and Agnes share a glance. "No," Lena says. "But now that you've mentioned them, please tell me about them." She wonders if John deals in stolen goods, or if 'radiators' is slang for something else.

"John tweaked them," the man explains. "For the flowers."

"What?" Lena asks.

"He made them hotter; otherwise the cold would kill the flowers. In summer, he changes them back to normal. They're his hobby. I like them too, and the landlord's okay with them. But I told him he'd get in trouble if he tinkered with the plumbing."

"These are John's flowers?" Lena asks. "All of them?"

The man nods. "He waters them nearly every day. Well, nights. He works late shifts."

"I see," Lena says. "And no, we wouldn't be here because he's tampered with the plumbing."

She hands the man her card and wonders what kind of advertisement agency did night shifts. In her experience, people in that business hung around vodka bars and cafés with menus in Italian.

"Let me know if you see John again," she says, "or if you think of something else that can help us."

"I will." He nods and closes the door.

Lena looks at John's door and at the flowers around her. They had been nursed by a man in love. A man who smiled a lot and looked after his neighbours' kids. Now that man was running without shoes through the snow, gone along with footage of a probable killer.

A murderer whose face perhaps only John knows.

"What do you want to do?" Agnes asks.

"We've got the warrant," Lena says, "so we're taking a look inside. I need to get the bead on John. Find some clue as to where he is, what he'll do, and who he is."

Or was, she adds quietly to herself.

The lock clicks open.

"Done," the locksmith says. "All yours."

*

CHAPTER 8

The other John

Snow on the rails is slowing the train to a crawl, making the two-minute journey take more than ten. Next stop is Stora Mossen, near a high school, a handful of flats, and a busy roundabout.

The three men exchange glances again: this is the ideal location. It is unlikely that there will be any security staff, and outside the station are dozens of unlit bicycle paths, parkways and paths. They can clear the stairs or jump the fence if they end up chased. After that, the storm will hide them.

When the speakers announce the upcoming station, John does not stir. After a few seconds, the train stops and opens the doors, venting the warm air into the night.

The men spring into action.

Their routine is rehearsed to perfection. Each man knows his role. The outcome is inevitable and unconditional; only the tools and the size of the targets change. The rush, though, is always fresh, always worth the risk.

The largest of the three men stands up and bars the passage between the groups of seats. At the end of the train car, there is only one way to guard, so he opens his jacket to block the view and pretends to search a pocket. No one looks at him or his friends. Everyone is lost in his or her phone, bent over a free newspaper, or drifting off to sleep.

The ginger man and his tall comrade move in on John, low and fast.

Pinning John's arm to the wall with his knee, the ginger man flashes his knife in John's face and then holds it to John's stomach. Its tip pokes a hole in John's shirt. The other man grabs John's jacket, flips it open and reaches for the wad of notes.

"Don't fucking move," the ginger man hisses. His voice is quiet and confident.

"Stop." John's eyes open, and he clutches his money.

"What the fuck?" The ginger man who holds the knife stares at John. "Let go, or I'll gut you. I'll fucking do it." He presses the knife deeper. "Let go of the cash, you fuckwit. Are you slow?"

Unbeknownst to each other, the three men share a collective thought: this is not right. They have skidded off the road of routine and swerved out into the dark woods.

"Hurry up," hisses the man who is blocking the corridor.

"Don't," John says. "You can't. Not yet." He holds on to his jacket while the ginger man tries to dislodge John's hand.

"What the fuck's wrong with you?" the ginger man growls. "Do you have a death wish? Do you *want* me to fuck you up?"

"I don't want to die," John answers, "but I need the money."

"This is bullshit," the black-haired man spits. "Cut him. Slice him open. *Come on.*"

The ginger man hesitates. "Man, I don't know. They've got cameras in here–"

"His fingers," the dark man says. "Cut them off."

"*Will you get a fucking move on?*" The man who bars the corridor slams his hand into the wall in frustration. "The doors are closing."

"Hold them open," shouts the dark-haired man. There is no longer any point in trying to be discreet; this has already gone all kinds of wrong.

He snatches the knife from the ginger man and slashes at John's hand once, twice. The two gashes make a deep cross on John's hand. Blood jets away and paints patterns on clothes and seats.

John still holds on to the money. He tilts his head and studies the dark-haired man's eyes, as if measuring him up.

The ginger man shakes his head and pulls at his friend. "He's stoned," he screams. "Fuck him. Let's go."

The train car shakes as the doors begin to close, but the man on lookout moves between them and holds them open. "Fucking hell," he moans. "*Let's go.*"

The dark-haired man stabs at John's hand again, but a moment before the blade hits, John lets go of his jacket and flings it sideways, making the knife go through empty air.

"What the—" The attacker loses his balance, stumbles backwards and falls down on his back.

The car shakes again. Its speakers rasp, and the voice of the irritated driver booms throughout the train as she instructs all passengers to move away from the doors. Startled shouts come from farther down the car; people stand up and back away from the fight.

The large man and his ginger friend look at each other. They are at a breaking point: Their prey is irrational, and there is no time left. It is a matter of moments before someone calls the police.

As one, the two men run out and away, fleeing the train and the easy-hit-turned-disaster. The doors shut, and the train leaves the platform.

Left behind inside the train, the man with the knife is on his back. Blood seeps through his clothes; he can feel its warmth against his skin. His jacket is ruined. His pants are stained beyond salvation. And he is alone, abandoned by his so-called mates.

But he has his knife, and in his other hand is the money, finally torn away from John's grip. Two fistfuls of power and possibilities. Now only to disable the crazed junkie and escape.

Teeth clenched, he wriggles out of John's hold, gets up onto his knees, and strikes again, aiming for the centre of John's abdomen. For a moment, it seems as if his aim is true, then John's foot shoots up and smacks into the man's groin.

Red suns burst in the dark-haired man's head. He sucks in air with a keening sound as nausea explodes in him, starting in his crotch and welling out into his limbs. All strength leaves him within the space of a second.

He falls onto his back between the groups of seats, in full view of the surveillance cameras. Only sheer pain makes him hold on to the knife and the money. When he manages to open his eyes, he stares down the length of another knife.

John holds the point of his knife millimetres from the man's face. Blood oozes between John's clenched fingers, and he uses both hands to keep the knife steady.

The man is bewildered but still furious. "Man, you're–"

John stamps hard on the man's arm until the man's knife clatters to the floor.

"Drop the money," John says when his opponent has stopped screaming.

"You're screwed," the dark-haired man wheezes and laughs hysterically. "When the train stops, I'm gone, and I'm keeping the money. *You're* the one holding the knife, you fucking idiot." He nods at the ceiling, implying the hidden CCTV camera.

For a long moment, John looks at the camera behind its protective plastic cover.

"That's right," the man says and grins. "What do you think they'll see? You with a knife. It's called armed assault. Now back the fuck away."

John turns back to the man and moves the point of his knife to the man's nostril, then pushes the knife up the man's nose a full three centimetres. Before the man has time to scream, John rips the knife up and away, slicing open the entire length of the man's nose.

Blood rises like a fine mist and rains over the man's face, clogging his eyes and flooding his mouth. The man gives up a panicked, gurgling shriek. John slides the tip of the knife into the man's other nostril and holds it there.

Searching the man's pockets, John finds a mobile phone in chrome and a leather wallet. He holds each item in front of the man's wild eyes, making sure the man understands the implications.

I have your name. I have your number. I have your friends' numbers.

"I repeat," John says, "let go of my money."

Howling in pain, the dark-haired man clings to the bloodied stack of notes as if they were a rope that could pull him out of his terror.

John leans closer until his lips touch the man's ear, and while the train slows down, he describes what he will do with the knife unless the man releases the money. The man wails, and the money falls from his shaking hand.

Finally, the train stops. John takes the money, the phone and the wallet, and runs out.

The other passengers, who had retreated to the other end of the car, rush out and back away from John. Parents carrying their children jog towards the exits. Men and women shout at their phones to make themselves heard over the wind and those around them: *Yes, a fight. On the train. I think someone's dead.*

John looks along the tracks. They continue onto a soaring bridge that connects the suburbs with the city. He hefts his bag, jumps down onto the tracks, and steps over the live rail to reach the maintenance walkway wedged between the rail and a thirty-metre drop down to the frozen strait. Two fences on each side provide a handhold.

John enters the walkway and runs up on the bridge, towards the city.

*

CHAPTER 9

John Andersson

To John's surprise, he's lying on a large field.

A weak, ambient light bathes him in the pale glow of a moonlit night. What he thought was dirt beneath him turns out to be ice, smooth and hard, partially covered by shallow droves of snow and filled with large shadows.

Farther away is a wall, dark and forbidding, like a vertical mountainside draped in a silky gloom. The wall curves away left and right.

The bitter cold stings his skin. His clothes are nowhere in sight. This fierce cold should render him immobile, yet for some reason he can still think, even move. Although for how long is anyone's guess.

I'm dreaming, he thinks, but knows he isn't.

This icy ground, the snow on his arms and the howling wind are all real. So are his memories of what transpired a few minutes ago.

Molly. She's dead. Murdered.

Grief fills him like acid, sloshing around inside him.

Throughout his life, he tried to capture ideas in oil, acrylics and gouache. Day after day, hour upon hour when he wasn't working or sleeping, attempting to catch beauty, despair or dedication in the two-dimensional cage of a canvas. Sometimes he imagined reaching a point when he'd be able to capture any sensation.

He was wrong. This pain defies any attempt of representation. It's not a feeling or an experience, but a colossal weight, smothering, crushing, and impossible to shrug off. Were it not for the urgency that burns in his mind, he would lie down and cease to be.

It's what he's meant to do. His feeble struggle is an anomaly. He must fight the temptation to give in.

John pushes himself up to stand on his knees. He's lost and confused, unprotected and isolated, and he may have minutes left before the cold or fear claims him.

But he's not dead.

Not yet.

*

CHAPTER 10

Lena

The locksmith tucks away his tools with practised speed and wipes sweat from his face. Lena hands him a card for him to forward to his manager. He takes it, nods, heads down the stairs and out into the blizzard.

Lena moves to the side of the door and motions for Agnes to be ready to open it, then reaches for the small torch in her belt clip. The torch is shorter and not much thicker than her thumb, but it is enough to illuminate most rooms.

She runs her tongue over her teeth, forms her fingers around the grip of her gun, and grits her teeth. Memories spring to her mind quicker than she can push them away.

Sirens, shouts, and dark, fleshy holes. The stink of sanitizers.

Amplified pleas, screamed accusations, crying children.

The gun, jolting like an animal in her hands.

Flashes of bright orange.

"Lena?" Agnes looks at her and frowns. "Are you all right?"

"Wait," Lena says. "I thought I heard something."

She hates lying, and she knows she does not do it well, but Agnes does not look suspicious. Then she does hear a sound from inside the flat: two rapid thuds, muted but still distinct. They sound like footsteps. Agnes's eyes widen.

"I'll call for backup," Agnes says and reaches for her radio.

"No." Lena shakes her head. "We can't wait. He might jump through a window, and we won't spot him in this weather."

So much for her hopes that John would not be around. It could be a friend, but that was unlikely. She pulls the pistol free from its holster and glances down at the weapon. Its weight outside the shooting range always surprises her.

A colleague had once told her he thought of his weapon as an extension of his hand. Another officer had claimed his gun felt like a necessary evil, an unreliable lump of steel and plastic, prone to breaking down at the worst of times.

Lena disagrees with those views. To her, a gun is a dangerous catalyst, amplifying whispers to roars. The sensation makes itself known right at that moment: submerged beneath concentration and schedules, the honey-sweet urge stirs and reaches out, loosening the reins on her conscience.

"Now," Lena says.

Agnes nods and opens the door.

Lena's torch reveals a cramped hall, part of a small kitchen on her right, and a larger room ahead. She holds her gun parallel to the beam of light. Agnes switches on her torch, forcing the shadows back.

There is no sound or movement, but the noise came from inside these rooms. She peers at the silhouettes of furniture, the walls, the shadows. Someone is hiding in there.

"Police," Lena calls out. "We're coming in. Put your hands on your head and stay still." She breathes out and swallows. The air is thick with the scent of oil and chemicals.

Once they move past the doorway, they can see most of the flat. Hall, kitchen, a tiny bathroom and a single living room. The small kitchen allows for only one person at a time. The cupboards are the size of bar fridges. No hiding spaces in there.

The bathroom door is wide open. She takes a quick step inside and checks the bathtub. Empty. Only one room remains.

Lena and Agnes turn to the living room and pause in the doorway.

There is no one in the room, but its walls are covered with paintings. Most are the size of regular paper, some are several square metres, others are small as postcards. Stacks of canvases and cardboards lean against the wall and lay in knee-high piles. Drawings and sketches are heaped around the floor. Along the right-hand wall is a table littered with brushes, tubes of oil colour and bottles of acrylic paint. Wooden rulers and sharpened charcoal sticks jut out from teacups in different sizes.

Some of the paintings portray people, alone or in groups, wandering among looming cityscapes or huddled in open fields and mountain ranges under wide skies. Others depict open landscapes, horses, mansions and gardens. Many of the smaller paintings are detailed renderings of small objects: flowers and lush trees, intricate symbols and trinkets, candlestick holders and ornate lamps. Art is not Lena's strong point, but many of the paintings look photorealistic. She assumes John made them.

"Huh," Lena says and edges into the room. She must have imagined the noise.

On the opposite wall is a window, its drawn blinds turned into a glowing grey square by the street lights outside. Below the window is a bed covered partially by a blanket. Next to the bed is a three-way spotlight floor lamp, and beside that two IKEA sideboards.

On Lena's right is an easel with a large unpainted canvas. No TV, sofa, or couch. A bedside alarm clock blinks midnight in bright red to the soundtrack of its radio spitting soft static. She sweeps her light over the cluttered walls; the light switch has to be somewhere.

The sheets move.

Lena whips her torch back to the bed. Something under the blanket. Too small for a man. A child, perhaps. An infant.

Before Lena has more time to reflect on what is hiding in the bed, Agnes walks across the room and lifts the corner of the blanket. A cat peeks out, hisses and shows off its tiny fangs before retreating deeper under the blanket.

Lena exhales. "There's our bump in the dark," she says. "Let's get some light in here." For the second time that day, she longs to be back in the blizzard; her hands are so clammy she can barely hold on to her pistol.

Agnes finds a dimmer control behind an easel. As soft light fills the room, she holsters her gun and unzips her jacket. "Are you looking for something specific?" she asks.

"Anything that might point to where he is." Lena brushes a tangle of hair from her face. Someday soon, she promises herself, she will get a navy cut. "Notebooks, postcards, envelopes with different addresses."

"Would he hide in a place where we're bound to look?"

"Possibly," Lena says. "He's scared, and he's cold. I wonder why the clock is reset?" The noise of static is grating on her concentration, so she walks over to the bedside clock and turns the power off.

"Maybe there's been a blackout?" Agnes suggests.

Lena nods absently and leans close to some of the smaller paintings to study them. A young woman carrying a large key and walking down a dark tunnel. An open silver locket holding a tuft of blond hair. Something that looks like a black Rubik's Cube. All three paintings are as small as pocketbooks and so meticulously painted they look almost lifelike.

"He's good," Lena says quietly.

"What?" Agnes looks up from the table.

"At painting. He knows this stuff."

"He works for an advertisement company. Maybe it's part of his job."

Lena grimaces. "Perhaps."

"But you don't think so."

"How often do you see paintings in ads?" Lena asks.

"Good point."

"Work or hobby, this place is absolutely crammed." Lena gestures at the room. "Let's have a look around. I'll call the animal welfare people about the cat."

Agnes nods, glances down, and frowns momentarily before she turns to search the room. Lena looks down and realizes she is still holding her gun. She shoves the weapon back in its holster, snaps the security strap in place, and investigates the desk.

She soon finds an order in the chaos. The mess is the kind of untidiness that stems from inspiration, not disinterest in cleaning: a continual wake of disorder behind someone with an idea in sight. Or perhaps she sees patterns because she wants them to be there.

It would not be the first time. Shivering, she thinks of her own chaotic flat.

Her phone rings. The office. She takes the call.

"Franke."

"This is Wiknell from the information department. I have the mobile phone records you requested. They're for a man called John Andersson."

"Go on." Lena parts the blinds and peers at the parking lot. No one there.

"There's only one company, but lots of matching calls. I'll email the list."

"Anything that stands out?"

"Not really. Most calls were made evenings, all within the past three months."

"When's the latest call?"

"This afternoon, just after two o'clock."

"Right." She looks at a painting of clouded sky, layer upon layer of deep grey and blue. "I've got to go."

She ends the call, turns to Agnes and briefs her. As Agnes scribbles in her small leather-bound notebook, Lena watches the woman's concentrated face and wonders if Agnes takes notes when watching the morning weather forecast.

Once Agnes is done, she returns to checking the drawers. "Clothes and paints," she calls over her shoulder to Lena. "Some papers, mostly bills. Blue overalls." Agnes holds them close to her face. "Smells funny. Paint, I think."

Agnes turns to searching the kitchen while Lena gets down on one knee and looks under the table.

Underneath the tabletop is a pet cage with a tattered toy mouse stuck through the fenced door. Next to the cage are rows of paint bottles, spray cans, a folded rug, and two large plastic bottles of solvent.

Behind the bottles is a phone cord nailed along the skirting board. She follows the cord to the plug and finds a plain red telephone behind an empty canvas.

"I found the phone," Lena says, "but there's no modem." She hears Agnes rummaging through cupboards, lifting plates and moving packets around.

"He might use a neighbour's connection," Agnes replies from the kitchen. "Or a mobile phone. Useful if you're doing something illegal. Hard to trace."

Agnes comes back from the kitchen and shakes her head. "Nothing in there. What do you want to do now?"

Lena runs her thumb along the edge of the canvas on the easel. "We'll go back to the station. I'll brief Gren, and I'll make sure the warrant's been forwarded to the other stations. And to the underground security companies, too." Looking at the canvas, she notices the motif and takes a step back.

"I'll be damned," she says under her breath. "Look at this." She takes a step back to let Agnes get a better view.

The portrait depicts a woman in a deep green dress. Sitting next to a blossoming tree on a hill, she looks wistful and at peace, her face turned to a setting sun outside the frame. Her hands are resting in the tall billowing grass around the base of the tree.

In the background are mountain tops, grey waves blending with an equally ashen sky. Some way away from the tree, the ground seems to end, as if the grass hides a vertical cliff. The scene is both vast and detailed.

"It's her," Agnes says quietly, "isn't it?"

"I think so," Lena replies.

She saw the same face less than an hour before, though then it was only a shell, void of anything resembling life. In this painting, caught in thick oil and precise brushstrokes, Molly looks fully alive. The grass appears to wait for a gust of wind to caress it. She cannot make out the woman's expression, but she seems to be smiling.

Lena's radio beeps. She pulls back from the canvas and answers. "Franke here."

"This is Nordström from patrol one. We've just completed a third sweep of the area."

"Any sign of John Andersson?"

"No, but he's definitely out there. People have seen him down by the station. Although the station's security is absolutely sure that he hasn't passed through the turnstiles. We also have a confirmed sighting from the owner of a corner shop near the crime scene, but the man said you've already talked to him. And there are some others who say they've seen him, too."

"Who?"

"A few people around the station. Commuters and retail staff. One man saw John use a nearby cash machine. The most definite statement is by a woman who works at the gas station near the roundabout."

"I think I know which gas station you mean. What did she say?"

"John bought shoes and a lot of chocolate bars. The woman said he looked at her in a creepy way. Not dirty, but weird."

"Do they have any cameras?" Lena asks.

"Yes, but they don't record anything."

Lena looks at the ceiling, closes her eyes, and exhales hard in frustration.

"So John didn't catch a train," she says, summing it up to herself. "Instead he bought shoes, withdrew money, and went back to the scene to buy a computer."

"It seems so. But there's another thing."

The coil of worry in Lena's stomach stirs. "Go on."

"There's a strong possibility that another man ran from the flat. Or one more, that is. Not just John Andersson."

"Proceed." Lena opens her eyes. She had been right: this was not a case of a boyfriend gone off the rails. It was more complicated and could soon become far worse.

"Many disagreed on the victim's neighbour's description of how John was dressed. We compared our notes, and like I said, it's likely that there's another man involved. He wore a grey sweater, had dark hair and was unshaved. Black trainers and blue trousers. Maybe a bag or a backpack. Some witnesses say the first suspect also had a bag. It's confusing, I know."

"How sure are you that the second man is part of this?" Lena asks. "Have people seen him near the victim's flat?"

"Yes. A woman walking her baby even saw him leave the building. Running as if he were on fire, she said."

"In the same direction as John Andersson."

"Correct."

"Any trace of him?" Lena looks at Agnes, who is talking to someone on her own radio.

"He got to the train station and then disappeared. Just like John, really. He could've made it onto a train, for all we know. Security don't remember seeing him."

"Get the footage from the station," Lena says. "We know roughly when he was there."

"We'll try."

"Don't try, just – look, we need that fucking image, understood? I'm going to the station now. Out."

Lena thrusts her radio back into her pocket before she loses her temper completely. She can tell by a glance at Agnes's face that Agnes has bad news.

"What?" Lena asks.

"There's been an assault on the underground," Agnes says. "At Alvik. That's only three stops from Abrahamsberg."

"What happened?"

"Someone attacked a passenger with a knife."

"That doesn't have to be related to John," Lena says. "Molly's murderer has a gun."

"It's unclear what happened, but the description of one of the men sounds vaguely like John."

"Oh." Lena runs her hands through her hair and tries to think. Neither man would want to get into a fight; both of them would hope to stay unnoticed, out of sight and mind. "Is anyone in custody?"

Agnes shakes her head. "So far, only the underground security is on the scene, but two police patrols are on their way. Do you want to go there?"

Still holding her hair back, Lena sighs. She wants to run to her car, speed to the scene, and get to the bottom of what is going on. At the same time, she needs to ensure they get the footage of the mysterious second man. The tangled leads pull and spin her in different directions. And instead of following up on either lead, she must run a briefing at the police headquarters.

"We're going back to the station," Lena says and walks out of the room.

Agnes pockets her notepad and follows Lena out into the stairwell. "I overheard some of what you said on the radio," she says. "Are we looking for the wrong man?"

"I don't know. At any rate, we have two suspects: John, and the man who ran from the flat just before him."

They seal the door with a strip of crime scene tape, and leave the humid stairwell for the biting winter night. Moments later, Lena's car swerves out onto the road. Agnes's car follows close behind.

Agnes calls just as Lena clears the roundabout.

"Could the other man have been someone she saw on the side?" Agnes asks.

"I've thought about it," Lena admits and winces as a cloud of snow eclipses her sight of the road. "But do you remember the wine glasses and the candle in the kitchen?"

"Sure."

"If I were cheating on my partner, I wouldn't do so next to a window. She planned to eat with John. Only someone else came knocking first."

She stares down the tunnel of churning snow, checks her speedometer, and forces herself to slow down. Crashing now would see her lose hours, and she was already too far behind her quarry.

"Then what's John doing?" she asks. "Why is he running?"

The traffic lights ahead turn yellow, and Lena shoots across the intersection just as the lights turn red.

"I'm not so sure he's running," Lena says. "I'm starting to think he's doing the opposite. The shopkeeper near Molly's place believes the same."

"Oh." Agnes is silent for a few seconds. "I see. What do we do now?"

"I need to think. We'll talk at the station."

*

CHAPTER 11

John Andersson

John stays conscious despite the ferocious cold.

He recalls the words of the ghost who'd taunted him back in Molly's flat. It'd been full of vicious intent, but the creature who stole Molly's face had not been after him.

There'd been someone else it wanted to snare. A woman called Lena Franke, who was on her way to Molly's home. For some reason, the ghost-like entity hates her.

The kernel of anger inside him blooms. Weak and desperate, he caved in to the ghost's promises of revenge and abandoned his own flesh. There'd been a pang of emptiness followed by a seemingly endless fall. Then he'd slept, until he woke up.

But he feels *too* awake. This isn't a place for reflection or coherent thought. Here, one is meant to cower and suffer, mutely and obediently, in a state of continual stricken dread.

Fighting against the impulse to surrender is an abnormality. He's pushing against an unseen current. Somehow, this worries him as much as the cold.

Stranger still, not all of him departed his body. If he's right, the blind rage, all the thoughtless bloodlust he felt at seeing Molly dead stayed behind, like the captain of a soulless ship with only hate in its hold. That kind of fury is capable of anything.

The ghost's plan becomes clear to him: his body is bait.

It wanted to unleash John's unflinching, uncaring husk on the streets, where it can cause any amount of damage. That's how the phantom expects to catch its prey.

Somewhere beyond this outlandish dungeon, there'll be more suffering and violence, all because of his naivety.

He has traded his pain for a prison.
Anger swells up, thawing his limbs, clearing his mind.
I'm not dead yet.

*

CHAPTER 12

The other John

The steam of John's breaths trail behind him as he runs over the bridge.

Far below is the strait, frozen solid for weeks, a wrinkled field covered by wisps of snow sailing over the dunes like clouds. Two trains pass, but no passengers look at him except a boy who presses his face against the window. A police car heading in the other direction swishes past, its sirens baying. In front of him is Stockholm city, a glittering mound behind the curtain of snow.

He passes the crest of the bridge and continues down. Far ahead at the next station are the tail lights of a train. Just before the station, the bridge touches land, and the railing is flanked by fences and barbed wire. Near the station is a door in the fence that leads out to a street.

He slows down and walks up to the door. It is locked with a large padlock shielded from rain by a cover of brushed steel. John lowers his bag to the ground, takes out his keys, selects one and opens the lock. Once outside, he shuts the door and looks around.

Kristineberg, a suburb-cum-part-of-the-city, is a cluster of tall blocks of flats divided by a long park and the underground rail. Most buildings are huddled close together, their forties-era fronts overlooking the strait below. Wedged in between the blocks are rows of streets that run towards a high-rise.

Normally a busy area, tonight there a few in sight. A man pulling a reluctant dog. Farther away, a group of people carrying plastic bags full of clinking bottles. On his left, a couple marching hand in hand towards the station, their heads bent against the wind.

John chooses one of the streets and runs up the incline. In the distance are sirens calling from the depth of the storm. He runs faster, past parties, closed shops, and snowed-in cars, past music, laughter, coughs and cries. He crosses a street, turns a corner and stops, resting with his hands on his knees.

The sirens are coming closer. Around another corner are a few concrete steps that lead down to a brown metal door leading to a windowless basement. A sign on the door reads *Argenti Advertising*.

John unlocks the door with his keys, shuts it behind him, and locks it again. Strip lights splutter in the ceiling and light up the room.

The basement holds racks with leftover posters, shelves stacked with cans of glue, boxes full of solvents, rollers, sticky tape, cutters, and a pair of large halogen torches. On his left is the door to a small bathroom. In a corner stand three aluminium ladders.

Along a wall, jackets and caps are draped over a row of hooks. Facing him is a large cracked mirror. In another corner are piles of blue overalls. Green plastic bins brim with cigarette packets and polystyrene cups. Unwashed coffee cups line a metal sink next to a bench with an old filter coffee brewer. A rusted bicycle leans against one wall.

In a corner is a desk teeming with Post-it notes, cheap pens, worn folders and phone books. Next to the desk are a grey office chair and a double-door metal cabinet locked by a small padlock. John chooses a key from his key ring and opens the lock.

The cabinet is packed with equipment. On the lower shelves, toolboxes and batteries stand side by side between rows of headlights for helmets and walkie-talkies. On the top shelf, next to a tangle of computer cables, is an inkjet printer.

John puts the printer on the desk, sweeps away a layer of dust, and plugs in the power cord. He turns the printer on and places a stack of schedules upside down in the paper tray. The printer hums and whirrs and stops. A red light blinks on its front.

He rummages among the cables, selects one and connects it to the printer. He takes out the laptop and, after a few tries, connects the other end of the cable to the computer and switches it on.

When the computer has booted up, he sits down on the chair and browses the files on its hard drive.

After nearly twenty minutes, he pauses at an image of a running man who is facing the camera. The image is small, but the quality is good. A lean, pale man, perhaps thirty years old. His face is a mask of stress. Thick stubble, dark hair, blue eyes. In his right ear is a small ring. John prints the image and puts it on the desk.

There is a knock on the door.

John slips one of the images into a plastic folder and puts the folder in his bag.

Another knock, this time long and insistent.

He rises from the chair, takes one of the knives from his bag, stands next to the door, and flicks the light switch. Darkness fills the room.

A key rasps in the door's lock, and the door swings open. Pale street lights illuminate the snowflakes blown inside. Hesitantly, a man steps into the room and stamps hard on the floor to shake the snow off his boots.

"Anyone here?" the man asks as he fiddles with a dark cylinder in his hand.

Standing at an angle behind the man, John moves forward with the knife held low, but his planned strike misses as the beam of a flashlight explodes in his face.

The man who has entered staggers backwards with a choked scream. John trips over a toolbox and slams back-first into the ladders, which topple and fall down around him with piercing bangs.

As John pushes the ladders away and rises, the strip lights come back on.

"John?" The man with the torch leans against the opposite wall. "It's me, Nils. I almost had a heart attack, for God's sake. Didn't you recognize me?"

"I thought someone was trying to break in," John says. "I'm so sorry. Are you all right?"

"You nearly scared me to death," Nils says and laughs nervously. "Why weren't the lights on?"

"I wanted to hide. I guess I panicked a little." John makes a sheepish grimace and shrugs.

"You're paranoid, mate." Nils peers at John. "Actually, you look terrible. Have you slept at all lately? And is that blood on your face?"

"It's gouache," John says. "I've been painting."

"What about that?" Nils points at the gash on John's hand.

"I slipped with a knife back home. It looks much worse than it is. I'm going to clean it up in a bit."

"If you say so," Nils says, sounding unconvinced. "Are you working tonight? I thought you were off to see your girlfriend."

"I'll see her later. There's something I need to fix first."

"Well, lucky you." Nils shakes his head. "I've got shifts the whole weekend, and the tunnels are fucking freezing. I'm just going to grab a few batteries, then I'm off. As soon as I get my breath back," he adds with a forced laugh.

Nils sits down in the office chair with a heavy thump and points at the computer. "Is that yours?"

John nods. "I'm printing a birthday card for my girlfriend."

"On this?" Nils taps the printer. "I'm surprised it works. It's as old as my son." A ringtone beeps from his pocket. He checks the screen and rolls his eyes.

"It's the boss," he says. "Probably thinks I'm in a pub." Sighing, he takes the call.

John turns away and pretends to examine his damaged jacket while he watches Nils in the mirror.

"No, I'm at Kristineberg," Nils says to the person on the other end of the conversation. "My torch gave up. I'll be at the site in fifteen minutes. What?" He frowns and presses his phone to his ear. "Yes, I have. Why?"

Behind Nils's back, John takes a step closer to Nils.

"Oh," Nils says. He scratches at his neck and swallows. "Look, can I call you back in a few minutes? The reception's bad."

Slowly, John crouches and reaches for a toolbox next to his feet.

*

CHAPTER 13

Lena

Lena scoops up water from the sink, splashes it over her face and gasps; the water is chilled from travelling through near-frozen pipes. She's alone in the bathroom. Her only company is the odour of disinfectants, the humming pipes, and the wind rattling windows coated with frost.

She looks up at her reflection in the mirror. Her eyes are bloodshot, her skin pasty. Her thoughts are constantly derailed by flashbacks bobbing to the surface of her consciousness. Molly's flat, John's paintings, the shopkeeper's concerned look. The wine glasses and the burning candle. Forgetting to put away her gun.

She has to find these men. Before she cracks, she will catch a killer and stop another man from becoming one. The missions will be the glue that keeps her together, permanently or merely a little longer. *Please, let it be so.*

The reports from the underground station at Alvik have complicated an already tangled mess. A knife fight, a bloodied train car, and more confused statements. On the plus side were definite sightings of John, but he disappeared again, most likely running over the bridge and into the city.

She looks at her mobile phone. Twenty past eight. Agnes and Gren will be waiting for her to run the briefing. Shaking her head, she grabs her notes and leaves the bathroom.

The seventies still cling to the police headquarters' veneer doors and carpeted floors. Most walls are painted an immaculate non-colour, as if the painter had been unable to choose between yellow and orange and settled for a compromise that defies words. Over time, grey linoleum had replaced some of the carpets, large maps of the city had given way to LCD screens, and the *taptaptap* of typewriters had changed to the soft plastic whisper of keyboards.

But the past lingers like a lecturing spirit: *work harder, act faster, be smarter.* Forty years of hard thought, night shifts, and desperate puzzling left marks that faded slowly. The less time she has to spend in the oppressive corridors, the better.

She walks past rooms filled with discussions, ringing phones, radio calls and news broadcasts. Pausing at a vending machine outside the room, she chooses between two varieties of sandwiches she does not want, picks the cheapest, and enters the meeting room.

A dozen officers sit around a rectangular table, their faces cast in blue and white by a ceiling-mounted projector. On a wall are flickering images of John's driver's licence photo and a dot-point list of facts. Three small windows frame the night outside. The room smells of strong coffee and hot plastic. Everyone is silent.

Gren stands at the far back, a white folder in hand, his face in deep shadow. Agnes is waiting just inside the door.

Lena is thankful for the half-gloom as everyone turns to look at her; the spotlight is not her favourite location. Someone must coordinate and sum up the ongoing investigation, but she would rather get back to work.

"Any news before we start?" Lena asks the room.

Gren clears his throat and shakes his head. "Nothing since you came back."

"Right." Lena walks to the end of the table. As she passes the water cooler, she reaches out to turn it off, but someone has already done so.

Agnes catches Lena's eye and nods once, almost imperceptibly.

Frowning, Lena winces in the light from the projector. She tries to remember if she has ever told Agnes that she hates the sound the water cooler makes, but she is sure she never has.

Lena clears her throat. "As you all know by now, we're looking for two men. The person for whom we put out the first warrant is John Peter Andersson."

She points to the wall behind her where an image of John is projected. "He's forty-two years old and lives in Grimsta, a small suburb west of the city. Unmarried, no criminal record. His employer is a company called Argenti Advertising. We've left a message with their manager and asked him to report back if he hears from John."

"Does he have any family?" an officer asks.

"None living," Lena answers. "His parents have passed away. No siblings."

She changes the image. "This is a copy of the attendance record at John's high school," she continues. "It seems John went to counselling, but the counsellor's journals have been archived, so I have nothing that explains why he went there. Seeing a counsellor hardly makes John an exception, but I still want to know why he did."

"I'm quite sure those records still exist," Gren says. "They're probably kept in some department. Almost definitely as actual papers, although we should be able to get hold of them quickly if the right office is staffed."

"See if you can get them," Lena says to Agnes, who makes a note on her phone.

"What was John's relation to the victim?" Gren asks.

"I'm getting there." Lena sifts through her notes. "John's believed to have been the victim's partner for some time. We initially thought he was involved in the murder, but there's nothing specific that ties him to it. I take it we haven't found the weapon yet?" She looks up at an officer, who shakes his head.

"We have prints from John," Lena continues, "and the victim. I requested another sweep, and the lab's working on some partial prints they've found."

Lena walks over to the laptop that controls the projector, taps with her finger on the screen, and waits for the software to load. She resists the urge to shake the slow computer. Every second that passes is another moment for John to go deeper or run farther. Or closer.

When a map replaces the projected photo on the wall, Lena zooms in on the western suburbs.

"John has done a number of unusual moves since he was sighted at the scene," she says. "Soon after the murder, he withdrew money from a cash machine at Brommaplan." She points at coloured areas and dotted lines that illustrate John's supposed route. "He left his shoes behind in the flat, probably to avoid leaving tracks. His car was parked outside. He probably realised that he wouldn't have made it far in the blizzard."

"The bank says he got as much cash as he could in a single day," she continues. "He went on to buy shoes and chocolate bars from a gas station at Brommaplan. After that, he returned to the corner shop across the street from the scene and bought a second-hand computer from the owner."

"A computer?" an officer asks.

"Yes," Lena says. "After that, we think he ran to another station, probably Abrahamsberg, where he got on a train. One stop later, he gets in a fight. Again, the statements on what happened are all over the place, but we're pretty sure it's him. One of the involved men matches the description of John, and the timing is right. Three other people were part of the fight too, one of which was wounded. There was blood in the train car. Lots of blood."

"Was it the suspect's?" an officer asks.

"We're not sure. From what I've been told, the surveillance camera filmed John holding the knife and fighting someone else, and apparently it looks as if John is stabbing the other man in his face. I haven't seen the tape, but I will soon. And we're going to match the blood with DNA samples from the shoes."

"After that," Lena continues, "John climbed down onto the tracks and ran over the bridge, towards the city. A passenger on a passing train reported seeing a man on the maintenance track. That's the last sighting we can link to John. What else have we got?"

An officer at the back waves a paper. "I've talked to the tax authorities. His record is spotless, but we found that John owns another property. A house in Drottningholm. It's about fifteen minutes from Brommaplan by car when it isn't rush hour. Or a blizzard."

"Drottningholm?" Another officer turns to look at the paper. "That's an expensive address. And his other place is a tiny flat in Grimsta?"

"The property in Drottningholm isn't big," says the officer who holds the paper. "I looked it up. It's a family property. The land's worth a lot, but the house is old and small."

"I want to have a look," Lena says. "Has any patrol been out there yet?"

The officer shakes his head. "It'd take forever to reach the place," he says. "The ploughs are focussing on busier areas. I'm sure the main road in the district is cleared, but from there, it must be at least an hour's walk. And that's without the snow. Right now, it'd take half the night to trudge there."

Lena pinches the bridge of her nose. "We still need to see it. Gren?"

"I'll put in a request for a helicopter," Gren says. "Don't expect miracles, though. They're needed everywhere right now. And that's those that are cleared for flight in this weather."

"I see," Lena says. "That's not in the direction John was heading, though. Unless he doubled back." Lena pauses. "But I don't think he did."

"Why not?" Gren asks.

Lena looks at him and braces herself. "He's got an agenda," she says. "Food, money, and the computer. It sounds random, but it's not random enough. John Andersson has a plan."

This is the critical part: she needs to let them work through the options and exclude dead ends. If she simply states her idea that John has turned into an avenger, her reputation is going to trigger denial and immediate scepticism. Logic is no match for brute cynicism.

Gren puts his palms together in thought and looks at Lena. "What has the computer got to do with this?" he asks. "Do you know why he bought it?"

"I think so," Lena replies. "It's got footage from the corner shop's surveillance cam."

"You think John is trying to cover his tracks?" Gren asks.

Lena shakes her head. "He risked too much for that by going back."

"Unless he's panicked and isn't thinking clearly."

"Unlikely," Lena replies. "The shopkeeper said John was calm and composed."

Gren gestures with his papers. "Then what's your theory?"

Lena flexes her hands. The projector glares at her like an interrogator's light. "The camera is mounted outside the shop. It caught John, but it might have filmed the other man, too."

Gren pauses, then curses and sits back in his chair. "You think John is going after him," he says after a moment.

"Yes."

A moment passes while the notion sinks in. Heads turn, looks are exchanged. A murmur rises. Someone sighs. An officer curses. Lena holds her trembling hands behind her back to hide them; if she is right, John is heading down a dark path. And she will follow him.

Lena's phone buzzes. When she sees the number from the police's laboratory, she takes the call.

"Tell me you have what I need?" she asks.

"Hello to you too," says a man in a deep, tired voice. The caller is Liam Swan, a young and ambitious forensic who works too late and smokes too much. "I'm calling to let you know we've pieced together a set of prints from the front door of the victim's flat. They were made very recently."

"Were there any matches in the database?" Lena asks.

"Oh yes," Swan says.

Lena suppresses a relieved sigh. At bloody last.

"I'll put you on loudspeaker," she says. "We're in the middle of the brief. I'm hanging up, so call back on this number." She runs through the number twice and ends the call just as the man on the other end starts to speak.

Across the room, Agnes's phone rings. Agnes checks the phone, looks at Lena, mouths a word Lena does not catch, and then slips out of the room.

The speakers beep. Lena pushes a button, and the sound of the lab technician clearing his throat booms in the stifled room. Lena lowers the volume.

"We can hear you," she says. "Proceed."

"As I was about to say before I was cut off, we ran the new set through the scanner and have a positive match. Niklas Petterson, born 1971 in Sala, just outside of Stockholm. He's got a long criminal record. I'll read you a summary. The rest is in the email."

"Go on," Lena says.

"Thirteen cases of assault, nine cases of robbery, two of which were armed. He was taken in for a botched-up burglary when he was fourteen. After that, he's been picked up five times for possession of marijuana and amphetamine. He's done two years for grievous bodily harm, another two for three robberies."

The technician clears his throat. "There's also charges of possession of guns, knives, axes, and tear gas. Explosives, too. He was released from prison a year ago. His current address is unknown, but most previous arrests took place west of the city."

Lena closes her eyes. An armed, brutal psychopath junkie, a furious, devastated man on his tail, and she was hunting both. The confined space of the room is smothering her. She wants to walk away, run out into the storm to breathe, clear her head and think. Her hands shake so much she can barely hold on to her papers.

"Thank you," Gren says to the technician. "That's very valuable."

Lena's eyes shoot open. "Yes, thank you," she echoes. "Let me know if you find anything else."

The call ends with a click. Lena switches the projector off and turns on the lights. Eyes blink in the sudden pearl-white glow.

"I want to search the area around the foot of the bridge," she says. "Starting with Kristineberg and its adjacent stations," she says. "Two patrols, more if any are available."

"Not very likely on Friday night," a man murmurs. Two other officers nod.

Lena wants to throw her papers at all of them. They do not need two patrols; they need twenty, a hundred, a regiment. They should have an army of volunteers. They need to search every square metre of the city until they find John, because there is no telling what he will do next, only that it will be bad.

"We might get lucky," Lena says. "I need one more patrol to start looking around Brommaplan for Niklas. I don't think he's there, but we might find people who know him, or at least about him. Check with the security companies and make sure they get the photos. I'll sort out the new warrant as soon as we're done here."

Lena pauses. "If anyone finds him," she continues, "be careful. That goes for both men. As you heard, Niklas has an ugly history and may have access to weapons. As for John, just be prepared."

Agnes waves at Lena from the doorway.

"Yes?" Lena asks.

"I had a call from John's manager. He's tried to get hold of John but only got to talk to his voicemail, so he called around to his team and started asking questions."

Lena slaps the table with her notes. "But for fuck's sake," she shouts. "That's exactly what I told him not to do. He'll scare John into hiding."

"I think he got worried," Agnes says. "But there's something else."

"What?" Lena feels the adrenaline trickle into her blood. With luck, this is the lead she is hoping for.

"The manager has just talked to one of his staff," Agnes says. "A man who was in one of their storage depots. The manager said that the conversation was odd."

"Odd how?" Lena asks.

"According to the manager, the man sounded strange. And the man in question said he'd call the manager back."

"Did he?" Lena asks.

"No. And now that man's phone is switched off."

A detail picks at Lena's attention. "Agnes, you said 'depot'. I thought John worked for an advertisement agency?"

"He does, of a sort. I looked them up just before the meeting. They put up underground advertisements. Those big posters at the stations."

Lena's mouth goes dry. *Of course.* The van. That jacket. The night shifts.

"Do you know if John's got keys to the underground network?" Lena asks. "That would be a nightmare." At any rate, John knows the tunnels inside out, including a hundred places where one could hide and stay hidden.

"I'll find out." Agnes reaches for her phone again.

"Where is this depot?" Lena asks.

"Kristineberg," Agnes says. "I've got the address."

"That's John," Lena says and snatches up her jacket. "It's too close to Alvik to be a coincidence." The trickle of adrenaline grows into a stream.

"I'll arrange backup," Gren calls after Lena as she runs out the door. "And Lena?" he shouts. "Call me. Keep me informed."

Lena doesn't reply. Her mind is set on reaching Kristineberg in time and stopping John. Nothing else matters.

*

CHAPTER 14

John Andersson

John plants his hands against the ground and pushes away until he stands up.

His palms burn as if they were on fire; strips of skin remain stuck to the ground, as if he'd been sinking down into the ice. The snow is grey as concrete and viciously cold, as if each flake were studded with tiny blades.

He's naked and alone, stranded in a blizzard on a frozen lake at the bottom of a ravine. Nothing makes any sense. He's colder than he's ever been. The chill alone should already have killed him.

Yet he remains conscious. Able to think, move around, perhaps even walk. By all that is right, this should be a dream. Although dreams never feel so real.

The cliff is even taller than he thought. Arching up into the snowfall, it traces the rim of the lake, as if he were standing at the bottom of a giant cauldron. The sky is a churning, restless sea of dark grey.

High above, buried inside the clouds, is a patch of brightness, maybe the moon or possibly the sun. He can't say if it's day or night. What little light there is appears to have no source.

John tries to walk towards the cliff, but his leg is trapped. Frowning, he looks down. Pale, icy fingers are clenched around his ankle.

Someone buried in the snow is holding on to him.

*

CHAPTER 15

The other John

Snow crunches under John's shoes as he crosses the frozen strait.

A carpet of perfect white covers the metre-thick ice, temporarily bridging the fringe of the inner city with jetties along the suburban shorelines. John has swapped his old jacket for the one he took from the depot, crisp and clean, smelling of artificial lavender. His bag bounces against his back as he walks.

On his right, the strait broadens and splits into several frozen channels. On his left is the bridge, a looming arc behind the curtain of snow. The lights of the passing trains are too feeble to reach John. Even the street lights' glow is too weak to illuminate the strait. Down here, he is invisible, veiled by the snow.

He heads for Alvik again, although he has no intention to enter any station again tonight. Walking is safer. The cameras in the train cars caught him bloodied and armed. People will be looking for him, hoping to snare him and lock him in. Question, secure, and restrain. He cannot allow that to happen yet.

The map in his mind dictates his course. The chain of events stretches on into the distance, but the next link is clear, and there is time. Morning is hours away.

John reaches the far side of the strait and enters the suburbs. He walks down empty walkways and roads, zigzags between roadwork machines and follows a path that curves up and west, around the blocks and away from Alvik.

His walk takes him past three underground stations surrounded by large houses and low blocks of flats in yellow brick. After he has left Alvik behind him, he follows the road towards Brommaplan.

Half an hour later, he reaches the gas station where he bought his shoes.

The traffic has calmed; only the occasional car crawls past through the snow. Snowploughs rumble on nearby roads.

He continues to the bus stops near the underground train and looks around. A few commuters brave the weather and wait outside, but most stay in the warmth of the station hall and rush to their buses as they emerge out of the blizzard. A police car is parked at an angle just outside the doors.

John's hands are numb. His face is stiff, his feet sluggish. He must find shelter for the night. Tomorrow the printed image will help him find his target, and then he needs to be alert, ready to use his last strength to reset the scales. All Molly's suffering will be visited upon the one who caused her pain. All her fear, hurt, and damage.

Keeping his face turned down, he crosses the area, walks past a hotel and continues in behind a row of shops that separate the residential blocks from traffic. Ploughs have pushed snow off the street and onto the sidewalk, leaving pedestrians with a slippery path littered with cigarette packs and dog faeces.

At the end of the street are the stairs he ran up and down earlier that night. He uses them again and soon trudges past the first red-brick flats of Abrahamsberg.

He pauses at the top and looks around. No ploughs have made their way here yet. Every street is buried in a knee-deep blanket of snow. Swells reach halfway up to roofs of cars parked along the sidewalks. Looking along the street, he makes sure no one is watching him, and lowers his heavy bag to the ground.

Inside it are several tools from the toolbox at the storage depot, including an electric drill, a short crowbar, a blowtorch, pliers, and screwdrivers. They will be useful, but they are heavy; carrying them this far has exhausted him.

Minutes pass while John stands still and waits.

A front door opens farther down the street. Yellow light spills out past a man in a grey coat, pausing on the doorstep to put on his gloves. The man looks up and walks out, shuffling through the snow, away from John. Behind him, the front door swings back, grating against sand and ice.

John grabs his bag and runs towards the door. A moment before it will close, he puts his hand in the gap and pulls the door open, then stumbles in and closes the door behind him.

He moves to the side and stands still, looking around and listening.

Narrow stairs curve up and down from the entrance landing. Pale green walls, lime green ceiling, black iron railings. Three storeys, two flats on each floor. The stairs leading down end at a basement door. Water hums in pipes. The distant booms of a video game echo around him. Someone sneezes.

John unzips his bag, takes out his knife, and rams the hilt into the plastic light switch on the wall. The plastic splinters and clatters to the floor. He punches it again and shatters its circuits, then uses his feet to sweep the splinters down the stairs. No one will be able to switch the light on again tonight, and the shadows near the basement door are thick enough to hide him.

After a quick look out through the door to make sure there is no one outside, he walks down to the basement door, sits back in a corner, and sets the alarm on his wristwatch. It is time to rest and recover.

His next task will require all the strength he has.

*

CHAPTER 16

Lena

Lena hisses and snatches her hand back as the coffee machine spits its brew in all directions. The human race can build smart phones, perfect brain surgery and launch satellites, but it cannot create a machine that makes decent coffee, let alone one that aims the substitute straight into a cup.

When Agnes received the call about the depot, Lena and a dozen other officers raced the short distance from the headquarters to the location, a ten-minute journey that seemed to take hours. Police cars or not, drivers are slow to give way when the roads are coated in slick ice, but she had zipped past the crawling traffic and hoped oncoming cars would spot her in time.

Once they arrived, six patrol cars surrounded the depot to cut off all escape routes. Guns drawn, Lena and the officers left the cars and advanced up the streets, past windows full of open-mouthed people. Her mouth was dry and sour by the time she turned a corner and saw the closed metal door.

She had hoped John would be inside. She had pictured him giving up peacefully. No drama, no blood, no fight. But something, perhaps the complete stillness of the scene, told her they were too late again.

To her surprise, the door had been unlocked, and when the officers stormed in, their torches found Nils gagged and tied to an office chair. A strip of duct tape covered his eyes and mouth. Given how frantic Nils had been at that point, it was just as well he could not see the guns aimed at him.

They rushed Nils back to the headquarters and to the nurse in residence, a calm, elderly man who had dealt with the most unnerved people. Once Nils was deemed fit to be interviewed,

Gren brought him to a small conference room near Lena's office, where they wait for Lena to join them.

Lena waits for the brown trickle to stop and takes the plastic cup. When she turns around, Agnes is walking down the corridor.

"I just received a call from the national agency for education," Agnes says. "They've found John's school's counselling files."

"That fast?" Lena is surprised. "On a Friday night?"

"It seems they have a diligent intern doing serious overtime. He's sorting through old archives and was happy to chase down the files we wanted. I think he appreciated the distraction."

"Sum it up for me," Lena asks. The files may be important. Old, rank bubbles of teenage sins can have echoes, returning many years later as much darker acts.

"We got the contents of John's folder by fax," Agnes says. "I've only skimmed the files, so I may have missed details, but I think I've got the gist of John's problems."

"Uncontrollable behaviour?" Lena guesses.

Agnes shakes her head. "A teacher."

"Did John abuse one of the staff?"

"Possibly," Agnes replies. "John certainly wasn't happy with him. But the counsellor's documents included copies of more than three dozen complaints filed against John. Stubborn disobedience, upsetting the classroom, and so on."

"Those records must have shown up in our registry?" Lena says. Having to dig up important information that should have been on her desk long ago was a perfect waste of time. She wonders what other secrets hide in John's past.

"They would have," Agnes says, "if the school had sent the reports on, but they sat on them. The agency for education had the files only because the school's board was restructured years ago. It seems the school decided to hush the affair up."

"They hid every report?" Lena asks. "That's ridiculous, and also criminal. Which teachers complained?"

"I'll get back to the man in the archives," Agnes says. "Perhaps he's willing to do some more research. There are more records from John's school years. The head teacher's journal, the school nurse, and so on."

"He better be interested," Lena says. "If he doesn't comply, I'll talk to him."

"The information will be on paper and also confidential. Do you want him to send it over by courier?"

"As fast as he can."

Agnes nods. "I'll get to it as soon as I've checked up on the patrols."

Lena nods, says goodbye to Agnes, and continues to the cramped, airless debriefing room where Gren and Nils, John Andersson's colleague, sit around a small square table. The light is turned down to a gloom that is meant to be soothing, but it is also unnerving; the shadows are much deeper than they have any right to be in a room this small.

Stifling a yawn, she places the drink on the table in front of Nils, who nods in thanks and sips before Lena can warn him the coffee is hot. Nils winces, gingerly puts the cup down, and gives in to a coughing fit. Gren steadies the cup while Nils regains his composure.

Lena sits down on a chair next to Nils. "Are you all right?"

Nils nods and wipes his mouth. "I'm fine. Really. It's just – no, I'm okay."

Lena looks at Gren, who raises his eyebrows at her. Nils is anything but okay.

Sitting shivering under an orange blanket, the man is almost physically unharmed. His only visible wounds are the bruises where cable ties have dug into his arms and legs, and the sore rectangle the duct tape over his mouth has left. But the unseen damage is much worse: shock has left Nils bewildered on a deep, primitive level. His face has a sickly, yellowish tint, and his eyes flicker around the room.

"There's no rush," Lena lies; John is already an ongoing disaster. She wants to be in her car, out on the streets and looking for him, no matter how futile her chances of finding him. Four cars – as many as the force can spare – are scouting for John, and another four patrols track the other man. It is all they have, and it is nowhere near enough.

Nils tells them what happened up until his manager called and then dwindles off. Lena knows why; Nils wants to say more, but the words will raise the spectre of what happened at the depot. He needs time to brace himself. Time they do not have.

Lena runs her hand through her hair and pulls it back from her face. All this guessing. What is John doing right now? Will she sleep tonight, and if she does, what will she dream?

When, and how, will this hunt end?

Gren smiles. "We understand that you're ill at ease, but we need only a few more answers."

"Can I go home once we're done?" Nils asks.

"If you want to," Gren says. "Otherwise, there's a room here. The nurse will check up on you again as soon as we're done. If you decide to leave, we'll need your contact details."

Lena clears her throat, pushes a button on the panel on the table, and adjusts the angle of a small microphone next to the panel.

"Please tell us what happened after your boss called," she asks. "Try to recall things John did or said that were out of character."

"Such as tying me to a chair?" Nils says. "That's pretty strange, isn't it?" His laugh comes out as a broken stutter.

"I mean more specific details," Lena says. "Especially anything that points to where John went next."

"I get it." Nils reaches for the coffee cup again but bangs his hand on the edge of the table. He grimaces, shifts in his chair, and rubs his left hand.

"Well," he says, "when I was on the phone, I couldn't tell my boss that John was there, so I tried to stall. I planned to say the reception was bad and head outside. My boss was kind of cagey about why he wanted to know if I'd seen John, but I could tell from his tone that it was bad."

"Just as I was about to rise from the chair," Nils continues, "John slapped the phone from my hand down on the floor and stamped on it. Then he turned around and held a big damn knife to my face."

"Go on," Lena says.

"He told me to be quiet, or he'd cut one of my eyes out. I still can't believe he said that. We've worked together for five bloody years, and I never once thought he was a bloody psychopath."

"How did you respond?" Lena asks.

"I didn't say anything. I just gaped like an idiot."

"Do you think he would have hurt you?"

Nils stares at the coffee cup and nods. "John's voice was, I don't know. Not hoarse, but level. Completely flat. I should've known something was wrong, the way he acted when I first got there."

"This isn't something you expect to happen," Gren says. "What happened next?"

"John tied me to the chair with cable ties, tight as hell. I thought my arms would fall off. Then he slapped that tape over my eyes and mouth. I don't know for sure what happened after that," Nils says.

Lena looks at Nils's bruised arms. If Nils had been tied for a while longer, his arms would have been lost. John had almost turned his friend into an amputee. She wonders if John had pulled the ties so tight by accident or design.

"You must have heard sounds," Lena says.

"I was in a panic," Nils says. "But I heard him use the computer. There were a couple of printed papers on the desk when I got there."

Lena leans closer. "What was on them?" she asks. "This might be very important."

"A man's face," Nils answers. "Pale, kind of gaunt. That's all I saw. I had no reason to take a closer look."

"Hair colour?" Lena urges. "Eyes? His age?"

Gren raises his hands a fraction, and Lena presses her lips together.

Nils shakes his head. "I'm sorry."

"That's all right," Gren says. "Please continue."

Nils takes a deep breath. "A minute or so later, I heard him pull a cable from the socket in the wall. He shuffled his bag around on the floor. Then I heard him search the toolbox. It took forever. I almost pissed myself; I thought he was going to torture me. You know, like in those movies."

"Do you think John took any tools with him?" Lena asks.

Nils shrugs. "He might have put some of them in his bag."

Lena studies the microphone on the table and wonders why John needs tools.

"And I heard the clink of bottles," Nils continues. "Did you find my bag? There were two bottles of Lord Calvert in it. Whiskey."

Nils and Gren look at Lena, who shakes her head. "John must have taken them," she says.

"Oh," Nils says. "Bastard."

Lena taps her fingers on the table. If John gets drunk, he would be careless and easier to find, but that does not fit with her idea of his behaviour. He took the alcohol for some other reason. Perhaps for sterilizing a wound or to set something on fire.

"Did John sound or act stressed?" she asks.

Nils shakes his head. "Just disinterested. Bored, almost. But he never talked to me after he taped my eyes, except to say–" Nils falls silent and closes his eyes.

Lena and Gren look at each other. "What?" Lena urges.

"I can't tell. Sorry. I just can't." Tears work their way out from behind Nils's closed eyes.

Lena rephrases her question. "Was it about where he was going?" If it was, she has to know. There are no alternatives.

Nils shakes his head and rubs at his eyes. "He told me what he'd do if I called the police. But he won't, right? Because I never called you."

"We know you didn't," Gren assures him. "Did he threaten you?"

"Not me." Nils pauses. "I have a son. He lives with his mother. My ex-wife."

"He threatened your son?" Lena asks.

"Please," Nils begs and looks at Lena. "You must protect him. Send police to the house, make sure John doesn't get to him."

"Of course," Gren says, "but–"

Nils's voice climbs to a hoarse scream. "John can't harm him. He has no bloody reason now. You have to tell him. *Please, you have to let him know.*"

*

CHAPTER 17

John Andersson

John curses and pulls his foot out of the hand's grip.

The blizzard hid whoever crept up on him. He's startled and scared, but also relieved: until now, he thought he was alone. If others are present in this outlandish place, he has a better chance at understanding what's happening, and how to get out.

Slowly, John walks back to the spot where he'd been snared. Drifts of snow cover the ground around the hand. Someone is buried in the snow. His or her fingers still grasp in the air, as if searching for something else to clutch. They remind him of pale, withered roots animated by a slow wind.

John takes the hand and pulls as hard as he can, but can't move the person. Confused, he brushes away more of the snow.

The arm to which the hand belongs is inside the ice. So is the body of its owner. A naked, elderly woman locked in a twisted position beneath the surface, as if flash-frozen while swimming.

Deeper down in the ice is the shape of another body. Around it are other shadows: more women and men, young and old, all naked, contorted, and encased in the ice.

John drops the hand in horror and backs away. This is not a lake, the site of an accident, or a cemetery.

He's trapped inside something far worse.

*

CHAPTER 18

Lena

Lena slumps back in her chair while Gren tries to calm Nils down.

"There's no reason to shout," Lena says weakly.

"Can I go now?" Nils wipes away tears from his face. "I've got a headache. I want to make sure my son's all right."

"Absolutely." Gren rises but motions for Lena to stay seated. "I'll get the nurse. He'll be here in a moment."

A minute passes while Lena stares at visions far beyond the room's walls. Tools. Threats. Torture. John on his way to the devil knows where, carrying a picture, a knife and whatever else he has in his bag.

The nurse arrives and leads Nils away. Gren waits outside until they are out of sight, then goes back into the room, closes the door, and sits down next to Lena. He crosses his arms and looks at her.

Lena meets his eyes and wonders if it is her turn to be debriefed.

"How are you holding up?" Gren asks.

Lena sighs. "Good," she lies. "Tired and worried, but otherwise fine."

Gren puts his fingertips on the edge of the table and nods.

"I'm glad you're doing all right," he says. "I've got my eyes on you." He chuckles and shakes his head. "That came out wrong."

Studying her commander, Lena wonders if his words had not been exactly what he meant. "You meant to say you're looking after me?" she says. "I appreciate it."

"You know I am." He pauses. "This is a strange case."

"Agreed." Lena picks at a callus on her palm. She could kill for a session in the gym. "I should get back to my desk."

Gren waves away her concern. "There's nothing you can do right now."

"There's always something. You know that."

"You're pushing yourself too hard."

"Look who's talking–" Lena catches Gren's look, breathes deep, and refocuses. "Sure. I'll get some rest soon. I promise."

"When?"

Lena scratches her nose. No other path is open to her except honesty. "When John is brought in," she says. "We can only guess what he'll do next."

Their eyes meet in a moment's silence.

"Will you be upset," Gren asks, "if I tell you the department's psychologist has advised me to make sure you don't get too involved?"

Even though Lena is not surprised, she cannot resist making a disgusted face. She pictures them discussing her mental health. "No." Lena sighs. "I won't be upset."

"We care about you. It's that simple. Your accident wasn't that long ago." He clears his throat and pokes at some invisible dent in the table. This is why Lena respects Gren, at least most of the time: He knows when to shut up. It is a rare quality in anyone.

Lena decides to end the silence with a question. "Does she know?" She looks closely at Gren for any sign of a lie. She has wanted to ask this for a long time.

"Does who know what?" Gren asks and stops prodding at the table.

Lena lowers her voice. "Does Agnes know why we're having this chat? Is she aware of why the psychologist is breathing down my neck?"

"Of course not. It's classified."

"I know, but Agnes's a rookie. I thought maybe she'd been warned unofficially. I know there are rumours."

Gren shrugs. "I certainly haven't said anything, and I'd give anyone who did a hard time. Trust me on that."

"Can I tell her?"

Gren looks troubled. "I can't order you not to. Even if I thought that'd help." He pauses. "Do you want to?"

"I'm not sure. Are we done here?"

Gren nods. "Take a break," he says. "Get some rest. We'll find the men. But not tonight."

"You're right." Lena lowers her eyes. "I'm running on empty. We got no leads until a patrol comes up with one or we get the footage. Right?"

Gren nods again.

"Right," she says. "I'll be back at eight tomorrow. It's only eleven thirty now. That'll give me enough sleep."

Gren smiles and stands up. "I'm glad you see my point."

"It's a shiny point. Hard to miss in the gloom."

He rubs his back. "Two officers are at the victim's flat to go over it thoroughly. If there's anything that gives us a new lead, I'll let you know straight away. It's your case. But you must sleep. That's an order."

"I got it."

"That's all for now. The roads are getting worse by the minute. If this keeps up, you won't be able to drive home."

"I can sleep here." In the corner of her eye, Lena sees Agnes outside the door, looking away.

Gren shakes his head. "All rest rooms are full. The few trains that are running are hours behind their schedules. We're hosting officers from the whole city."

"Ah."

"So you better hurry while the roads are still open," Gren says. "By the way, can Agnes ride with you? Her train's delayed, and there's no knowing if it'll leave the Central Station at all. She lives not too far from your place, but I suppose you know that."

Lena wants to slam her fist down on the table. There goes her last chance to dodge Gren's request and get back to the suburb for another look at the flat. "Of course," she says.

"Thank you." Gren shuffles his papers into a neat stack. "See you tomorrow morning."

When Lena walks out of the room, Agnes straightens up and brushes a stray hair from her face.

"Hi," Agnes says. "Can I–"

"Let's go," Lena says.

"Oh. That's great. Thanks."

Agnes follows Lena towards the elevators. "I've heard back from our helpful intern at the Ministry of Education," she says. "A car has picked up a boxful of paper for us. A removal box. Their office is nearby, so the papers will be here soon, despite this weather. Do you want me to wait here and have a look?"

"Absolutely not," Lena says. "Call Gren and tell him to instruct someone here to start browsing. We want to know more about what kind of trouble John caused. And the names of the teachers who filed complaints about John."

They arrive at the steel doors of the elevator. The scents of cold coffee and damp carpets fill the air. Agnes reads something on her phone while Lena watches the reflection of them both in the metal doors.

"I appreciate this, Lena. I just checked, and my train is still stuck."

"Not a problem." Lena stifles a yawn. "Gren said that you live near me."

Agnes nods and tells Lena her address. It is minutes from Lena's flat, though tonight, that distance could be an hour. The elevator doors open, and a minute later they are walking through the freezing underground garage.

"I'm parked over here," Lena says. "Before I forget, I'm going back tomorrow at seven. Do you want a ride?"

"If it isn't inconvenient," Agnes says.

"Of course not." Lena pauses with her hand on the car door handle. "Wait. You're not on duty tomorrow."

"I know, but I want – I'd like to come in anyway. Is that all right? This case is–" Agnes's eyes meet Lena's over the car roof.

Lena knows what Agnes thinks: This chase has its claws in her. It is her first bad case, and it doesn't look to improve anytime soon.

"It's fine with me. I'll talk to Gren."

"Thank you. I mean it."

To Lena's amazement, the roads are less crowded than she feared. She turns on the radio to listen to the news, but interference makes the report sound like a broken transmission from a war front. Agnes is silent, apparently lost in thought, her eyes on the road ahead. Lena feels sorry for her; Agnes is keen, bright, and precise, always doing things by the book and the numbers. This mess must be agonizing for her too.

Agnes's phone chimes. She looks down, reads, and turns to Lena. "I just received an email from the office about the files."

"That was quick. We've been gone only forty-five minutes."

"Gren put five officers on going through the documents. I didn't think he would do that."

"He's bright," Lena says. "And the poor man trusts me. What's the verdict?"

Agnes scrolls through the email. "This is interesting."

"Talk to me, or I swear I will confiscate your phone."

"All complaints were filed by John's art teacher."

"Maybe they didn't get along," Lena suggests. "Hell knows I wasn't best friends with many of my tutors. Anything more on what John actually did?"

"Nothing, I'm afraid. But as we thought, no files were forwarded from the school. John's troubles were kept completely quiet."

"Wonderful." Lena sighs. "Leave it for now."

Glancing at Agnes's intent eyes and perfect uniform, Lena realises she knows nothing about the woman's background. Agnes's accent suggests she is from northern Sweden, but she cannot tell from where.

What she does know is that choosing Lena as a mentor was a moronic decision. Someone among the brass must hate Agnes. Teaming up an officer just out of the academy with a senior detective whom many thought should go into mandatory retirement was strange, not to mention cruel. Perhaps they had thought Lena and Agnes would balance each other out.

Lena hopes she will not ruin the woman's career; sometimes Agnes looks up at her with an eagerness that makes her want to scream. A medicated squirrel with insomnia would lead by better example. If Agnes knew about Lena's history, she would agree. Instead, the woman depends on Lena for guidance and protection. And, worse, for advice. It is pure madness.

She wants to talk to Agnes, only that may spook her, perhaps so much that Agnes will want a different partner. That would be a disaster. Agnes is crucial to the case; bringing someone else up to speed will take too long. And even if Agnes says she does not care, she would see Lena in a new light. Every slight slip would be seen as a sign of going off the rails. Eventually, Agnes's voice will join the choir of crows that caw behind Lena's back.

The alternative is to keep quiet and let Agnes continue to see Lena as a pillar. A charade that will work for a time. But Lena's mask will pale, perhaps crumble altogether at the wrong time, and that could get Agnes in trouble. It may get her killed.

Lena glares at the road while the crux burns in her mind. Coming clean to Agnes can cost Lena her job, and not warning her can cost the woman more than that.

"Have you eaten?" Lena asks.

"What?" Agnes says, startled out of her reverie. "Not dinner, no. Never had time this evening. But I've got food at home."

"I'm sure you do." Lena brakes and veers into another lane.

"The exit to where I live is–"

"I know where you live. We're not going there."

"Oh." Agnes smiles nervously. "Then where are we going?"

"My flat," Lena says. "We'll eat there."

She can tell Agnes is anxious, but there is no going back. This is something she should've done weeks ago. Ideally, it should've happened the day they first met.

"Why?" Agnes asks.

"We need to talk."

*

CHAPTER 19

John Andersson

Terror almost paralyzes John as he staggers towards the cliff.

Everywhere he looks, bodies are encased in the ice. Women and men, more than he can count, some buried just beneath the surface, others so deep down he can barely make out their silhouettes.

What little comfort he felt is gone. How these wretched souls ended up here is a mystery. Perhaps they fell from the top of the cliff, wandered through a tunnel he has yet to find, or plummeted from the sky.

Maybe they all began like him. First stunned and bewildered, then paralyzed by despair, devoured by this hostile place, and ultimately preserved like stuffed animals on display for those who are yet to arrive.

The scene is as unreal as it is ghastly. No place on the planet can be this horrific.

Once he reaches the cliff, he runs his hands over the rock. It's coarse and black, like petrified charcoal, and as cold as the frozen lake. The top is lost in the murk above. Crevices and small outcrops make for possible footholds, although a fall onto the ice is likely to cripple him, even from a low height.

John reaches for a promising crack in the wall when a hint of movement under the ice beneath his feet catches his eye.

He's standing right above the body of an old woman embedded an arm's length below, her corpse wrangled as if twisted by a careless giant.

One of the woman's fingers twitches. A moment later, her torso turns slowly on its axis, as if rotating on a skewer.

"What the–" John's gaze strays from the grotesque sight to the other bodies.

There's movement everywhere he looks. Here is a shuddering arm, there a shifting leg, a shudder, a flinch or a tremble.

The woman's head turns and faces him. To his surprise, her eyes are intact and filled with savage hysteria. Her lips mouth words lost inside the ice, but he doesn't need to hear them to understand what she's saying.

Help me.

*

CHAPTER 20

The other John

Curled up in the shadows at the bottom of the stairwell, John sleeps, breathing gently while the hushed sounds of the suburban winter night echo around him: TV sets on cautious volumes, water rushing through pipes, crying children refusing to go to sleep.

But he is not entirely at rest; deep in his determination is a persistent disturbance, a nuisance that refuses to go away: a spark of remorse and grace steadily gaining in strength. It is only an insignificant speck of trouble, but trouble nonetheless. One loose thread can be enough to unravel his carefully woven path towards justice and revenge.

That must not happen.

He needs a tool that can extinguish this small flame.

John visits the most distant reaches of his soul, the remote corners where the most hurtful memories have been brushed away, and soon finds what he needs: A resurrected memory brought back from the grave. Bringing it to life is easy; after all, it is what the nuisance inside him is looking for.

All he needs to do is give it a voice.

*

CHAPTER 21

John Andersson

John presses his back against the cliff and stares at the ice: the people inside it are alive.

Hundreds of women and men, maybe thousands; it's impossible to tell how deep the frozen lake is. Everyone broken, wrangled and trapped in a contorted position, without air to breathe or clothes to protect them. And still, they're not dead. He didn't imagine that a hand clutched his foot. Its owner had reached for him, perhaps in hope of aid. Or maybe hoping to drag him down.

He turns around, drives his fingertips into a horizontal crack, and heaves himself up. Any longer down here and his mind will crumble under the onslaught of sheer dread. He's battling against dread as well as gravity, but revulsion also drives him on, as if the snow below him were flames.

The horror has escalated every moment since he came to in this pit. First, the confusion and the biting cold. A hand reaching for him. Discovering a body in the ice. Finding more of them, so many he quickly lost count. Realising that the bodies are alive and, no doubt, in unimaginable pain.

It's impossible to say how long they've been here. A safe guess is probably longer than the few minutes he has spent awake. Maybe much longer.

It's a nightmare, he tells himself.

I'm in shock.

That must be it.

Somewhere outside of here, back where things make sense, my subconscious is flooding me with these wild visions.

Perhaps I'm catatonic and strapped to a bed in a hospital ward. It's the best explanation.

Please, let it be the only one.

His instincts snuff out the idea like a fist closing around a lit candle.

The stone against his hands is hard and unyielding. This cold gnaws at his skin as if he were standing in flames. The darkness above is as thick as an upside down sea, and those poor people embedded inside the ice are far too detailed. If he were to look down, the bodies will still be there, squirming like a mass of larvae trapped underneath a slab of dirty glass.

He can't will himself awake. If he's right, there's nothing to which he can wake up.

This place is real. And he's *here*, cast down into this abyss.

It can mean only one thing. Perhaps hearing the truth spoken out loud will give him strength to continue climbing. Pushing each syllable through clenched teeth, he forces himself to say the words.

"I'm John Andersson," he says. "And I am in Hell."

*

CHAPTER 22

Lena

Lena parks her car in the parking lot. With luck, she will not wake up and find it buried under a mountain of snow, although that is wishful thinking.

"Twenty-four flats and ten parking spots," she says to Agnes and turns off the engine. "It makes you wonder what they were thinking. Let's go before we're snowed in."

Lena turns the car alarm on and trudges to the entrance of a three-storey block of flats. Squares slabs of concrete painted white and grey, square windows, square tiles in the stairwells. The building always reminds her of a chessboard gone mad. She would not be surprised if the architect had argued for square doors as well.

Two flights of stairs later, Lena and Agnes stop outside Lena's front door. Lena kicks the concrete wall to get the snow off her shoes, opens the door, and flicks the light on. "Enter at your own risk," she says. "It's even more chaotic than usual."

Most of the flat is visible from the doorstep: yellow walls, worn wooden floor, stacks of fitness magazines, piles of pocketbooks and sideboards laden with folded clothes. A mountain bike is leaning against a wall. Behind it are rows of protein supplement jars.

Agnes walks into the hall and pauses at a four-storey shoe rack filled with neatly paired shoes.

"You collect shoes?" Agnes cannot hide her surprise.

"Don't tell anyone," Lena says. "That would ruin my she-man image at the office. Let's eat." She squeezes past Agnes, walks into the kitchen, and drops her coat on a chair at the kitchen table. Agnes follows and sits down hesitantly by the table.

"I'm making tea," Lena says. "I'd rather have coffee, but seeing as I've been ordered not to work, I might as well catch some sleep. Do you want some? Tea, I mean. Not sleep." She runs a hand through her hair and opens the fridge.

"If it isn't too much trouble," Agnes says.

"There's a coat hanger in the bedroom," Lena says from the other side of the open fridge door. "The light switch is on the left, near the desk. Just leave your jacket on the floor if you can't find it. Living room's in there; bathroom's through that door."

Agnes's phone chimes, and she looks down. "The team going over the files in the box just emailed me."

"Have they found out what John did yet?"

Agnes frowns slightly while she reads. "I replied on our way here and asked them to widen the search, and they've found more complaint records. Over forty of them, in fact."

"Christ." Lena braces herself for more news on John's unknown past. The box of files was a huge cardboard can of worms. "Let me guess," she says. "John's behaviour spiralled out of control?"

Agnes looks up. "It's not John," she says. "All these complaints are about the art teacher. The one who tried to get John kicked out. His name was Lennart Holm."

"Past tense," Lena notes. "Has he passed away?"

Agnes nods. "Cancer, eight years ago. The team looked him up against the tax authorities."

"So John made objections of his own," Lena says. "I suppose they were engaged in some kind of vendetta. A student gets on the nerves of a teacher, the teacher wants the kid gone, and the boy blames the teacher back. That can't be unique, so I can't see why the school would've kept silent about that?"

"Because it was other teachers who complained," Agnes says. "Not John."

"Oh." Lena looks at Agnes for a long moment while her image of John is realigned. There had been a problem at the school, but perhaps she had the victim wrong. "Go on."

"Lennart's colleagues thought Lennart was unfit for his job," Agnes says. "They described him as overly authoritative, condescending, and prone to anger. They also accused him of actively trying to damage his students' self-esteem. He regularly took works he didn't like and tore them to pieces, even threw some of them out the window."

"So in short," Lena says, "he was a tyrant. And he singled John out as his pincushion, probably because he couldn't take that John was talented. What a fucking bastard." She imagines John's boot camp for adult life: daily fear of a man twice his size who couldn't handle bright children.

"He didn't sound like a pleasant man." Agnes pockets her phone and looks up at Lena. "But did he really make a murderer out of John?"

"No," Lena says. "Not yet. Did you want tea?"

"Yes, please. Black, if you have it."

"Tea comes in colours?" Lena frowns at the box of tea bags in her cupboard. "I've got Pricesmart extra, and that's it. I'm not much of a tea person."

"Any tea is good, really." Agnes flashes a smile.

"Pity." Lena turns on the gas stove and fills a saucepan with water. "I was hoping you'd demand coffee. That would've given me an excuse to have some too."

"If you want, I could–"

"Never mind. Help yourself to anything in the fridge if you're hungry. I'm having this." Lena holds up a small metal bowl. "Tuna and cottage cheese. Emergency food."

Agnes watches in silence as Lena spreads the mix on slices of dark bread. "I'm good, thank you."

"If you want some," Lena says, "you know where to look." She turns the blinds open and nods at the curtain of snowflakes outside. "Would you look at this? I could've slept on a sofa at the office, but no, I need to rest at home. Gren's fussing is driving me insane." She yawns so wide her jaws ache.

"I think he means well," Agnes says. "He cares about you."

"He fusses." Lena gestures at the snow with the sandwich in her hand. "We could've stayed at the headquarters and gone over our data. Maybe we missed something important. In fact, we can go over all we know right here. I know you won't tell Gren. I think your tea's ready."

"Thank you." Agnes uses a fork to fish the tea bag out of her cup.

"The bin's over there. Ignore the obvious need to take it out. Do you have any new ideas about John?"

Agnes shakes her head. "I think he's still near the crime scene, looking for the other man."

"That's my thought too." Lena takes another bite of her sandwich and looks at the parking lot below the window. "But John must be indoors, or he'd die."

"Lena?"

"What?" Lena turns from the window, takes another bite from her sandwich, and raises her eyebrows at Agnes.

Agnes sits perfectly still and holds her cup in both hands. "Why am I here?"

Lena stops chewing. She looks away, out the window, down at the floor and at the kitchen table. There is no escape. Then again, she had chosen this battle the moment she took Agnes here. She moves piles of advertising and post from the table to make room for her cup and her sandwich, then sits down with her arms crossed and looks at her tea.

"Why do I have this feeling you already know what I'm going to say?" Lena asks.

Agnes looks perplexed, but Lena continues to watch her, waiting for an answer. "You're going to tell me not to worry about you?" Agnes hazards.

Lena blinks. "Why would you do that?" she asks. "Gren is already troubled enough for ten people. No, that's not it."

"I'm listening."

Lena nods. Agnes always listens. She often feels as if she babbles in the younger officer's company. No matter how she tries, she cannot remember anyone else having that effect on her. Despite the weather, the kitchen is warm and stuffy; her back is prickled with sweat.

She opens the window a fraction. When the air has cooled, she reaches for her coat, takes out her badge, and puts it on the table. After a moment, she tentatively places her gun next to the badge. The leather-encased weapon seems to suck in the light from the low lamp above the table.

Lena takes a deep breath. "We talked about nicknames before," she says. "When we were outside John's flat."

"I remember."

"And you've heard them," Lena says.

Agnes grimaces, but she has the grace to nod. "Yes. But like I said, I don't care."

"I do, although I don't let it show very often. I want to tell you the reason behind some of those names."

"I already know you're not queer."

"Not that." Lena pushes the window open a little more and watches the snow. "The reason for the other nicknames." She ticks them off on her fingers. "She-man, Bella bicep, bag lady.

"The first two are easy," Lena says. "They're coined by idiots who can't cope with women who work hard or work out. Or have any brains at all. The last one, though, has a history. And you need to know."

"Are you sure?" Agnes asks.

"I'm definite." Lena's gaze flutter to the gun and back to Agnes. *Keep your voice steady. Just talk.*

"Five years ago," Lena says, "in October, I was in a raid outside Stockholm. Gren was in charge. It was part of Operation Guardian. You look as if you remember it?"

"That child abuse ring?" Agnes asks.

"Child porn. Things you would not believe. Thousands of photos, hours of film, all swapped around on a secret website. They'd been running it for years before we learned about them. If you scraped the bottom of human nature, you'd still have to drill down to find the like of these people."

Lena rises from her chair, fills a glass with water, and sits back down. "But we found them out, and we got them. Part of the gang was Swedish. I was on the team set to bring them in, only the raid didn't go as planned.

"The house was an old, large one-storey villa. Red walls, tiled roof, small backyard shed. Surrounded by fields and woods, almost a kilometre to the nearest neighbour. A little idyllic place full of rot and horror. The house is gone now. Someone torched it.

"We knew from recon that the suspect was in the house, but we didn't know about his friends. No one had come or left for days, and there was only one car outside, so we thought he'd be alone. As it turned out, the suspect was running a little molesting party for five of his friends."

"Oh, God." Agnes's face goes stiff. "There were children there?"

"No children, but films and photos. It was an orgy. They had even rigged a projector. I had been naïve enough to think these perverts did their thing alone, in private. I was wrong.

"Just before we were meant to go in, minutes before our reinforcements and our helicopter got there, they started to leave. To this day, I don't know if they had an alarm set up. The bastards were sophisticated. We had to move."

Lena clears her throat and continues. "There were twelve officers, including me. A two-to-one ratio, as it turned out. Most of the time, that's enough, but these men fled and fought like possessed. They knew what they faced, the prison sentences and the media attention. Maybe they knew what happens to their ilk in prison, too. I've heard stories about inmates who use pins and shards of glass to get creative on rapists."

"So they ran," Agnes says.

"Our suspect's friends did. It was the middle of the night, and the whole area was a circus of torches, shadows and shouts. At that point, we didn't know how many there were. The helicopter was nowhere near and had no infrared scanners.

"While the other officers ran after the people who fled," Lena continues, "a colleague and I went to the house to search for anyone hiding and to seize evidence. The house was dark; the only light was our torches and a film projected on the wall. One of their films."

Lena pauses to refill her glass. She has to use both hands to keep it from shaking under the tap. Agnes is sitting even more still than she was before Lena began to speak.

"We came upon two men in the living room," Lena says and sits down. "They were throwing hard drives and DVDs into a wood-fired stove. When we ordered them to lie down, one of them tried to tackle my colleague, and they both tumbled into the room next door, wrestling and shouting. I was left with the last man.

"He was in his fifties, almost bald, small glasses, bright blue hooded sweater, new trainers. Your classic office grunt on downtime. He stands there and screams nonsense at me, backlit by that film. The projector was in the ceiling, and I couldn't reach it to switch it off.

"The man I faced was the main suspect, but I didn't realise that in the chaos. I told him again to drop down on the floor, but instead he walked closer, pointed at his chest, and screamed about rights and warrants, lawyers and laws, how he's going to sue me. And so on."

"You must have been so furious," Agnes says quietly.

Lena nods. "I wanted to rip his tongue out. I wanted to point at the film behind him and ask him what fucking rights he thought he had. I wanted to see what happened to him in prison, every minute of it. But I didn't.

"All I did was keep my pistol trained on the floor, in front of his feet, and tell him to back away, to lie down, over and over. But he didn't. He was too busy justifying what he was doing and telling me I had no right. Breaking into his house was against the law; this was his private property, et cetera."

Lena shakes her head. "I pointed to the movie and screamed at him, 'Do you think I'm blind? That's a *child*.' I may have added something about what he could expect in prison. He looked over his shoulder as if he'd never seen the film before, turned back to me and said, 'He likes it. You all do.'"

Agnes pales a shade. "He said that?"

"Exactly that," Lena says. "And more."

"That's unbelievable."

"Then he tried to take my gun. Maybe he thought I didn't have the guts to shoot, or perhaps he hoped he'd be faster than I was. He almost succeeded. I was distracted by the fighting in the other room, and I almost lost hold of my pistol when he made a grab for it. I tried to shove him away, but he was frantic. He even bit my hand." She holds up her right hand and points at a pale curved line below her little finger.

"When that didn't work," Lena continues, "he tried to punch me but lost his balance. We stumbled around the room, fighting over the gun. Right when the pistol happens to point at his head, he manages to hook his thumb inside the trigger guard and pull the trigger. The gun went off, right into his mouth."

Agnes raises her hands to her mouth. "So that's why," she whispers.

"Why what?"

"Why they call you that name. *Bag lady*. As in a body bag?"

Lena nods, unsurprised by how fast Agnes made the connection. "It's strange how those with no sense of humour always are the loudest. But there's more. And this is where I need you to believe me." She leans forward. "When he was shot, a spasm went through him, and he pulled the trigger again. I couldn't stop him. His thumb was stuck, and he was flailing like a ragdoll on strings."

"He was shot more than once?" Agnes asks.

"Four times. My colleague tried to revive him, but the first shot took most of the man's neck with it."

Agnes looks down at her untouched tea. "What happened then?"

"Standard procedure. I briefed the others, called in to report, and bagged the gun. Our backup arrived, and the other men were arrested. Apparently the shots made them give up. The helicopter finally came and took me back to the office, where I did the paperwork and slept on a couch. Enter five years of fretting bosses and nice nicknames. Gren is stuck between blaming me for the disaster and feeling sorry for me."

A long silence settles in the kitchen. The two women look at each other while the wind pushes against the window. Agnes looks devastated, which catches Lena off guard; she had expected disgust or disbelief. That was easier to deal with. Compassion always left her embarrassed and flustered.

Agnes shakes her head. "I don't know what to say."

"There's no need to say anything," Lena says. "But I can see you have questions. Ask them."

Agnes opens and closes her mouth several times. "Is this why you work so hard?" she asks. "Does it help with the memories?"

Lena shakes her head and pokes at a non-existent spot on the table.

"I do my job because I want to help," Lena says. "It's that simple. But you're right, in a way; I've done longer shifts and slept less since that night, because I need to keep busy."

Agnes peers at Lena. "You want to make amends," she says softly. "You're wearing yourself thin because you feel guilty."

"Of course I'm guilty," Lena snaps. "I screwed up and shot a man. There are no excuses. And yes," she adds, "the reason I want to catch John is to stop him from damning himself too."

Agnes shakes her head. "Damnation is intent, to hurt on purpose. Or so I choose to believe. But even the best of people make mistakes, and what happened to you was an accident."

"I lost control," Lena says. "That's not an accident. There was a moment when I should have reined myself in, but I didn't. I was too furious."

Lena clears her throat. Talking to Agnes is unsettlingly easy, and the urge to share more information is almost overwhelming.

"All I can do now," Lena continues, "is try to stop other people from repeating my mistake. Few realise how steep and slippery the slope is. If a similar thing happens to me again, I'd–" She grimaces and looks away. "It would definitely get me fired, and probably leave me in an asylum."

"And would not finding John in time be such a mistake?" Agnes asks.

Still looking away, Lena nods. "I can't let that happen. Saving him won't change my past, but it's my only road ahead."

After a long moment, Lena sighs and turns back to face Agnes. "You needed to know," she says, "so you can decide if you still want to work together with me."

"Of course I do." Agnes pauses. "I just wish there was something I could do to help you."

Lena shrugs. "You listen. That's a lot right there. And you don't call me names, at least not to my face."

"I'd never–"

"I know." Lena yawns. "But now you know why I see a psychologist, why Gren is concerned, and why he thinks it's a good idea that I waste time sleeping instead of doing my job."

Agnes sits still and watches the table. "Can I ask you something?"

"Sure."

"It's not about what you told me now."

"Just ask."

"I've noticed that you always switch off the water coolers when you're in the conference rooms, but I've never asked why?"

"Ah." Lena puts her elbows on the table and rests her face in her hands. "In fact, that is related to what I told you. It's the sound. That thick, awful gurgle the air bubbles inside the canister make when you tap water from it."

"You don't like that noise?"

"That's exactly how the man in the house sounded when he died." Lena makes a grimace. "A great cough of blood, beer and bile before he stopped breathing. That bastard. I wish I were religious, because then I'd know where he'd be right now."

Lena stands up and pushes her chair back. "I need to sleep. You can take my car, but if you don't want to drive home, there's a sofa in the living room. Push whatever is on it down on the floor. There are blankets in the wardrobe in the hallway."

Agnes stands up too. "I'll go. I don't want to be an inconvenience."

"If you end up in a pile-up on the highway, then you'd be an inconvenience. And I'd be mad at you, too. It's your call. See you tomorrow."

Lena locks herself inside the bathroom and exhales. After a moment in the dark, she flicks the switch and blinks in the white glare. Her reflection makes her shudder. Her eyes are bloodshot, her skin pasty. There are crumbs of bread at the corners of her mouth.

She brushes her teeth, rinses her face, and presses a towel against her cheeks, wondering if anyone ever truly feels as if their thoughts race. Hers never do. The more tired or stressed she is, the slower her brain works.

Lena pauses in front of the bathroom mirror and studies herself in the unforgiving light. Speaking silently, she lets her mouth form the lies she told Agnes a few minutes earlier. The words come with ease. They have been well rehearsed. Practise makes perfect.

Agnes deserves better, but she cannot lose the woman's trust. Not before John is brought in. She needs Agnes and the woman's eagerness and ambition, so once again, she has to twist part of her past into a plausible story. A wrong to make a right.

She turns out the light, walks to the bed, and lies down. Less than a minute later, Lena sleeps.

*

CHAPTER 23

Agnes

Moving softly around Lena's living room, Agnes carefully moves Lena's crumpled clothes and fitness magazines from the short leather sofa onto the floor. When the sofa is visible, she lies down and waits for Lena to fall asleep.

The screen of snow outside the window makes the light on the ceiling wave and flutter. Across the room is the television set's standby light, a distant blue star in the near-dark. The wind is an urgent whistle.

When Agnes has not heard a sound from Lena for half an hour, she cautiously rises from the sofa, pausing at every creak of leather, and pads quietly into Lena's bedroom.

Lena is asleep, lying on her side with her legs pulled up and her hands crossed over her stomach. Her eyes flutter and dart behind her eyelids. She is still dressed. On a bedside table is a textbook on criminal profiling, a mobile phone manual, and a birdwatching guide. A low bookshelf is half-filled with workout magazines and newspapers. A thick grey curtain hides a large window.

Agnes looks around the room and takes in its bare blue walls, the pale wooden floor. A heavy security lock is mounted on the window. Goosebumps cover Lena's wrists; even though the small radiator under the window is hot, the room is cool, almost cold.

Taking care not to wake her, Agnes spreads a blanket over Lena and stands back. For several minutes, she stands still and watches Lena sleep while winter pushes at the window.

Agnes starts to cry.

Sobbing mutedly, she hugs herself as her tears fall on the blanket she has placed over Lena. She watches the bright red minutes on Lena's alarm clock tick away, one by one.

When a door slams far away, she starts and dries her face with her hands. When the tears have stopped and her face is dry, she leans down over Lena, hesitates, and kisses the nape of Lena's neck.

Lena sighs, mumbles, and smiles in her sleep.

Agnes shivers and bites her lip. She makes sure the blanket covers Lena's hands, slowly rises from the bed, and leaves the apartment.

*

CHAPTER 24

John Andersson

John drives his fingers into another crevice in the wall and drags himself up. Another hand's breadth closer to the top. If there is one.

I am in Hell.

His feet scrape away patches of frost that are carried away by the wind. Sooner or later, it'll land on the ice and bury the not-quite-dead people below a fraction deeper.

Keep climbing, he reminds himself.

There's no telling when the other people arrived here. It's impossible to guess how long they'll remain, but probably a very long time. If the concept of time is relevant in this place, that is.

He's meant to become one of them. This much he can anticipate. He was supposed to submit to the pain, stay prone, and become iced over, part of the macabre exhibition of entombed souls. Imprisoned in a state of indescribable pain, restrained and mute.

It's the natural course for all who find themselves here. His slow ascent is not only a battle against the vicious arctic climate; he's also challenging fate itself. He may be doomed on a level beyond his comprehension.

Keep climbing.

The patch of light above is his fix-star. His eyes are locked on the fuzzy brightness while he claws for a new handhold for his aching hands, another slit into which he can fit his numb toes.

If he doesn't push on, find an exit, and get out, more people will die.

That's not who he is. That isn't the man Molly knew.

Keep climbing.

*

CHAPTER 25

The other John

John wakes up seven minutes before his alarm is set to go off.

When he is certain no one is in the stairwell, he leaves the stairwell and enters the pale and still Saturday morning. The clouds have shed most of their burden and are content to sprinkle a fine shower of glittering snowflakes over the suburb. The hum of traffic is gone. Few move on the streets; while the blizzard has settled, the cold continues to keep people indoors.

He walks back to Brommaplan and finds that his assumption was right: One of the men who had seen John's quarry is sitting on the bench where he had sat yesterday, waiting for the nearby liquor store to open. It is one of the men, but not the right one.

John goes to a bus stop and watches the man. Yesterday's milling lines of commuters have been replaced by people drifting home from Friday night revelries or heading towards their weekend jobs. Taxis pick up huddled groups of tourists leaving the single-storey budget hotel. Red buses negotiate snow-filled lanes.

After a while, another man, red-faced, bearded and obese, joins the first man on the bench. He is the one whom his friends interrupted when John spoke to them yesterday.

Close to the two men, half-hidden under a cluster of trees, is a public toilet: a green metal booth almost too small for a single person. Its door faces towards John, away from the men. He moves closer to the toilet and waits behind a tree.

After half an hour, one of the men walks to the wine shop and returns ten minutes later with a plastic bag filled with bottles. A moment later, the bearded man on the bench rises and walks towards the public toilet. John waits until the man is inside and moves around the toilet, keeping out of the other man's view.

When John hears the man inside the toilet unlock the door, he walks up to the door and waits. The door opens, and the two men stand face to face outside the toilet's entrance.

"Wha–" the man blurts.

John pushes the man back inside the toilet. The man staggers backwards, thuds back-first into the wall, and John follows, pulling the door shut behind him.

With two men inside the booth, there is almost no space to move. The air reeks of disinfectants, cheap soap and urine. The bearded man's eyes are bloodshot and his breath is foul, but he is more alert than John has anticipated.

The man grabs John's jacket and pulls John close. "What the hell d'you think you're–"

John drives his fist into the man's left temple. The man moans and raises his hands, but John strikes again, this time ramming his other fist deep into the man's stomach.

For a long moment, the man leans on the wall, bent over in agony, spitting and wheezing. John stands silent beside him. When the man can talk again, he looks up at John.

"What have I done to you?" the man asks, shaking as he speaks.

"Do you remember me?" John asks.

"Yes, but I haven't–"

John takes the printed image from his pocket and holds it under the man's face.

The man looks at it and turns away. "Oh, fuck," he mumbles.

"Where does the man in the picture score?" John asks. "Who does he buy from?"

"I've no idea," the bearded man mumbles. "I don't know him. It could be anyone."

"Yesterday you said you knew. I want his dealer's name and address."

The man groans. "Are you fucking stoned?" he rasps. "They're not the kind of people you rat on."

"I am not stoned," John says, "but I'm in a hurry." He folds the image, puts it back in his pocket and takes out his knife. The fluorescent light in the ceiling tints the blade green.

The man's pupils balloon at the sight of the blade. "Don't," he says and raises his hands. Names, numbers and addresses tumble off his tongue as if the words crowded his mouth.

John stands still, knife in hand, and listens for key details among the trickle of slurred syllables. He memorizes the important details. Once he knows all he needs to know, he tells the man to be quiet.

The man breathes hard. Sweat covers his forehead. "Can I go now? I just want to leave. Please."

"You can leave in a minute." John uses his free hand to take a large bottle from his bag. He hands it to the man and orders him to drink it.

The man's face is slack with incomprehension. "Why?" he asks in a broken voice. "What is it?"

"Read the label."

"Whiskey?" the man says, confused. "Why would you give me that? It's poison, isn't it?" he whimpers. "You're going to poison me."

"It's not poison. Drink, or I will cut your throat open."

The man takes the bottle with a quivering hand and drinks.

When the bottle is empty, John puts the knife away and tells the man to sit down. The man obeys sluggishly. John exits the public toilet, closes the door, and leaves for the underground.

*

CHAPTER 26

The other John

Twenty minutes later, John arrives in Hässelby.

The train wheezes to a halt at the end of the line and opens its doors. Wind and snow rush into the car, followed by a handful of frozen people. A voice announces the remaining time until the train leaves for the city.

John rises, grabs his bag, leans out and looks around.

The open-air platform is flanked by tower blocks, their windows like bright mosaic tiles against the dim morning light. Deep in the gentle snowfall, on the other side of a small outdoor shopping centre, a red light pulses at the top of a soaring chimney. It marks the end of the suburb; past the power plant is the waterfront, beyond that a wide strait where the snow blends with the sky into grey nothingness. The wind plucks at John's clothes.

He walks down a sloping tunnel in the middle of the platform and looks over the turnstiles. A handful of people wait for their buses. No security staff. On his right, outside the station, a local bus empties passengers who march with determined steps towards the station.

John crosses the street, plods through the snow past a grocery shop, and turns a corner. He pauses in a roofed area lined with empty cigarette packets and beer cans. The thick snow muffles the sounds of voices and cars.

He has been here many times.

The area, its contours, all the lights are familiar. So are the criss-crossing parkways, the parking lots and the sparse patches of pine trees. Most streets in this suburb are named after fruits that would not last a minute in the climate.

The man he looks for lives on one of them.

John doubles back along a road parallel to the underground rail. He is heading towards the previous underground train station, located closer to John's destination but also closer to local offices and diners. It often has security staff. The end station, like this morning, does not.

When he nears the station, he turns and follows a pathway towards a massive block of flats, a towering rectangle in red brick with hundreds of windows. Apart from a man walking his dog in the distance, he passes no one.

He follows the façade to the end of the block. Along the ground floor are metal meshes over the windows, all dark except one where huge aquariums light them in a shimmering green. When he reaches the end of the block, he stops outside a door in glass and pale wood.

Inside is a dim stairwell with walls in yellow and brown. He tries to glance at the list of names inside, but the light is too weak for him to make out the numbers.

John tries the door. It is locked.

He takes a step back and looks up at the windows above the stairwell. All of them are dark. He moves back and puts the bag down on the ground, then stops as a woman in a brown coat opens the front door. At her feet is a small dog on a pink lead. When she sees John, she stops and peers at him.

John nods and smiles while he catches the door to stop it from closing. The woman's dog barks furiously, its claws scrabbling on the icy ground as it tries to reach John. The woman frowns, shakes her head, and walks off towards a park, half-dragging her dog behind her.

He watches her disappear around a corner. When the woman is out of sight, he walks through the door and closes it behind him.

Inside the stairwell, everything is silent. The thick smell of deep-fried oil fills the air. He looks at the list of names and finds the flat he is looking for: ground floor, the first on his left, inside a corridor.

John considers the number of doors, the location of windows. If he is correct, the flat is a small studio apartment with one window set low in the building's front, just outside the front door. Anyone inside the flat could have seen him.

He puts the bag down on the granite floor and takes out a small axe. Its head is heavy and full-sized while its wooden shaft is as short as a wine bottle. After a look around to make sure he is alone, he tucks the axe under his jacket and presses his left arm to his side to keep it in place. When he is certain he will not drop it, he walks up to the flat and looks at the dark peephole.

The man who lives behind the door is the next link in the chain, another component that separates John from resetting the balance. One way or another, he will get the information from the dealer and find his ultimate target.

He knocks on the door.

Silence.

He waits for a minute and knocks again.

Nothing.

John raises his hand to try a third time when he hears something scrape against the floor inside the flat. A muffled curse follows the sound. A shadow passes in front of the peephole.

"Who's there?" a male voice asks from inside the flat.

"Jerry," John whispers. "Are you Mick?"

"I don't know any Jerry. Piss off."

"I'm – I'm sorry," John says and coughs. "Someone said I could buy from you. He gave me the address."

"Who the fuck said that?" the man inside hisses.

John gives the name of the man John left near-unconscious in the public toilet at Brommaplan.

Another curse sounds from inside the flat. "That fuckhead sent you here?" the unseen man asks. "I'll knock his teeth out. This isn't a bloody corner shop. I don't sell anything. Now, sod off."

John hears another male voice inside the flat. There are two men behind the door.

"Please," John says and raises his voice. "Let me in. I've got cash." He flashes the wad of bills in front of the peephole and puts the money away.

A long silence follows. "Show me your face," the man inside says.

John leans close to the peephole. He licks his lips, looks to his sides, and stammers another plea.

"Fucking junkie," the man mutters. "This is bullshit." He raises his voice. "Let me see your hands."

John raises his hands, careful not to drop the axe squeezed tight in his armpit.

"Fine," the man says. "Get inside, quick."

The other voice behind the door makes a protesting sound, but the first man with whom John has spoken hushes him. There is a dull metal thud as a bolt slides back, followed by the rustle of a security chain. The door opens a hand's breadth.

John looks into a pale, narrow face pocked with acne scars. The man is in his late twenties and wears a red hooded jumper, black jeans and orange trainers. His hands are out of John's sight, hidden by the door and the wall.

The man is a head shorter than John; behind him, John sees a dim flat crowded with boxes and plastic bags. An open built-in wardrobe houses a stationary computer, its monitor glowing with a racing car waiting at the start line. Green shabby curtains cover a window on the opposite wall.

On the floor are plastic bags, blankets, pizza boxes, piles of crumpled tissue and empty cans. A candlestick holder balances on an old portable TV with streaks of paraffin tracing its sides.

The man nods at John. "Give me the money. Quickly."

Just as John reaches for the shaft of his axe, the other man inside the flat looks around the door.

Behind Mick is the man who fled from Molly's house.

Even though the printed image from the surveillance camera is poor, John has studied the photo long enough to be sure. The man has the correct features, the right hair, the matching clothes. John came to the flat looking for a link in the chain, but now the chain has rushed through his hands and reached its end.

"Come on," the man in the doorway urges. "I haven't got all day."

"That's correct," John says.

"What's that supposed to mean?" the man demands.

"And my name is not Jerry," John adds.

The man frowns and looks John up and down. "Then who the fuck are you?"

"I am Molly Berglund's lover," John says, and rams the blunt end of the axe head into the man's face.

*

CHAPTER 27

Lena

Lena wakes up to the frantic beeping of her alarm clock.

Her first thoughts are on her dreams: Surrounded by large birds, she had soared through clouds, not knowing where she was going but feeling that she needed to go faster. The echo of beating wings lingers in her head.

She grimaces, reaches over to stop the beeping, and falls back onto the bed. Only the bedside clock and the street lights outside illuminate the room. The sun is an hour from rising. Disconnected thoughts whirl in her mind; were it not for the time displayed on the clock, she would think she had slept only a few minutes.

She sighs, stares at the ceiling, and closes her eyes. Now Agnes knows the truth. At least, she knows all that Lena has told her. It is good enough for now. She rises from the bed and frowns at the blanket, wondering when she pulled it over her. Perhaps she was more tired than she had thought.

That does not matter; five hours of sleep is enough. She has booked the basement gym and needs a quick session. Cool iron and gravity never fail to clear her head, and her thoughts are a dense pack of loose ends.

But there is no time this morning. She needs to get back to the office. John will soon move again, if he has not already, and he must be tired. He will leave a trace. When he does, she will be ready.

She is making sandwiches when her mobile phone rings. She takes a bite and looks at the display. It is Agnes.

Lena takes the call. "Any news?" she asks, speaking as she chews.

"The footage is ready," Agnes says. "It came in only minutes ago. They've been working on it all through the night. It's at the office."

"Perfect."

Lena remembers that Agnes had been in the flat when she fell asleep. The younger officer must have slept less than Lena, yet she sounds alert and wide awake. There's also a new inflection in the woman's voice. Almost anger, but not quite. Closer to a cool, oddly disquieting determination.

"Or we can go to John's house at Drottningholm," Agnes suggests. "Gren has got hold of a helicopter."

"First the film," Lena says. "It's unlikely that John's gone to the house if the road out there's blocked by snow. And if he has, he'll probably stay put."

"I understand."

"We need to find the other man. Wherever he is, that's where John's heading. What took them so long to get the film ready?" Lena asks.

"The quality was bad, so Gren got some company to go over the footage and do what they could to improve it."

"Ah."

"The full brief is in the system. It's a lot of reading. I borrowed a car. Do you want me to meet you up?"

"Sure." Lena tears another bite from her sandwich. "I'm ready in ten minutes."

"Are you all right? You sound like you're choking."

"Ten minutes," Lena says again. "I'll see you soon."

Lena hangs up and does her round through her flat: Quick shower, coat, gun, notepad, phone, keys. She pauses when brushing her teeth, takes a short wildlife knife from a drawer, and puts it in the pocket of her coat. She is almost done with the mascara when Agnes calls again.

"I'm in the parking lot," Agnes says. "Have you seen your car today?"

"No," Lena replies. "Why?"

"It's ploughed in. I can see only the roof."

"I bloody knew it." Lena sighs and crouches to tie her shoes. "Can I ride with you?"

"Of course."

"I'll be right down."

Forty-five minutes later, Lena and Agnes walk out of the elevator at the police headquarters. "The DVD is in room twelve," Agnes says. "I'll get Gren."

Lena nods and continues down a corridor. She gets black coffee from a coffee vending machine, takes three bananas from another department's fruit basket, walks into the room, and closes the door behind her.

She puts her food on the table and sits down in an office chair close to a whiteboard. Thirty seconds later, Agnes and Gren walk in.

"Morning," Gren says. "How are you feeling?"

Lena peels her banana. "Never better. Run the film from the station first. I want to see this second suspect."

Agnes switches on the projector and walks over to a computer at the back. Gren, unshaved and dressed in a grey, wrinkled shirt, sits down next to Lena. He smells sharply of deodorant. Lena wonders if he slept in the office.

A white rectangle lights up the whiteboard and changes into an image of a station floor. It is centred on the turnstiles, with the steel-and-Plexiglas ticket box on the right and the doors in the distance. Two security guards in green overalls lean on one of the turnstiles. Fluorescent lights in the high ceiling light the room. People frozen in mid-step cover the dark, wet floor.

The camera is mounted in a corner high above the floor and reveals only part of the faces of the people passing below.

"Is this the best angle we could get?" Lena asks.

"I'm afraid so." Agnes starts the film, and people snap into movement.

Lena leans close to the screen and peers at the faces passing past the camera's view. "This is like looking for a fish in a river," she mumbles.

Minutes pass while she scrutinizes every man. Her eyes water with the effort. She is about to ask Agnes to take a break when she spots the man.

"That's him," she shouts. "Stop the bloody film. That's our man."

Agnes rewinds the footage a few seconds and presses play again. A man slams the station doors open and stalks across the floor, towards the turnstiles. The security guards look up. A woman jumps out of the man's way. Agnes pauses the film just as the man fumbles for his money at the ticket stall. The picture flickers between two images, making the man's fingers quiver.

Lena looks at the man. If she is right, those hands had held a gun minutes before he was filmed. They cupped the cold metal, pulled the trigger, shook as the weapon fired. The man was small; the recoil must have shaken his entire frame.

She wishes she could rewind the tape and follow the man back to the flat, up the stairs, through the door, all the way to the moment after the bullet left the barrel. If only she could see his face, the size of his pupils, what words his mouth formed. Had he gaped in surprise, laughed, or cried.

The man in the film is probably guilty, but that is only half of the picture. Murdering Molly makes him a killer; his reaction determines what kind of killer.

Agnes rewinds and plays the footage in slow motion. The man zips from one position to the next as he moves through the turnstiles and farther down the station, towards the escalators. When he has left the picture frame, she rewinds the film again. After the third replay, she leaves it running at normal speed.

Ten minutes pass before the security staff snatch their radios from their belts, spring into activity, and stop people from passing. People grimace and raise their mobile phones.

"That's when the alert was sent out," Gren says. "The station was shut down. Looks like John never showed up."

Lena crosses her arms and sits back, still intent on the screen. "Have someone with good eyesight look through the tape again. Search for any sign of John, and get a usable image of the other man. I want to know where he went. Have we got footage from the platform?"

"Their camera up there is broken." Gren makes an apologetic face.

"You can't be serious. Who the hell is—" Lena raises a hand before Gren frowns at her. "Never mind," she says. "It's only ten minutes. They must be able to work out which trains stopped at the station during that time."

"Probably," Gren agrees.

Lena turns to Agnes. "Get them to send us the footage from all those trains. And tell them to do it fast. Agnes?"

Agnes flinches as Lena touches her arm. "What?"

"Are you all right?" Lena asks.

"Sorry." Agnes shakes her head. "I was distracted. Are we going looking again?"

"We haven't seen the other recording yet," Lena says.

"Oh. Of course." Agnes changes the disc, and the image flickers and changes into the interior of a train car distorted by the wide-angle lens.

Lena leans closer. The first film was key to finding the killer; this footage will tell her about John. She should prioritize finding the presumed killer, but she cannot exorcise the image of John from her thoughts. Frantic, alone, and armed.

"Where the hell is he?" Lena asks, squinting at the fish-eye picture.

"At the far end." Agnes points to the screen. "There."

Lena shakes her head. "This is rubbish. How are we meant to see what happens?"

Agnes fast-forwards a few minutes. "The tech team said they'd enhanced the sequence. Here we are."

The picture centres and zooms in on a man in the distance. Large and restless pixels resolve into a sharper picture: two groups of blue seats, pale green walls, advertisements for mobile phones above the backs of the seats. The image quality is good, but the light is too bright: everything is cast in a bluish glare, making the scene look as if it were filmed in an icy hospital.

Lena recognizes John straight away.

He is sitting by the window, his face blank, seemingly oblivious of the three men in the booth next to his. Lena can easily read their glances and their collective poise. Body language is as subtle as a megaphone when you know what signals to look for. She sees what will come next. For a moment, she is almost overcome with the urge to shout a warning.

The trains stops, and the men make their move: One moment they sit in the adjacent booth, then two of them stand in front of John while the third keeps watch, scowling at the other passengers and blocking Lena's view.

Agnes reads off her notepad. "We're not sure what happens here, but witness statements indicate that they tried to rob John. One witness said he saw a knife and heard threats. That's all we know."

Lena glances at the younger officer and wonders when Agnes found the time to read up on the witness statements. Probably when Lena looked away for a second. The woman is uncanny efficiency dressed in a uniform.

The men who moved in on John shuffle around and look over their shoulders. Lena can sense the tension. Their robbery is not going to plan.

Without warning, a plume of dark streaks appears on the advertisement on the wall above John.

Gren points at the lines. "What's that?"

"I'm not sure," Agnes says. "Perhaps some kind of discolouration from the digital enhancement."

"No." Lena shakes her head. "It's blood."

She read through as much as she could of the report on her way to the city. Notes on the crime scene described it as 'soaked'. Watching the red lines droop, she wonders how much of the blood was John's.

The scene changes in a flurry of movement. Two of the men move away from the booth while one remains bent over John with his back turned to the camera. The two men run out of the image and, Lena guesses, the train.

The last man looms over John, then doubles over and falls on his back between the two booths. Graceless but fast, John pounces on the fallen man and holds a knife to his face.

After a moment, John turns his head and looks directly at the camera, and for eight long seconds, he meets the eyes of Lena, Agnes and Gren.

"Bloody hell," Gren whispers. "He knows he's being filmed. He's looking right at us. What the hell?"

Lena is about to agree when John turns back to the man and slices his nose open.

"Christ," Agnes gasps.

Blood fountains from the wound and stains the nearby seats. The injured man twists manically on the floor, but John pins him down and leans down, his head close to the man's ear.

"He's talking," Lena says hoarsely; her throat is parched. "I think he's whispering." She would sacrifice days of her lifespan in return for knowing what John is saying.

John stands up, takes his bag, and walks out of the train car. Were it not for his bloodied shirt, he could have been on his way to work. But Lena knows that John is on his way to a storage depot, where he will assault and tie down a colleague so hard the man nearly lost limbs. John will make threats so vile Lena could not coax the details out of his former friend. And now John is gone. Again.

"Stop the tape." Lena presses the heels of her hands to the sides of her head. If she needed any confirmation that John is not their regular grieving relative, this is it. He is violent and callous, but calculating. His gaze has left her with a cold knot in her stomach: he had looked like an animal, stripped of compassion and hesitation.

The psychology department would have a field day with him. For all John's composedness, his actions are bold and irreversible. He knows the police are watching, and he does not care. The man is a burning fuse. When the detonation comes, John would be far past saving. As would more people.

"Any more news from the patrols?" Lena asks.

"Not yet," Gren says. "It's only a matter of time, though. John is leaving a strong trail."

"Not strong enough." Lena rises and turns to Agnes. "Call the lab and make sure they work on getting better pictures fast. Tell them to call me as soon as the image of the second man is in our system. John is a loose cannon heading for a disaster, and all we do is let him slip away. Gren?"

"Yes?"

"About that helicopter?"

*

CHAPTER 28

The other John

John's thrust with the axe is not precise, but hard enough to split Mick's cheek open. Mick stumbles backwards into the flat, trips on a low table, falls over and smashes the wooden tabletop in half. A small revolver falls from his hand and lands on the floor.

The door is partially open, still barred by the security chain. John sees the other man move inside the flat, towards the door, hoping to slam it shut in John's face.

John lifts the axe and hammers down on the security chain. The blade effortlessly cuts through the metal, and he shoulders the door wide open.

On John's left, Mick struggles to disentangle himself from the ruined table. White bone shows through the wound on his cheek. On John's right, the other man is backing away, one arm raised in defence while his other hand clutches a glass bottle by its neck. The man's eyes are wide, his skin pasty with sweat. The bottle quivers wildly in the man's grip.

John shuts the door, locks it from the inside, and turns to Mick, who tries to sit up, cursing and spitting blood. Before Mick can rise to his feet, John picks up a toaster from the floor, raises it high, and slams it into the side of Mick's head.

Mick slumps back and lies still. John drops the toaster, turns around, and faces his target.

The man has backed up to the wall. Shaking and whimpering, he holds the bottle in front of him as if it were a sword. When he realizes he has nowhere to escape, he charges at John.

John watches the man come towards him. The attack is savage but desperate, and the man's aim is off. He sidesteps the swing and drives the butt of his axe deep into the man's groin.

The man's mouth drops open. The bottle flies from his hands and lands on a stained couch. He tries to move away but buckles and collapses to the floor, gasping for breath.

John crouches and drives a knee deep into the man's chest, pinning him down. He raises the axe in the air and aims.

The man splutters and flails with his arms. "I can pay," he gasps. "I should've paid by now, I know, and I will. Got almost all of the money, just a few grand missing. I would never play Tom. He knows it's true. Ask him."

John says nothing. The axe is perfectly aligned; one quick twist of his arm and his hunt will be over.

"Or is it Marco?" the man rants on. "But I've paid him. He's got his money, right? I made the swap last week. No, you work for Tom, don't you? Call him. Tell him I'll make good. I just need another day. Something got in the way, is all. Shit got ugly yesterday."

John is silent.

"Real ugly," the man continues, his words spilling out as he bargains for mercy. "I was fucking blitzed, totally loaded, and I got it in my head to try doors. Some idiots don't lock them, you know?"

"Go on," John says.

"I find an open door," the man croaks. "I go in, and I find this bitch hiding in her bedroom. When I pulled my piece and took her bag, she clings to it. So I shoot her. Fucking dumb, I know, but I needed the cash. I needed to pay Tom. That's it. Had to get the money."

John finds himself at a watershed. He has to destroy the squirming anomaly under him, obliterate this source of injustice, but the axe does not fall. Hesitation has checked his final attack. His imagined chain of actions is incomplete.

He may have found the instrument that took Molly from him, but he has not located the hand that guided it. Another link in the chain beckons from farther away: The man who sold Molly's murderer the drugs. The finger on the trigger. The ultimate prey.

John lowers the axe and scans the room. Crumpled clothes, bins brimming with empty fast-food boxes, mounds of cigarette packs next to the broken table. A sleeping bag on a foam mattress. Towers of DVD movies on the floor. A wide flat-screen TV balancing on a small fridge. Glossy movie posters nailed to the worn wallpaper. Cigarette butts pressed into the vent of a radiator. A mobile phone on the floor. Cheap boxes of chocolate on a low table by the window.

John opens the lid of one of the boxes. Inside are dozens of small transparent bags filled with yellow powder.

He turns back to the man under him. Mick does not move; his head rests in a pool of blood. It is a complication. He did not expect the need to prolong his search, and there are those who want to stop him.

In moments, he knows the steps he must take to truly end his chase. Plans and options arrange themselves in his mind. Primarily, he needs more information, and he needs to move.

Slowly, he lowers the axe.

"Bloody hell," the man on the floor gasps, then laughs hysterically. "I thought you'd kill me. You know I'm honest, right? Tom trusts me. He can always trust me."

"If you scream," John says, "or make any noise, I will cleave your face in half. Do you understand?"

"I got it. I got it, man. Do you want cash? Over there, the yellow bag, under the bed. Take the shoebox too; that alone is worth all I owe him and then some."

"I need information," John says. "Not money."

"You want what?"

"Tell me about Tom. His full name and his address. Everything you know."

"I thought you meant – man, I can't tell you that. You don't know Tom. He'd kill me."

John drives the axe into the floor right next to the man's head and raises it again.

"*Stop. Please.*" Tears flood the man's eyes. "Jesus fuck. I'm going to die. He'll torture me, and then he'll kill me."

"Tom's full name," John says. "Addresses, phone numbers, names of his friends." The axe hovers in the air above the man's face.

"Shit," the man whimpers and then speaks.

After a few minutes, John knows all he needs to know. He is almost ready to move on.

But he is not finished here. His next step will not bring him closer to his new goal, but his quest for balance requires it. A part to fit in the greater picture. The man under John's knee might be a tool, but he is part of the disturbance John looks to quiet.

There is a bill to settle. An anguish for an agony.

"Keep quiet," John says and unzips his bag.

"Right. I'm quiet, I'm quiet."

"Close your eyes."

"What?" the man stutters. "Why should I close my eyes? I don't want to close my eyes. I'm not – hey, what's that? You're going to paint something? No, that's – *oh hell, no, don't–*"

*

CHAPTER 29

The other John

John puts his equipment back in his bag and looks at Molly's murderer. At last, the man's eyes are closed. He will not give any more excuses or tell more lies.

He examines the phone. Half charged, no security code required. He pockets it, continues to search the room, and finds under the bed a green canvas bag and a large shoebox.

Kneeling down, he pulls the shoebox out and opens the lid. Once he has inspected the contents, he pulls out the bag, unzips it, and looks inside. A distant radio murmurs a weather forecast while he thinks.

His own bag is full, so he pulls out his bedroll to make room for the box. After today, he will not need to sleep, but the contents of the box and the rest of the items he has brought may prove useful. At the bottom of the shoebox are three folded printouts of web pages. He leafs through the papers and puts them in his pocket.

Last into the bag goes an advertisement for a local pizzeria. On its back, he has noted down key details about the man who supplied Molly's killer with drugs: Names, addresses, telephone numbers, descriptions.

John closes the bag and leaves the flat. One more task. One more chase. A different breed of prey, more dangerous, but less prepared.

And he knows where it nests.

*

CHAPTER 30

Lena

The helicopter whips up a small cyclone of snow as Lena lands on a meadow close to John's countryside property. They are near a narrow, winding road that cuts between barns, stables and fenced fields.

Before she left the city headquarters, Gren learned that residents near John's cabin had teamed up and cleared the roads as much as they could. Some farmers had brought tractors with ploughs and opened up kilometres. That meant cars could reach the house, but Lena insisted on going in the helicopter; she had wasted enough time already.

While she was in the helicopter, Gren called. Two words into the conversation, she could tell from his tone that he was about to give her bad news, and she was right: Lena was no longer in charge of the hunt of the second man, now also the presumed murderer. That task had been transferred to another detective at another department.

It had happened for administrative purposes, Gren assured her three times over. She knew he was lying, or had been lied to.

When Lena did not blow up over the phone, Gren sounded surprised. She offered a small rant to suggest she was upset, but in truth, the decision helped her: it meant she could turn her full attention to John. In practise, she already had.

Lena told Gren there was no need for backup when she searched John's house. Most likely, she argued, John would not be there, and if the infrared sweep hinted at anything bigger than a rat inside the house, they would land far away and wait for reinforcements.

"It's possible he's there," Lena admitted over the phone when talking to Gren. "The buses go straight to the area from where his girlfriend lived. But unless he's got a car or a ride waiting to pick him up, he'd have to walk. All bus drivers along those routes have been briefed. They'd call in straight away if they saw him."

"I'm not sure," Gren said.

Lena wondered what Gren had been unsure about: John's whereabouts or Lena's judgement.

"Even if he went by car," Lena continued, "the roads weren't ploughed last night. Besides, he must know we're aware of the property. Isolating himself there makes no sense."

"Do you really think John is that rational?" Gren asked.

"In his own way, yes. And he doesn't want to be caught. That profile doesn't rhyme with John at all."

Gren caved in, but only in part: He authorised Lena to take a look around, but she had to wait for backup before she went close to the house, regardless of what the sweep found.

"I'll arrange the search warrant," he said. "And you will wait before going in." His command came out as a half-plea.

"I won't go close," Lena promised.

Twenty-five minutes later, stepping out of the helicopter while the rotor blades spin like a misty disc above her head, she wonders why Gren forgot to define 'close'. It was his loss and her gain.

Three sweeps with the infrared scanner before they landed had not shown any sign of life in the house. Lena had also had time for an aerial view of the property.

A small house, a tiny outhouse, and a small overgrown garden surrendered to the whims of nature. A thick forest surrounded the house. The larger road ran some hundred metres away, while the road leading up to the house was so narrow it was more a big path.

"I've been called back to the airport," the pilot calls to Lena when she steps out. "You'll have to ride back with the backup. Sorry."

Lena nods and jogs away from the helicopter. Seconds later, she is alone.

The air nips at her face; the blizzard is over, but the temperature has dropped. At least the air is fresh and clean, carrying the scent of woodlands and horses even at this arctic temperature.

When the helicopter has shot away in the grey sky, she looks around to get her bearings.

The field on which she stands is the size of a soccer field. Patches of woods and boulders left behind by the inland ice break up the rolling hills. To the east and south are dense copses of pine trees. There are no people or moving cars nearby. A few kilometres from where she stands, beyond private woodland and large villas with sprawling grounds, is the home of the Swedish royal family. People like John are rare in these parts of Stockholm.

She turns east. John's house is located behind a small forest at the other end of the field. The wind is picking up. Pulling up the lapel of her jacket, she walks towards the trees, trying to tread where the blanket of snow is the thinnest.

When she is halfway across the field, she calls Agnes. "I'm near John's property," she says. "Gren wants me to be a good girl and stay away from the house."

"Will you do that?" Agnes asks. "Please, take care."

Under other, less disastrous circumstances, Lena would have smiled. Agnes is starting to know her well.

"I won't go too close," Lena says. "Like I promised."

"We're at the bridge," Agnes says. "The roads aren't good, but they're better than I expected. We should be with you in about twelve minutes. Did the sweep show anything?"

Lena shakes her head as she walks. Twelve minutes. Not fifteen, not ten. Twelve. Knowing Agnes, she will probably arrive exactly then. "We got nothing," she says. "If John's in the house, he's either dead or hiding in the fridge."

"Be careful."

"Call me when you get here." She hangs up.

Lena jogs towards the forest. She wants to see the cabin. Not that she expects the small house to hide a lead, but she cannot help imagine that this place holds a secret, some clue that will vanish like a bubble unless caught in time.

Once at the forest, she barely breaks pace. Branches flash by as she runs, ducking and twisting through the rock-riddled maze of boulders and trees, watching out for holes in the ground, roots, patches of ice, anything that could trip her and break her legs. She crawls over a large rock, slides down its side, runs sideways between two trees, and then she is there, next to the small outhouse she saw from the air.

Resting her hands on her knees, she stops and breathes hard. The house looks ordinary enough: Red-painted timber, probably almost a hundred years old. Low, square and quaint, complete with large snowflakes coasting down onto its roof.

It has three windows on the wall facing her, all covered by white wooden shutters. Halfway between the outhouse and house, in the middle of a clearing, is an old well visible above the snow only as a circle of round stones and grey mortar. It is a perfect Christmas card.

Before Lena left the headquarters, a colleague who had found building plans had informed her that the house has two rooms: One main room and a small kitchen. The small outhouse hides a modernized bathroom, if something built in the late seventies counts as modern.

Beyond the house is a short stretch of trees, behind them more fields and boulders. She hears no sounds except the soft rustle of branches and the distant barking of a dog. Three minutes have passed since she spoke with Agnes.

Lena flexes her fingers, sets her jaw, and draws her pistol. The plastic grip feels like heavy ice in her palms. For a moment, she stands still next to the outhouse and steers her attention away from the gun. It is a tool, nothing more. A dead weight, unthinking, unconscious. She has to focus on the task at hand. Inspect, think, move on.

"Come on," she whispers to herself.

Willing herself into action, she moves along the wall of the small outhouse and looks through its tiny window. No one inside. Wooden walls, sink, toilet, old bar of yellow soap. A thick wilted book balancing on the windowsill. She tilts her head to read the title, but the cover has been torn off.

She turns to the house. The shutters cover the windows almost entirely, leaving only a vertical crack. Someone inside could spy on her through the slit, so she advances crouching, staying in what she hopes is an angle obscured by the shutters.

Once she is at a corner, she pauses next to a large plastic barrel under the gutter and moves towards the door, keeping low to stay under the windows. At the door, she pauses again to listen. Nothing. No footprints on the single step in front of the narrow door. A thick string of snow balances on the handle.

She looks over her shoulder. There is no sign of life except for a crow watching her from a naked branch high above the house.

Breathing slowly, she studies the building. If Gren were able to read her thoughts at that moment, he would think she was distressed, but she is certain the house is vacant: There is a sense of hollowness to the location, a lack of life. A missing presence.

Still, she wants to look inside. There might be a clue to what John is doing.

The lock on the door is simple; the locksmith coming with the backup will open it in the blink of an eye, and she herself can probably pry the door open if she found a tool lying around the yard. But if she does, she risks having to explain her actions to Gren. It is better to wait.

She checks the time. Five minutes until Agnes said she'd arrive.

Keeping her gun pointed at the ground, she retraces her steps and walks over to the well. Way back, before the island changed from rural nowhere to sanctuary for the wealthy, the water supply would have been used by the house's residents. The circle of mortared stones is less than a metre across, and its edge reaches only up to her knees.

Two rusty boards of corrugated steel held in place by a large stone cover the opening. The crow caws and flies to another branch as she leans down and pushes at the steel boards. They shift easily.

"A quick look can't hurt," she mumbles under her breath.

She slides one of the boards off the well, leans forward to look down, and stumbles back when the well screams in her face.

*

CHAPTER 31

John Andersson

John squeezes his bare foot into a crack in the rock and pushes himself up.

The chill is still a blanket of nails scraping against his skin, but less brutal than on the lake. His fingers are stiffened into whitish claws. He can no longer feel his toes, or much else beyond the piercing chill.

The frozen lake far below is a smudge of sickly pale, almost obscured by whirling snow. Roaring gusts of wind chase around him and threaten to pluck him from the wall. Far above him, the cliff wall blends with the clouds to a tar-like, restless soup, interrupted only by the spot of faint light.

For all he knows, the wall might be endless. It may be part of his own, private purgatory. If he's stuck in a bespoke torture chamber, designed to torture him for whatever sins he's committed and forgotten, he's facing a perpetual climb.

Perhaps he's destined to struggle until he slips, crashes down, despairs and attempts to flee again. With time, he may be reduced to a collection of animated broken bones, destined to claw for freedom until the end of time, or even longer.

Even so, he must keep climbing.

It is all that remains to do. For the sake of those he might harm. *For Molly's sake.*

Still staring at the clouds, he reaches out and feels around for a new grip, but the wall is gone. A sharp line just above his head marks the edge of the cliff.

He's reached the top.

*

CHAPTER 32

Lena

The furious roar rises from the hole in the ground like an anguished plea. Teeth gritted, Lena throws herself backwards and aims her gun at the air above the well, prepared to fire at whatever unthinkable nightmare she has unleashed.

The scream goes on unabated. She pushes herself farther away from the well, trying to hold her gun and cover her ears at the same time, but the snow holds her in place. Blackness creeps into view like curtains closing a performance; she is being constricted by terror and shock. As if sensing her helplessness, the relentless wail rises in pitch and wakes the ghouls that usually stalk her by night.

She blinks –

– and she is back in the house, in the chaos.

On the wall is the projected film, a tapestry of horror she has tried and failed to forget. Noises invade her: sirens and protests, screams and tortured whimpering, furniture breaking in the adjacent room where her colleague fights another man. In front of her stands the suspect, defiant and indignant, scorning and ranting. No hint of remorse.

She relives the fury that crashed through her that night: a quick tide of adrenaline and, underneath, the sensation of sudden company. Her thoughts run parallel with those of another entity evoked by revulsion and unrestrained hate. She was not alone in her head.

When she faltered for words to scream at the suspect, the alien, storming presence inside took over. It did not lack imagination, and it knew exactly what to say.

"Do you know what happens to paedophiles in prison?" she asked, lowering her voice. "I have first-hand sources." In truth, she had not known. She had never heard any stories. The words she spoke had not been hers.

"Fuck you," the man sneered, still screaming. "Get the hell out."

"They'll come for you at night. First they'll gag you; then they get the cable ties out. One is all it takes."

"Shut up."

Lena continued, glee creeping into her voice. "They pull it as tight as they can, right at the base of your ball sack. Then they knock you out."

"Shut *up*."

"The guards know what's happening, but they don't care. They know you deserve it."

"Lying cunt," the man roared. "Get the fuck out of my house."

"When you wake up, the surgery is already over. There's nothing left but a plastic tube and a scar."

The man hesitated. His eyes narrowed.

"And that's just the start," she said, grinning widely. "After that, it gets really bad."

Silent, she stared at him, willing him to move, begging him to fight.

And the man moved.

Once again, she feels the convulsions of the gun, the metallic smacks of bullets parting from their casings to twist through the air. Her fingers have a will of their own; her thoughts are far behind, racing behind much stronger and faster impulses.

The first pull of the trigger had been reflexive: She had been so close to firing that a tremor was all it took.

The second had been in shock. Had she been in control of herself, she would have stopped, but when her bubble of astonishment popped, vengeance waited outside.

The third shot had been in determination: This subhuman creature would never return. She could and would banish him to permanent silence. The means were in her hands, and she used them with the casual concentration of a carpenter driving down a nail into a floorboard.

144

But the fourth shot had been different.

Without warning, the need to cause more damage took hold of her. Killing the man was not enough; he deserved to experience the same level of suffering displayed on the wall behind him. But her target was already damaged beyond repair, so she concentrated on the pleasure of destruction, the sweet pang of bringing pain and ruin to the man's flesh and bone.

Laughing under her breath, she had felt a profound, sensual stab of joy as she pulled the trigger and with great precision sent a bullet through the man's brain. And so, she had crossed the line and become what she loathed more than anything.

A bad cop.

The ghost of that particular shot still wakes her at night. Gasping for breath, it jerks her upright, nods in recognition, and fades away. She remains behind, sweating and famished for the guilt that always fails to come.

Every time that happens, before she can sleep again, she touches her own face to make sure she is not smiling the way she had done in the house.

*

CHAPTER 33

Lena

The moment passes, and Lena is back in the yard, staring down the barrel of her gun at the old well. All is quiet apart from a faint hum in the air. The crow still sits on its branch and looks down on her, speculative and condescending.

"Jesus Christ," Lena whispers.

She lies back and rests her head on the snow. It must have been the wind. There had to be a passage down in the well, some form of natural duct. When she removed the corrugated steel boards, the wind had torn unhindered through the channel and caused the piercing screech.

Noticing the gun in her hand, she tosses the weapon away. The sky above is a white ocean sprinkling its jagged drops over her face. It is snowing again.

She thinks of Agnes. Caring and trusting, she had listened to her amended story and believed her. She should have told her the truth. The constant lying and secrecy are erasing Lena's sanity.

Her phone rings. She starts, makes her trembling hands find her phone, and looks at the display. It is Agnes. Lena takes the call and realises she hears cars nearby.

"We're almost at the house," Agnes says. "Where are you?"

Lena stands up and quickly picks up her gun. "Meet me at the front door."

She returns to the house and waits. The flashback is a raw wound; she wants to sit down, bury her face in her hands and shut out the world, but she must look professional, or at least operational. Agnes is relying on her.

The slams of car doors echo through the forest. After a minute, Agnes appears, trudging through the snow along the road that leads up to the house. Six other officers follow in her wake, five men and one woman. Behind them walks a man in orange trousers and a green insulated jacket. The officers are tense; rumours about John and what he has done are flying wild.

Agnes looks around the yard and turns to Lena. The young officer could pull off the impressive feat of scowling without a shadow of a frown.

"I haven't touched the house," Lena says. "But I will, now that you're here." She bangs on the door with her fist. "Police. Open up."

No answer. Lena points at the man in the green jacket and jerks her thumb at the door behind her. "Get going. It's not getting any warmer."

The man blows his cheeks and lowers his toolbox down on the step. "Yes, I'm the locksmith, thanks for asking."

"You don't look like an undercover officer to me, so who else would you be?" Lena shakes her tousled hair and pulls it back up in a tighter ponytail. Agnes looks pained; she too must be freezing. Hopefully the locksmith is not an amateur.

"Any news?" Lena asks Agnes.

"No sign of John or the other man," Agnes answers, "and no incidents that point to either of them. They're working on the recording at the station. Oh, and Gren is getting busy. Details about the case have leaked to the press, and the media is hounding him. He's been ordered to brief the senior command later today."

"So we're on our own." Lena turns to the locksmith. "Is the door open yet?"

The locksmith mutters something under his breath while he works on the lock.

"What was that?" Lena asks.

"I said," he replies slowly, "I'll be done in a few seconds." A sharp clunk sounds from the lock. "There. It's open. You're welcome."

As soon as the locksmith moves out of the way, Lena walks up to the door, pulls her gun, and switches her torch on. She closes her hand around the gun's grip. "On three," she says.

The other officers move in closer to Lena and draw their pistols. Lena counts down, swings the door open, and peers inside.

The door opens to a square room that takes up most of the space in the house. On her left is a cluttered working bench that runs almost the entire length of the room. Under the bench are small paint buckets, a toolbox and a pile of neatly stacked unused canvases still in their plastic wrappings.

On her right is a large and old orange sofa, and next to it a small table with a sound system. A stack of CDs balances precariously on a speaker. Under the table stands a hot air radiator. On the opposite wall is a narrow door, which, if she remembers correctly, leads to a miniature kitchen.

Next to the door, along the wall, are three deep rows of paintings. Bright colours hint under the sheet thrown over the canvases. The air smells heavily of oil paint and solvents. The cracks between the wooden shutters form vertical lines of light on the walls. A damp silence rests inside the house.

While the officers fan out across the room, Lena walks over to the bench and shines her torch on its contents.

Glass jars brim with worn brushes, plastic bottles with acrylic paint, piled boxes with oil colour tubes. Scalpels, rulers and scourers. Mounds of old newspapers, most of them cut to pieces. Enough sticky tape, pencils and erasers to supply a small school.

No TV, no game consoles. A houseful of colours, creations and music. John's little refuge from the world. By and large, it is an extension of John's flat, only more peaceful. When she realises the tools on the workbench are centred around a wide canvas, she turns her light to the painting and looks closer.

The motif is of the back of a man walking away from a calm lake in the foreground and towards a tower-like silhouette that blocks out a setting sun. Between the lake and the tower, right in the man's path, is a mass of trees with long interweaving branches. The sky is a wild blend of deep browns and stark yellows. A depiction of a dusk the like of which Lena has never seen.

Underneath the motif, almost concealed by the thick layer of colours, is a collage of newspaper clippings. She squints and tries to read some of them, but the oil paint has blurred the words.

"The guy's a real fanatic," an officer behind Lena says.

"He was," Lena replies. "I'm pretty sure he won't return to these."

Not if he continues down his current path of choice. Only John did not choose it, she reminds herself; someone else started John's downward spiral.

She looks at Agnes and nods at the second door. "Kitchen."

Lena and Agnes move to each side of the kitchen door. When Agnes nods, Lena opens the door and glances around the corner.

No one inside. The open cupboard holds a few tins of food, instant coffee, tomato sauce and three boxes of dry cat food. She pulls out the drawers and finds mismatched cutlery and tableware. A coffee cup rests in the sink. The bar fridge hides a bar of chocolate and a package of hot dogs.

One of the officers looks in and makes a disgusted face. "I can tell he's more a painter than a chef."

"The only thing we can tell," Lena says and slams the fridge shut, "is that John's still out there. We'll go back to the office and – hold on." Her phone buzzes.

"Lena."

"Gren here. Have there been any developments?"

"If there'd been, I would've called. We've got nothing other than more proof that John really likes to paint."

"Walls or paintings?"

"The latter. We're going back now. What did you want?"

"The lab got a usable image from the footage of the second suspect. We put it out on the system and sent off priority alerts to greater Stockholm. The security manager at Vällingby called two minutes after we sent out the alert."

"What did he say?" Lena clenches the phone hard in her hand. If they can find the murderer, sooner or later they will locate John too.

"One on the manager's staff recognized the man straight away. The suspect has been seen around Hässelby Gård lately. That's two stops away from Vällingby, towards the end of the line."

"I know where it is. Have they started to search yet?"

"All patrols in the area have been alerted," Gren says. "We'll talk to the staff around the station as soon as we can get more people out there."

"Call me if something happens. I know I'm no longer leading that case, but he's our key to John."

"You still think so?"

"I know it. Make sure the suspect doesn't board a train, or I will strangle someone."

"If he's out there, he won't leave that way."

"I'm going to Hässelby Gård."

"Understood. I'll call if I hear more. Please remember–"

"Gren," Lena snaps.

"Just keep it in mind."

Lena ends the call. The other officers look at her and wait. They think they are wasting time in John's picturesque, freezing painting studio.

"Right," Lena says. "John lives near Vällingby. The other man has been spotted in the same area. If John knows that man's identity, there's a chance John is near."

"How would John know whom to look for?" an officer asks.

"He's got a photo," Lena says. "And just after the murder, witnesses said John was asking around for a man dressed in clothes that match those of the suspect. We knew that when we saw the footage from the station. My guess is John's somewhere between Vällingby and the end of the line."

The officer shakes his head. "That's a weak lead."

"It's still a lead," Lena says, "and we're using it. I'll do one last check here, and then we're off. Agnes?"

"Yes?"

"Go to your car, check the reports from that area, and let me know if something out of the ordinary has happened. People might have noticed John. If nothing else, his clothes could be bloodied."

"There'll be hundreds of posts," Agnes says. "It's the weekend. What do you want me to look for more specifically?"

"Anything that catches your eye. I'll go through the list myself once I get to your car."

When Agnes has left, Lena bends down and peers underneath the sofa. A layer of dust and an old paintbrush. She stands back up and chews on her lips. If John has any secrets hidden here, she cannot find them. The house is a cold trail. All the paintings here were part of the John who existed before his girlfriend was murdered. The John they are searching for now is another creature entirely.

Lena's phone rings. She looks at the screen and blinks when she sees Agnes's name. Agnes's car is ten seconds away; there was no reason to call. Outside the house, a car starts.

Lena takes the call. "What's going on?"

"John's been spotted in Hässelby." Agnes's voice is almost drowned out by the growl of her car's engine.

Lena runs out of the house. Brushing past the other officers, she slams John's door shut and sprints down the road, towards where the other officers have parked their cars. Behind her, her colleagues scramble to catch up.

She reaches Agnes's car, throws the door open, and jumps into the passenger seat. Two officers get in the back seat a moment before Agnes accelerates. The other police cars start behind Agnes's car.

Lena throws her gloves on the floor and fumbles for her phone. "Tell me."

"An elderly woman called in to the local police station," Agnes says. "She met a man at the front door of her block. She thought he acted strange, so she got worried."

"When?"

"She just called. An officer realized the description matched the one from the train footage, down to the bag he carries. They got back to the old woman and told her to stay indoors. John apparently went into the block of flats where she lives."

"Perfect." Lena flicks on the heater; her hands are numb with cold. "Let's hope he's still there."

"Yes." Agnes turns onto a larger road and speeds up. She looks troubled.

"What's wrong?" Lena asks.

Agnes grimaces. "The woman called five minutes ago, but it's been over an hour since she saw John."

"What?"

"She wasn't sure it was necessary to trouble the police, so she waited until she got too worried. At least she called. The patrols are already there, and underground train security is keeping an eye out."

"Fuck." Lena slams the dashboard.

"Perhaps—"

"Just drive."

Lena is silent while the cars rip down the white road. One whole hour. A wealth of precious seconds gone to waste. John could be anywhere. Agnes thinks John might be lingering, but he will have vanished, turned into smoke again.

The other officers are blindfolded by textbook neatness; they think John's actions click to the grid of reason and predictability. She wishes she could tell them that she knows what is going through his head, although if she tried, she would flag herself for permanent desk duty. Or hospitalisation.

When her phone rings, Lena almost presses her thumb through the brittle thing. A number from the headquarters. "Franke."

"Is this Lena Franke?" A male voice. Loud voices in the background.

"Still here," Lena says. "Who is this?"

"This is Patrick Rahm. Krister Gren put me through to you."

Lena forces herself to stay calm. "How nice of him. How can I help? I'm busy."

"Gren said you're in charge of the investigation of John Andersson."

"Correct." Her pulse begins to drum in her ears.

The man clears his throat. "We responded to a tip-off from a woman who saw a man with matching clothes. We're at the address right now."

"Tell me you have him," Lena says before she can stop herself. "Please, tell me you got John."

A short silence. "I'm afraid not," Patrick says. "We're pretty sure he's been here, but–"

Lena wants to scream. They are late again. "Make sure no one touches anything," she says. "Start searching the area. John could still be nearby. The same goes for the murder suspect; he's been sighted in the district."

"You're talking about the man in the pictures we received this morning, right?" Patrick asks.

"Yes, he's the presumed murderer of–"

"He's here. We got him."

Lena falters from a sudden vertigo as the information sinks in. The sound of the siren on the car's roof turns into a single, drawn-out note. She wonders if she is imagining the words; perhaps she has grown so desperate to catch the men that she is hallucinating.

"Repeat," Lena says after a moment.

"We have the suspect, and also another man who was in the same flat. We've secured a large stash of drugs, too."

"Take them both to the station in Vällingby."

"I thought there was someone else running the investigation of–"

"There is," Lena says, "but right now, I'm talking to you, and I'm your superior. Find a room and keep the men there. We won't be long." Agnes flashes the fingers on one of her hands three times. "Fifteen minutes," Lena adds.

"We can't take them in," Patrick says.

"Will you bloody listen," Lena shouts at the phone. "I haven't got time to run through the whole procedure. I'll deal with the paperwork later. Those men have critical information, and I need it."

"It's not that," Patrick says hesitantly. "One of the men – not the suspect, but the other one – he must be taken to hospital. They're rolling him out now."

Lena goes cold. A thousand visions invade her mind. "Why?"

"The paramedics think his neck is fractured. And then some. His face is a mess."

"What of the suspect?" Lena asks. "Please tell me he's alive."

"He's alive, all right." Silence. "But he probably wishes he wasn't."

"Just tell me what the hell's wrong, will you?" Lena forces herself to keep her voice level. She ignores Agnes's concerned glance.

"I'm not sure how to explain," Patrick says. "You'd better see for yourself."

*

CHAPTER 34

The other John

John sits at the back of a bus and watches the suburbs pass by.

Moving at half its normal speed, the bus negotiates roads cleared by salt, warm underground conduits and lumbering ploughs. Beyond the snowfall are the soft outlines of cars covered by crisp layers of white.

Three other people are on the bus. All of them face the other way. The driver barely glanced at him and the ticket he bought from a corner shop. Everyone's mind is on the cold.

The route takes him through low blocks of flats and patches of small, one-storey villas. He passes large leafless trees, ruler-straight hedges, and staring snowmen. Trees filled with strings of lights glow like clusters of stars. The air inside the bus is hot and humid, but outside, the temperature is falling.

The bus will take him from Stockholm's western districts to the vast and closely huddled blocks of flats of the northern suburbs.

On his way to the bus stop, he stopped at a phone booth and called Tom's home landline number. A first step to find out where Tom is.

The person who answered the phone was not John's target, but a woman who curtly informed John that she was not Tom's damned secretary and added that John could try calling Tom's office or call again later.

He didn't know what company Tom works for, so he looked out the window and suggested a name that rhymed on a nearby supermarket. The woman asked what he was talking about and gave him the name of Tom's business.

"Thanks," John said. "You've been very helpful."

"Moron," the woman said and hung up.

John's second call had been to a directory enquiries service, from which he got Tom's company phone number and address. When he called Tom's office, a fast-speaking woman explained that Tom was busy in a meeting.

"Can I take a message for him?" she asked. "I'm sure he won't be long."

"It can wait," John replied. "But thank you."

Now John is on his way.

Once he reaches his destination, he will take the underground train to the city. The bus ride is long but necessary; police and security firms will be more alert on the underground. Three-quarters of an hour on the bus, half an hour on the train, and he will be at Tom's office. Then remains the question of how he will get close to Tom.

He will have to improvise.

Making sure his bag is out of sight, he unfolds the papers he found in the shoebox: Stapled web page printouts with data and pictures that describe the contents of the box. The information is new to him, and he has little time to prepare, so he reads carefully while the bus takes him closer to his target.

Semi-automatic. Eight rounds. Most effective within fifty metres. Safety switch location, recoil statistics, weight, dimensions.

John reaches into the box and fits his hand around the pistol's grip. The metal is cool and coarse. Two spare clips lie next to the weapon.

The bus stops. He puts the papers back, closes his bag, and leaves the bus. A short stroll across a park takes him to the underground train station. The ticket inspector is lost in a book half-hidden under a manual. No security in sight.

John rides down the escalator, stops on the platform, and looks along the tracks that lead to the city. The wind from the tunnel smells of soot and electricity.

He is closing in.

*

CHAPTER 35

Lena

As soon as Agnes's car has skidded to a stop outside the block in which John had been seen, Lena leaves the vehicle and runs past the police officers.

A plastic crime scene tape forms a barrier between the entrance to the apartment block and the mass of curious people. Twelve officers and an ambulance have sparked interest, and tweets and texts have attracted hundreds of people. The police are surrounded by wool hats, mittens and concerned whispers. There are at least fifty cameras pointed at the flat.

Flashing her police ID card over her shoulder, she ducks under the crime scene tape, dashes into the block of flats, and stops outside Mick's door.

Inside the small flat are over a dozen police officers and paramedics shuffling around the confined space and mumbling to each other. The air stinks of chemicals. The doors of the ambulance outside were open, so she expects to find the apprehended man inside the flat, but there is no one in the room except police officers and medical personnel.

Most paramedics and most of the officers are struggling with the built-in wardrobe door, but their backs block her view. A pool of blood has formed on the floor near a broken table. Motes of dust swirl in the light from an overturned lamp.

Despite the cold, sweat breaks out on Lena's back. Something bad has happened here. She can tell from the atmosphere alone.

She opens her mouth to tell everyone to leave before they ruin every useful trace, then glimpses the wardrobe.

Choking on her shout, she makes a strangled sound and begins to turn away, but she forces herself to look. A deep-seated remnant of her professional self knows this is a critical moment. She has to make sure she understands what she sees. After a few seconds, she walks away, fists clenched and her breath caught in her lungs.

Leaning against a wall, she waits for a paramedic to give her a rundown of what has happened to the two men inside the flat. She is fairly sure she knows, but she needs details to digest, facts she can break down to manageable pieces and isolated observations.

Hopefully, she will not have to go back inside the flat; the space might pull her into the pool of insanity that must fill John's head. The idea of saving him is shrivelling into a laughable dream. This is the second crime scene in two days with which she cannot cope, but she has to stay in case she spots a trace, a sign, anything to point her in the right direction.

The items Agnes and the officers find in the flat infuriate Lena as much as her inability to revisit the scene. They probably have Molly's murderer; the flat is covered in prints, and copies have been hurried to the headquarters for matching. The police have secured a major drug stash, too. On top of that, they have secured a large sum of money, numerous other fingerprints, and a tennis racket case with a disassembled automatic pistol.

A good find on any day except this, because what they need to find is a clue that tells them where John is. There is no landline or mobile phones in the flat. The men must have hidden their phones, unless they are buried in the mess on the floor.

Lena chews on her lip and glances at Agnes. The younger officer looks at ease as she helps the paramedics push a rolling stretcher through the block's narrow doorway. When they arrived, Agnes took a long look inside the flat, glanced at Lena, and jogged off to the underground station to buy Lena a cup of what the local kiosk called coffee.

The woman is hardening by the hour; there is no trace of anxiety on the woman's face, but she had been shaken by the scene in Molly's flat. Agnes's tenseness has been replaced by an irritating cool; as a senior officer, Lena is supposed to be a role model, not a nervous wreck. That is not happening.

And if they do not find John soon, Lena is afraid she might collapse altogether. She steadies her hand, sips from her coffee, and looks up at the sky. The snowflakes sting her eyes.

"Lena Franke?" a male voice addresses her.

Lena looks down and finds in front of her a young man in a green paramedic uniform. His face is round and soft, making his unyielding and watchful expression look out of place.

"Yes?" Lena says.

"I was told you wanted a summary before we leave. It'll have to be quick. The other officers want us to move the man on the door out; the sound is getting to them."

"The sound?"

"He's screaming, but you have to be close to hear him. Or maybe he's trying to speak. Don't get your hopes up; he won't be talking for a while. Perhaps he never will."

"I get it." Lena throws her empty coffee cup on the ground. "Give me the facts."

The man looks with disapproval at the cup and back at Lena. "We have two men, both in their late twenties. I saw the stuff in the flat, the drugs and all that, so I suppose you'll have their names soon. They'll have records."

"Maybe," Lena says, unwilling to speculate about details that do not matter now. "Tell me what happened."

The corner of the man's mouth twitches. "I can't tell exactly what went down in there, only the injuries. The man who's on his way to hospital has suffered severe trauma to his face. A hammer, I'd guess. His nose shattered, probable fractures to the surrounding bone. He's also got a trauma to the side of his head from some other tool, something sharp and heavy. We saw a bloodied toaster close to the broken table where he lay."

Lena swallows and bites her lip. John the placid painter almost braining a man with a toaster. The scenario is almost impossible to imagine. "How badly hurt is he?"

"He's lost lots of blood, and I wouldn't be surprised if he's suffered internal haemorrhages or damages to his brain, but—"

Lena presses the tips of her fingers to her forehead as a headache flashes into being. She squeezes her eyes shut, opens them again, and exhales through gritted teeth. "Right," she says. "Go on."

"Of course." The man's face is neutral while he waits for Lena to gather herself. "The other man," he says, "has been glued to the built-in wardrobe."

Lena nods; she thought she recognized the chemical smell, and the naked man on the wardrobe door had been covered by a semi-transparent film. Where it covered his face, it had fixed the man's contorted face into a hideous mask of acute pain.

"His legs are straight down," the paramedic continues, "his arms along his sides. Apart from his jeans, he's naked. He's still stuck there because the wardrobe is wooden. If he'd been glued to the wall, the paint would've come off and he would've fallen down. Wood just soaks it up. We have to saw him down."

"Bloody hell," Lena whispers.

"An officer found the glue can. It's some kind of spray-on instant super glue, industrial-strength stuff. It's been emptied over him, mostly over his face. He's breathing through his nose, so I think whoever did this covered the man's nostrils. But the guy's mouth, lips and teeth are practically fused together. The same with his eyes, his ears, and the rest of his face. The spray has dissolved much of his skin. Are you feeling all right?"

Lena leans against the wall while she stares at the ground. Her pulse booms in her head. Just as she thinks she understands how driven John is, he goes and does this. She wonders if there will be any trace of reason left in him when she finds him.

Even worse is the chance that John will not move again. What he has done here is different from the other incidents: he has taken his time to inflict a gruelling torture from which the victim, if he survives, never will recover.

And Lena is sure who the victim is. Even though he is encased in a shell of cement-hard glue, she knows him from the underground train surveillance footage. The prints will match. Gren will be relieved. One mission accomplished. Finding John will be the next priority, but a less urgent one. A stray lunatic is less dangerous than a killer on the loose, especially if he believes he has had his revenge.

But if John is done with his self-imposed mission, where is he?

Lena looks at the flat's opaque window. If Gren asks her to stand down, he will make a mistake. The murderer is alive. Deliberately kept breathing. Crippled, but not slain. John should not have held back; he wanted justice, and the woman he loved is gone. Her nemesis would need to meet the same fate.

Turning east, towards the city, she feels the conviction sink in. John is not finished; for all its horror, this scene lacks finality. The closure is yet to come.

"I'm okay," Lena says and straightens. She had tuned out the paramedic entirely. "What else?"

"Not much." The paramedic shrugs; he wants to get back to his work. "The glue is toxic, so as soon as we've got the man down, we need to take him in for a blood transfusion. If he survives that long."

"Should either of the men talk," Lena says, "call us straight away. They have important information."

The man studies Lena for a few seconds. "They've been abused to near death, and you are expecting to interview them?"

"Just let me know if it happens." Lena's phone buzzes in her pocket. She turns away from the paramedic and picks up her phone. Gren. She takes the call.

"I was just about to call," she lies. "Tell me you have good news."

"No sign of John on the trains," Gren answers. "The managers aren't happy, but we can hold the trains for a little longer. What's the status at the flat? All I have from the local police station is bits and pieces."

"The forensic team is going over the flat. I think you'll be glad to know that the primary suspect is here."

"Under arrest?" Gren asks quickly.

"What's left of him is under arrest. You'll need to send a patrol to keep watch at the hospital."

"Please explain."

Lena retells what the paramedic told her. As she expects, Gren is stunned; he replies only with taut questions and delayed hums. She suspects that this is beyond anything he has encountered too. They are in uncharted territory, and it is up to her to find the lighthouse.

"I'm going to see if there's any lead as to where John's gone," Lena finishes. "I'll be in touch soon."

When she has hung up, she looks around to see if she can catch John spying on them, but she doubts he is anywhere near. The crowd has grown to at least three hundred people. As far as she is concerned, mobile social networking is a curse.

Once again she turns east.

"Do something," she says under her breath. "Make some noise. But don't hurt anyone. No more pain."

She stands in the wake of John's deeds, surrounded by questions and riddles. This hunt will go on forever unless she changes the rules. In order to intercept John, she must tease out the *why* from the rampant confusion that is John's mind. She has to understand what drives him.

Walking towards the block's front door, she steels herself in preparation for going inside. There is no staying away any longer. Somewhere in the flat, there might be a critical lead, a subtle hint to John's next move.

Just as she is about to enter, the door opens and Molly's murderer is rolled out on a stretcher by two grim-looking paramedics.

A murmur rises from the crowd. The man on the stretcher racks so hard he threatens to throw off the blanket strapped over his body, so a third paramedic walking beside the stretcher does her best to keep the man covered from the cameras.

Lena is unsure why the man is shaking; perhaps because of toxins in the glue, or maybe from pain. The blanket is wrapped closely around the man, and as he passes in front of her, she sees a rectangular outline in one of his pockets. A phone.

She waits while the man is loaded into the ambulance to the sound of spectators gasping in wonder and revulsion. Once the man is inside, she quickly walks up to the vehicle and grabs one of the doors before a paramedic enters.

"Just a second," Lena says and climbs into the ambulance.

The confined space is packed with shelves, drawers, tubes, lights and switches. In the middle, the man strapped to the stretcher twitches and jerks like a doll pulled by strings in all directions.

She glimpses an arm and a leg, stiff and coloured bright red by the stiff layer of super-strength glue. Even if the doctors can get it off his skin and save his life, the man will at best end up a grotesque remnant of a human being.

A frantic humming sounds from the man's face under the blanket. Perhaps he knows Lena is near and wants to talk. Or perhaps he can sense her secret, hidden under her brittle front as an upholder of law and order. Maybe he feels what she is capable of and wants her to end his pain. One monster communicating with another on some silent, subconscious level.

But the actions of this man caught up with him. His punishment has been realized by John, peaceful painter turned avenging angel. No one has come for Lena yet. Until that happens, she will snatch her own kin back from the brink. And she'll start with John.

She turns her back to the protesting paramedic and pulls out her pocketknife, carves through the man's jeans, and pulls out the mobile phone. The screen is black. Blood seeps through the jeans; the knife is small, but she keeps it sharp. Grimacing, she stuffs the phone inside her jacket and turns around to face the scowling paramedic.

"Are you finished in there?" he asks. "There's no time for this. We have to take him in, right now."

Lena hops down from the ambulance and moves out of the flustered man's way. "All done," she says. "Let me know if he talks."

The paramedic looks at Lena, pulls the doors shut in her face, and the ambulance drives away, its siren blaring.

Agnes walks up to Lena's side. "What was that about?"

"I'll tell you in the car," Lena says.

*

163

CHAPTER 36

Lena

Four minutes later, Lena and Agnes exit a roundabout and leave the suburb. Lena sits in the passenger seat and prods the mobile phone. She hopes it will work without a code.

The sun is a faint disc struggling to rise over the rooftops. Inside the car, the air is hot and stifling; the heaters run on full effect. Agnes swerves from lane to lane between slower cars. Agnes drives with less caution than usual; Lena suspects that Agnes is shaken by John's macabre act.

Lena resists the urge to throw the phone to the floor. She has never been a fan of technology; everything with circuits is at odds with her lack of patience. After printers, phones are the worst.

She almost drops the phone in surprise when it obediently comes to life after she presses a small button. Thankfully, there is no code, and after a few minutes she finds the call log. She is reading through the list while Agnes brakes for a red light near Brommaplan.

Agnes glances at the phone. "Anything interesting?"

"Not yet." Lena frowns. "There's not a single text. He must wipe them regularly. There are plenty of calls, but no recent ones. Only numbers in the address book, no names. I bet most are to prepaid accounts anyway."

Not for the first time, Lena wishes Swedish legislation was as stringent as it was in many other countries, where you have to register to have a prepaid phone. She takes out her notepad and starts to copy the numbers.

"I'll have the office run the numbers through the system once we're back," Lena says. "I'll copy local officers in too. They might see a familiar number. You never know. I just have to get the numbers out of this phone at the office. I'll need your help."

"Can't the tech department do that for us?" Agnes asks.

"We don't have time to fill out the forms. Besides, someone might break the damn thing. This is important."

Agnes frowns. "Didn't you break your old phone—"

"That was an accident."

"Oh."

They pass another roundabout and turn onto a bridge. "Why are you doing that now?" Agnes asks.

"It's all I have to go on until John crops up somewhere else. I'm sick of chasing him. If there's anything in here that'll let me work out what he's up to, I will find it."

Agnes is quiet, then says, "Don't forget to check the phone's memory."

Lena looks at her. "What?"

"In case the numbers you got there are from only the SIM card."

"I know that," Lena lies and tries to figure out how to access the phone's internal memory. By the time she is done, they are driving down into the vast, damp garage underneath the police headquarters.

Eight minutes later, Lena is at her desk and types the numbers into an email to a technician. The office is filled with the drone of ringing phones, conversations, quick footsteps, coughs, the dull whirr of computers and the scraping of chairs. Outside the window, the clouds are a deep bluish black, heavy with the promise of more snow.

When she has sent off the list, she phones the recipient and tells her to report back immediately once the numbers have been checked. She hangs up and checks her email, her phone, the police's internal system, and her post box. No news about John.

She shrugs off her jacket over the back of her chair and walks to the canteen for a sandwich. Seeing the crawling queue, she returns to her desk. Somewhere in the chaos of her drawers, she is sure, a protein bar is hiding.

"Any luck with the phone?" Agnes says behind Lena.

Startled, Lena spins her chair around with her hands half raised in defence. Agnes takes a quick step back. In each of her hands is a steaming cup.

"Don't do that," Lena tells her. "You'll give someone a heart attack."

"I'm sorry." Agnes looks apologetic and offers Lena one of the cups. "I thought you might want more coffee. You didn't get much sleep last night."

Lena wants to groan as she takes the cup. "I thought you went back to your place?" She finds a half-eaten protein bar in the drawer. Not the meal she wished for, but a little is better than nothing.

"What I meant to say," Agnes says, "is you can't have slept more than six hours or so. I'm about to see if the patrols have any news. Call if you need me." She clears her throat, smiles, and walks away to her meticulously organized desk.

Lena's gaze lingers on Agnes for a moment, then turns back to her desk, and she shakes her head. The junior officer is babysitting her. It is the last thing she needs.

What she does need is a lead. She checks her inbox again. Nothing. Her phone is almost fully charged, but she plugs it in anyway. She begins on a report she must submit but finds she cannot string together a coherent sentence. Sweat prickles her back.

She calls Gren, hangs up on his voicemail, and moves the windows on her computer screen around. Anxiety constricts her lungs. She is still hungry; stress and concentration are burning off every calorie she eats. Against all odds, she finds another protein bar and tears away the wrapping.

A new email arrives: The numbers from the address book in the mobile phone have been checked. All names sent to her, along with text messages retrieved from the service providers.

Lena throws her half-eaten bar onto the clutter on her desk, opens the email, and skims through the list. Twenty-one calls made during the past two days, to and from fourteen different numbers.

Six outgoing, the rest incoming. Five of them to landlines.

She browses the text messages: Threats, questions, orders, agreed meeting times, locations, and prices. Some messages are in crackpot innuendo; others are misspelt pleas for drugs, typed by desperate and quivering thumbs. A wealth of leads for the narcotics department, but nothing that points to John.

She pinches the bridge of her nose and reads on, looking for clues in the thicket of acronyms, abbreviations, and butchered grammar. After a few seconds, she stops and rereads one of the messages.

Must come to your place. Got pigs after me.

Sent yesterday afternoon. The time closely matches that of the shooting. The reply makes her lean closer to the screen.

Don't. I'm meeting T soon. What the fuck have you done?

Another sent message:

I have to hide. I'll talk to T later. Stay at home. I'm coming there.

The reply:

Damn it. You better not be followed.

She presses her index finger to the *T* on the screen. Perhaps the letter is short for Niklas's dealer. If it is, then he or she could have been near the flat when John appeared there. The chance that the might-be dealer has seen John or anything else relevant to the case is small, but she will explore every clue no matter how weak.

She opens the list of calls made from Niklas's phone and scrolls down. Near the bottom is a mobile phone number that Niklas called moments after he got the first text message in which 'T' is mentioned. Mick had been supposed to meet him or her.

Had Niklas called his dealer?

She looks up the number and is unsurprised to find that it is anonymous; however unless the owner uses a military-grade secrecy screen, that is a small issue: if the phone is switched on, the police can trace it. But first she has to change into a new shirt; sweat makes the one she is wearing cling to her back.

"Agnes?" Lena calls and looks over her shoulder.

Agnes's head snaps up. "Yes?"

"I need you." Lena points to her monitor.

Agnes walks over and peers at Lena's screen, and Lena points at the *T.*

"The dealer?" Agnes asks after a moment.

"Probably. Tell the tech department to get a fix on that phone's location."

"I'll get right on it."

"And let's hope it isn't turned off," Lena says. "I'll be right back." She takes a spare T-shirt from a drawer, rises from her chair, and leaves for the bathroom.

*

CHAPTER 37

John Andersson

John drags himself up onto the flat rock and slumps down on his back. Seconds pass while he can do nothing but gulp down air. A blistering wind rips through his hair. His limbs are on fire after the climb, but the gale is quickly dispelling the warmth.

The bright spot on the sky beckons. It could be as distant as the moon. For all he knows, it may even be the sun, obscured by some ashen, unearthly fog. It remains the only anomaly he's seen so far. The clouds, if that's what they are, look somewhat closer, although that impression might be down to his imagination.

He rises to his knees and looks up.

Around him is an enormous field dotted by gaping holes. Everywhere he turns are deep pits, similar to the one he just escaped, as if he were standing on a giant blackened honeycomb. The plain stretches away in every direction until it bleeds into complete darkness. No sign of life or light. Apart from the glowing patch high above, he's surrounded by a featureless night filled with ferocious winds.

The sight bleeds him of strength. His long, harrowing ascent was worthless. He might as well have stayed on the ice and waited for his body to crumble under the cold, or the snow to suffocate him.

Only that is unlikely to happen. If he were to leap back down, he'd be kept alive and conscious, preserved to experience the full extent of the pain from his broken body, until he goes mad from pain, solitude, or sheer dread.

That's the ambition of this infernal place. Its foul intent is so palpable he should be able to taste it.

I am in Hell.

An impossible, absurd, laughable notion. And yet, it's all he has to go on.

Keep moving.

The edges between the pits are narrow, but wide enough to walk across. He walks up to the edge of the nearest pit and peers down. The bottom, a near-black disc dotted by shadows and almost lost under a cloud of whirling snow.

No closer look is needed to know the shadows are bodies. More people trapped on or under the ice of another frozen lake. If this is true for every hole in his sight, there must be a world of imprisoned souls before him.

He steps back from the edge and stops when he hears laughter.

*

CHAPTER 38

Lena

Lena enters the ladies-only bathroom, closes the door behind her, and sighs.

A brief breathing pause. Silence and cold water to sharpen her thoughts. When she feels a little more awake, she will head back to the office and wait for the techs to trace the mysterious phone. They have an hour. After that, she will take to the streets and walk while she waits for the call; the office is cramped and suffocating.

The bathroom is a tiled corridor with six stalls along the left wall and a row of porcelain sinks on the right. A long mirror above the sinks reflects the yellowish light from the fluorescent tubes high above. At the far end of the corridor, opposite the door, is a large frosted window that overlooks a landscape of rooftops. In a corner of the ceiling is a small air vent humming softly. She is alone; the doors to all the stalls are open.

Grimacing at the smell of disinfectants, she walks past the stalls and locks herself inside the last one. The blue T-shirt she has brought smells of dust, but it is dry and clean. Sweat, dirt and spots of blood stain the one she wears.

She takes off her shirt and slips into the T-shirt, wishing thoughts were as easy to swap. If they were, she would change her loop of anguish for the measured clarity that people expect from her. Not for the first time, she considers suggesting to Gren that Agnes could take over her role, and normal recruitment protocols be damned. Gren wants Lena in proper rehabilitation anyway. He may welcome the chance for a smooth transition.

The door to the bathroom opens and closes, and someone occupies the stall next to her, making only enough noise for Lena to know someone is using it. So much for a moment of privacy.

She takes her shirt under her arm, leaves her stall, and turns to the mirror in an effort to put her hair up. Pulling her hair back so hard she winces, she winds the elastic band hard around the tangled mass and studies her face in the mirror. Pasty skin, dirt on her forehead, bags under her eyes so dark she could have been in a fight. No wonder people fussed.

She needs more sleep, but that has to wait until John is found, brought in, sedated, and locked up. He has thrown the lid to her box of secrets open, and the contents are seeping out, making themselves known in her actions and words, even her face. Unless she finds John, he will destroy them both.

Breathing out, she cranes her neck and walks towards the exit, her dirty shirt clenched in her fist.

You were right, a male voice whispers.

Lena stops, frowns, and turns around. The voice was so hushed she barely caught the words. The stall adjacent to the one she used is still occupied, but she is sure the voice belonged to a man. No men use the ladies' bathroom here.

Walking down the bathroom, she checks the other stalls. All empty. She shakes her head and takes another step towards the exit.

There is a place for people like us, the voice whispers again. *A prison. A dead end. A home.*

Childish but deep, the voice trembles as if on the verge of laughter.

Lena faces the closed stall. Behind the door is a man, in the women's bathroom, whispering nonsense, raving to himself or someone on a phone.

Staring at the door, she tries to picture the man inside, but the notion feels contrived and false. The space where the vision would fit is already taken by another, more alarming sensation. Sweat trickles down her back again. The hum from the air vent seems to grow louder.

Do you understand the world now? The voice sighs. *You have lived like a bug on its surface, never crawled inside it. Until today.*

Lena backs away from the closed stall until her back is against the sink. Her eyes are fixed on the door. The voice is familiar: it belongs to a face that hovers on the threshold of her awareness, refusing to come into focus.

"Can I help you?" Lena demands in a weak voice.

Oh, but the chance to help has come and gone. It's too late for me, too late for him, and much too late for you.

"I haven't got time for this shit. If you want to—"

Such a swift journey, the voice giggles. *A pull, a slip and a twitch, and here we are. We bought the ticket, you and I, and we took the ride. We went all the way down. I just went a little faster than you.*

Finally, Lena recognises the voice. She drops her shirt and grips the sink so hard one of her fingernails cracks in half. Her eyes are so wide they fill with tears.

The voice laughs. *Is that disbelief on your face? How pathetic. Did you think your badge would save you? That a lacquer of virtue could hold the real you in a cage?*

Inside the stall is the paedophile she shot in the botched raid.

The first and last time she heard that voice, it accused her for bursting into its private domain of abuse and misery. She shut it up with a bullet sent straight through the man's words.

Your moral high ground can't keep your feet dry, the voice continues. *There's no stopping the flood, and it has come to wash you away.*

"Never," Lena whispers.

We're together at last. Didn't you know? A burst of dry laughter. *Of course you don't. You've never looked.* The voice gains in strength and makes the closed door shudder. *You never. Fucking. Looked.*

Panic closes in on Lena. This is a wind-up, an illusion, a nightmare reinforced by fatigue and fear. She has fallen asleep in the stall or at her desk, accidentally letting the demons in to taunt her. Still, her senses tell her otherwise. The sink is icy cold against her skin, the pain from her broken fingernail hot and vivid. The voice is real.

"Shut up." Lena's voice is a coarse murmur.

You ought to thank me. I've showed you what you've forgotten, or tried to forget.

"Go away." Her mouth is parched, her lungs empty. She swallows and draws a haggard breath. "You're not real."

I pulled your curtains of pretty ideals apart. A pause, followed by long, wheezing laughter. *How do you like the view?*

At last, Lena snaps. Adrenaline fountains like wildfire in her limbs. She has to look inside the stall, and when she does, she will see a man whose face she will ruin for pulling off this psychotic prank.

There is no slit under the door; the only way to see who hides in the stall is to peek over its walls, which means standing on the toilet in one of the adjacent stalls. She cannot will herself to do that, so instead she takes a step back and kicks the door with all her strength.

The thin door cracks down the middle with a sharp *bang* that makes her ears ring. Splinters and chipped wood explode into the stall. One part of the door remains hanging askew on a hinge while the other half falls down onto the tiled floor.

The stall is empty.

Standing in the doorway with her fists balled, she blinks with watering eyes into the stall. Toilet, brush, toilet roll, coat hanger. No man. The voice is gone. The small vacant space is a void where something had been a second ago.

She stumbles back to the sink, slumps down onto the floor, and rests her head in her hands, still keeping an eye on the stall. There is nowhere to hide or escape, but she did hear the words, every drawled syllable. It was not a hallucination.

Wiping away her tears, she coughs and bites back a sob. She cannot crack now. Not before she has found John. If she is destined to lose her sanity, she will do so only when the chase is over. Perhaps her saneness is not an essence she can keep bottled up by will alone, but she will try.

Slowly, she rises from the floor, picks up her shirt, and looks at the destroyed stall. Her breathing is shallow and rapid.

She gives the stall the finger, and leaves the bathroom.

*

CHAPTER 39

Lena

Agnes is waiting by Lena's desk. In her hand is a paper, but she lowers it as Lena approaches.

"Are you okay?" Agnes asks. "Someone just said they heard a crash from the ladies' room." She frowns at Lena's torn fingernail. "Is that blood?"

"The door was stuck. I broke it. Remind me to tell the janitor." Lena pulls a Band-Aid from a green plastic first-aid kit on the wall. "What is that in your hand?" she asks. "News?"

Agnes nods. "The phone is an anonymous prepaid account, but they got a good approximate location. It's in the system." She uses Lena's computer to open up the map.

A thumbnail-sized shadowed circle in the middle of the city marks the supposed location of the phone. The circle covers four blocks. There will be hundreds, if not thousands of people inside the area.

"We're lucky," Agnes continues. "The phone is in the city, so it was easy to triangulate."

"Great." Lena inspects her bandaged finger. "Have they got a call log for that phone?"

"It's in the system."

Lena sits down to open the file on her computer, but her hands shake so much she cannot type. Before she can say anything, Agnes leans over and uses Lena's mouse.

"Here." Agnes runs a finger down the list of incoming calls on the screen. "That's Niklas's number, third from the bottom."

Lena nods slowly and puts her hands in her lap to stop them from trembling. Hopefully, Agnes has not noticed how unsettled she is.

"Let's check all calls he made and received today and yesterday," Lena says. "Names, addresses for the landlines."

"I thought you would want to do that." Agnes moves the mouse and clicks. "Here. Eighteen calls, eleven to landlines."

Lena reads through the names and addresses of the landline phones that had called the anonymous mobile. This time, they were less lucky; the locations are across the entire city. She reads through the list again. "Fourth and eight addresses," she says. "Tobias Fryklund, Farsta, and Tom Lundberg in Bromma. One south, one west."

"You think one of them is him?"

"Their names start with T. It's a far shot, but worth testing." Lena enters one of the names in a criminal record search and shakes her head.

"Tobias was nabbed for bike theft at the age of fifteen, and that's that. It was also last year. Let's try Tom."

Lena expects a similar, useless record, but when the result whisks onto the screen, she raises her eyebrows.

"No recent activity," Lena reads out loud, "but he's got a string of old charges for minor possession of illegal substances, eight in total." She scrolls down. "He has also been in court for one charge of assault and fraud, and he did time in a juvenile prison. There's also a recent suspicion of tax evasion. No convictions, though."

"What do you think?" Agnes asks.

"Look at that." Lena points to another window. "He's filthy rich, too. I think Tom's our man."

"Do you want to bring him in? I can call the prosecutor."

"What I want," Lena says quietly while she browses Tom's details, "is to get everyone on the streets and scour the damn city for a trace of John. This is a good lead if we want to nail Tom for dealing, but we haven't got time for that. We need to make sure every taxi driver has a picture of John. He's running on empty now. John must be a wreck, and he must look like one too."

"Understood," Agnes says. "We can alert coaches and the national railway too, in case John tries to leave Stockholm."

"Good idea. I don't want to take any chances with either of the two. We might as well talk to the airports too and ask them to raise their alert."

"Do you think Gren will authorize it?"

"He'll agree after I've called them. Meanwhile, you can look up the call logs for Tom's landline."

Lena looks up the number to the national railways administration. Getting train staff and bus drivers involved means more people looking, and John will surface somewhere. The more eyes that search for him, the quicker she will know.

Someone will spot him. Someone must. She refuses to be shoved back to square one. They are tracing a bomb that should have gone off long ago.

She busies herself with filling out the necessary forms and makes a mental note to contact the search patrols again. After that, she will ask the forensic team if they found anything useful in the flat on their second visit.

Just as she submits the form, Agnes materializes by her side.

"I got the call logs like you asked me to," Agnes says.

"And?"

"I found something."

"Yes?" Lena motions for Agnes to continue.

"It's the call log from Tom's landline. A call was made to Tom's landline from a phone booth in Hässelby Gård, only minutes before someone at Tom's home called the mobile phone we traced in the city."

"Are you sure?" Lena asks. "What time was the call made?"

"About an hour after John was spotted in Hässelby."

Lena looks at Agnes. Thoughts and suspicions fly through her head, and she struggles to separate wishes borne by hope from conclusion based on logic.

"Anyone who's got the number to Tom's landline," Lena says, "could have Tom's mobile phone number too." Still, the timing disturbs her. Even if it had been one of Tom's friends who called, the message could have been related to John.

To find out who called Tom's landline, they have to ask the person who answered the call. Lena dials the landline number and waits while the phone rings on the other end.

"Marie," a sleepy woman's voice answers.

Lena considers activating the phone's loudspeaker but changes her mind.

"This is detective Lena Franke from the Stockholm County Police Department," she says. "We would like your help with a few brief questions. Thank you for taking your time."

"I don't–"

"You received a phone call at twenty to eleven this morning. We require the full name of the person who called you." Lena does not know if the woman on the other end took the call in question, but she hopes so. And if she does not cooperate, there are more suspicions she can test.

"I don't know what you're talking about." The woman's voice has gone from sleepy to tense in the space of a few seconds. "How do I even know you're the police?"

Lena wonders if people often called the woman and pretended they were someone else. She opts for some mild coercion.

"If you have a number display," Lena says mildly, "you will see that this call comes from the police department's exchange. Feel free to look up the number at your own leisure. If you're still in doubt, we're more than happy to come visit you."

"No, wait. I just–"

"There is a patrol car close to where you are, but we would rather do this over the phone to save time. It's your call."

The effort of polished formality makes Lena cringe, but she needs to play this straight. The woman will not want police officers in her home, and the more formal Lena sounds, the more she tightens the vice. Given the things found in Mick's flat, Tom's home will be turned upside down at some point anyway.

When the woman on the other end speaks again, she sounds fraught. "I don't have anything – shit, what has he done – look, can I call you back?"

"Absolutely, but there is no need. I'll send the officers up instead. They won't be a minute. Thank you for your–"

"No, wait. Hold on. What was it you wanted to know?"

"The full name of the person who called you at twenty to eleven this morning. And that person's residential address, if you know it."

"Let me think." A short pause. "I remember now. There was a man who called and asked for Tom. I told him Tom was still at the office. They had a big party yesterday. Tom always stays there when he's hungover," the woman explains with a note of hysteria in her voice.

"What was this man's name?" Lena asks.

"I don't know," the woman on the phone says. "Honestly, I have no idea. I've never seen the number before. He didn't even know the name of Tom's company. It's Lundberg Invest, but the guy who rang called it something else, like he was guessing."

Lena sits up straighter. "Are you suggesting that the man who called wasn't one of Tom's friends?"

"I thought he was. He never said so, though."

"Did he say anything else?"

"He thanked me for helping him. Sounded kind of weird, now that you ask."

"What did his voice sound like?"

"Not sure. Not young. Not old either. A bit stiff."

Lena stares into the distance. The room grows glacially cold.

"Hello?" the woman on the phone bleats nervously. "Are you still there? Are we done?"

Lena does not reply. She recalls what she thought when she stood outside Mick's flat: after what John had done there, he would want to get as far away as possible from the police, do anything to avoid getting caught, but also that he was not done.

A cold wave washes through her as she realises she was right. He was not done. John is still on the hunt.

"Did you give John the name of Tom's company?" Lena asks the woman weakly, hoping the answer would be no.

"Who's John?"

"Did you tell the man who rang you where Tom is?" Lena shouts.

"Jesus Christ, please calm down. Yes, I did. That's hardly a crime, is it?"

Lena slams the phone down and turns to Agnes. "Get the call log from that phone booth." Her throat hurts when she speaks.

While Agnes calls the telephone network, Lena turns to her computer and searches for Lundberg Invest. She finds the address: near Stureplan, right in the middle of Stockholm's fashion and banking district. An expensive office address. The pieces come together. She looks up the address on a map, and as she dreads, the address is exactly in the spot where Tom's mobile phone has been traced.

Agnes scribbles on a notepad, hangs up, and turns to Lena.

"Another call was made from the booth," Agnes says. "Just after the call to Tom's landline. It was to an office in the city."

"This one?" Lena points to the screen where the address is highlighted on a map. Her heartbeats are a rising thunder in her head. The police office is quiet; everyone is watching her.

"That's the one," Agnes says. "Do you think it's John?"

"I know it's him."

"How—"

"I just know." She rises from the chair so fast it falls over. So many things she needs to do, all of them screaming for attention. "Agnes, call that office and tell them to lock all their doors and stay there. Nobody leaves until we get there. If they ask why, say there's been a robbery next door."

While Agnes calls, Lena points at a colleague and then at her own computer screen. "Get every damn available car to this address. The suspect might be present and violent."

The officer nods and springs into action; the rumour of what Lena encountered at Mick's flat has spread.

Lena snatches her jacket from the back of her chair and runs towards the door. As she runs, she touches her gun waiting in its holster like a patient promise.

Just as she exits the room, Agnes catches up with her, and the two women jog down the corridor side by side, towards the elevators.

"There was no answer at the office," Agnes says. "Not even an answering machine."

"Damn it," Lena says under her breath and turns a corner. "It's John. He's there."

"Do you want me to call Gren?" Agnes asks.

"I'll do that," Lena replies. "As soon as we're in the car."

Less than a minute later, Lena and Agnes shoot out of the garage and into the white afternoon.

Three other police cars follow them from the garage. Snow drizzles down from the grey sky and reduces their sight to only a block ahead.

Agnes turns right, skids up on the pavement, swerves back on the road, and continues around an empty park on a hill. Lena turns the siren on and gets her safety belt on.

A moment later, one of their side view mirrors smacks into a parked truck and cracks. Until today, Agnes has always driven as she has acted: cool, gentle and controlled. This rough, reckless driving is new, and possibly lethal.

"Sorry." Agnes's hands grip the steering wheel hard. "I'm nervous."

Lena's phone rings while they turn another corner and continue downtown. "Franke," she answers while the city rushes past the window. Unless they slow down, they might not survive the short trip.

"This is Gren. Where are you?"

"I was just about to call," Lena says. "We're on our way to an office near Stureplan, and–"

"I know," Gren says. "I came in to the headquarters just after you left. Why do you think John is heading to this office?"

"It's complicated." Lena holds on to her seat while Agnes turns a corner and guns the car down a sloping street. "But it's not a wild guess. I promise."

"The tactical response team are on their way too. They'll probably be there before you."

Lena makes a disgusted sound. Bringing in the police's heavily armed response team makes sense, but the presence of more officers could cause John to run or send him deeper into his escalating madness.

Gren pauses before he continues. "Lena, listen to me."

"I have to–"

"Shut up and listen."

Lena goes quiet. Never before has she heard her commander so close to losing his temper. He was choosing the worst of moments to scold her. She wanted to tell him to go to hell, but he might order her back to the office.

"I'm listening," Lena says.

"I had a call from a paramedics manager about your visit inside an ambulance. He said you tried to interrogate a man who was on the brink of death. And someone here just mentioned your name in connection with a destroyed booth in the bathroom."

"The door was jammed."

"I appreciate that you're doing all you can to find John," Gren says, "but I can only do so much before you'll be taken off this case, or worse. More important people than me are watching. Do I make myself clear?"

"Crystal."

"When this is over, you and I will have a talk, and you will go on a brief leave. As I said, the response team might already be there, but do not proceed without them. Don't enter, don't call, don't do anything. That's an order."

"Anything else?"

He pauses again. "Be safe," Gren says, and hangs up.

Agnes glances at Lena. "What did he say?"

"Nothing helpful. Drive faster."

They shoot under first one overpass, then another, and accelerate down a broad street lined with theatres, bars and cinemas. In the distance, at the end of the street, is a mushroom-shaped sculpture, high as two men and ringed by pay phones. The other police cars are just behind Lena and Agnes. Cars in front veer left and right as they try to move out of the way. The sirens roar between the walls.

Agnes's eyes are concentrated on the street ahead. "Almost there."

*

CHAPTER 40

The other John

John stands in front of Tom's office.

The building is a wide six-storey block with spacious, century-old apartments converted to a maze of offices and conference rooms. Tall windows in the ochre façade reflect the grey-white sky. Most windows are dark, though a few are brightly lit by halogen spotlights inside.

John leans against the wall across the street and speaks into his mobile phone. His bag is slung over his shoulder, the remaining glue spray can is held tight in his right armpit, and the gun is tucked down the back of his trousers. He keeps his injured hand in his pocket; it can attract attention, and the hand is too swollen to hide inside a glove. If left untreated, he suspects the cuts will make the hand useless, but he will not need it much longer.

His hands, his feet, and his heart protest what he has put them through over the past day; however they have served their purpose. His organs have taken him and his tools here. This is where his mission will end. What he did to Niklas is not enough, but ending Tom will settle the debt.

He does not long for violence; his only goal is to restore the balance. The needle on the scales burns red in his mind. Justice for a crime committed. Pain for hurt inflicted. A life for a life lost.

Unless, of course, Tom's death reveals yet another part of the chain. If that were to happen, John will go on, link by link.

A group of women and men in suits and designer jackets leaves the building through its glass-and-steel entrance. They pause to zip up jackets and tighten wool scarves, then head towards the nearby plaza, walking slowly in the narrow path made by other pedestrians. Few cars pass outside; the street is wide but ends in a cul-de-sac currently used as a snow dump, making the street passable only by foot.

The entrance opens to a large marble hall. Inside is a spiral staircase to the left of the doors. Next to the staircase is a large lush plant in a terracotta pot, placed to conceal a fire extinguisher. On the opposite wall are a chrome bin and two elevators. To the right of the elevators is a curved desk in pale pine. Behind the desk, a receptionist watches a flat computer screen. She is a complication. He had not expected the entrance to be manned on a weekend.

John crosses the street and waits near the entrance. He continues to pretend to have a conversation over the phone. A sign next to the door lists the companies on each floor. Lundberg Invest is on the second floor.

After a few minutes, the doors to the elevator open. A man exits, walks towards the entrance, and opens the door. As the door swings back, John steps forward and keeps it open. When the man glances at John, he nods in greeting at the man and murmurs spurious details of an advertisement plan into his phone. The man frowns and walks away. John steps into the hall, closes the door behind him, and walks towards the stairs.

"Excuse me," the receptionist chirps.

John pauses with one foot on the stairs. He turns to face the receptionist.

"Can I help you?" she asks.

John walks up to her desk and studies her. Flawless make-up, early twenties, not a strand of hair straying from her blond ponytail. Blue business shirt, sleek black headset.

"I've come to see Tom Lundberg," John says. His voice echoes in the marble hall.

"Of course." She flashes a professional smile, taps at her screen, and frowns. "Have you made an appointment?"

"I'm afraid I haven't." John grimaces. "It's regarding a proposition I think Tom will be interested in. The deal is quite big, if you see what I mean. Which is why I'm here in person."

The receptionist nods but looks apologetic. "I understand, and I'm sure he would be interested, but unfortunately Tom is not in. Can I take a message?"

John pauses. "I don't understand," he says. "I called in earlier to make sure that Tom would be here. The woman who took the call confirmed that he was."

"Oh yes, I remember," she says. "You spoke with me. Tom was in at the time, but he's gone to Arlanda Airport for a business trip. He's due back early next week."

John stiffens and holds his breath. His prey has fled, perhaps too far to be caught before the police come too close. His head begins to throb. The muscles in his body ache with pent-up tension.

"I thought you wanted to talk to him over the phone," the receptionist continues. "But you hung up or were disconnected. If I'd known you wished to see him, I would have told you he would be leaving. I'm terribly sorry. Do you have his mobile phone number?"

"I do," John says, "but this is a matter I'd like to discuss face to face with Tom. Perhaps I can go to the airport and meet Tom there, if there's time?"

"I suppose you can," the receptionist says hesitantly. "His flight will leave early this afternoon, so he might already have gone through passport control. Let me give him a call and see where he is. Perhaps he can wait for you outside the security check." She beams at John and reaches for her keyboard.

John weighs risks in his mind. He asks if she knows exactly when Tom's plane is meant to take off.

"I have the details of the booking here, but–" The receptionist trails off and looks up.

John sees the wariness in her face, but she is too late. Three quick strides take him around her desk, where he crouches, close to the receptionist and out of sight from the entrance.

The receptionist stands up. "Excuse me, but this is a restricted space. You must move away."

When John fumbles inside his jacket instead of leaving, she takes a step back and reaches for the phone on her desk.

"If you don't leave, I'll have to–" she begins.

John aims his gun at her. "Keep still," he says. He must use both his hands to hold the weapon; its weight pulls his injured, tired fingers down.

The receptionist stares at the gun while her professional airs dissolve into naked fear. She points at a handbag that hangs on the back of her chair. "Take it," she stammers. "It's all I have."

"Sit down and face the entrance." When a faint ringtone sounds from the woman's headset, he instructs her to ignore the call and take off the headset. He grabs a handful of power cords on the floor and pulls the plugs out of the sockets. The computer and the telephone shut down with a series of clicks. Glancing above the desk, he looks at the front door. No one outside.

"Get down on the floor," John says.

The receptionist obeys, moving as if only in partial control of her limbs. Her face is pallid and clammy. This is a new problem; if the woman faints, he will have to find someone else who has the information he needs. Pain or fear might keep her conscious long enough.

He takes out his knife from his bag and explains what he will do with the knife if she passes out. He adds that he does not want to hurt her, but he must.

Tears well up in the woman's eyes. "What do you want?" she croaks.

"Information," John says. "Not money. Did you book Tom's ticket?"

"Yes."

"Do you have a copy?"

"Yes." She chokes back her tears and nods at the desk above her.

"Get the paper and show it to me."

"It's not a paper. The ticket's on the computer."

There is a small printer on the desk. "Print a copy of the ticket," John says.

"You turned it off." The receptionist points a trembling finger at the sockets. "You have to plug the cables back in."

John plugs the computer in again. "Hurry up."

The receptionist rises slowly, sits down on the chair, and starts up the computer. Minutes pass while she sobs and stares at the screen. Someone exits the elevator and leaves through the front door.

"Here," she says hoarsely. "Tom's itinerary and the other papers."

John looks at the columns and rows of information on the screen. "Print it."

The printer buzzes and spits out a stack of papers. Keeping his gun trained on the receptionist, John takes the papers and studies them. The flight leaves at three thirty.

One of the printouts shows a copy of Tom's passport: A man in his early thirties, fit and broad, white perfect teeth. Slightly raised chin, two-day stubble. Hard eyes focussed on the lens. Thick dark hair, perfect brush cut. Success with a dry smile.

John memorises gate, departure time, and flight number. He checks the time. The flight leaves in two hours. Quickly, he looks around the desk. Still no one outside.

He stands up and slams the butt of his gun into the monitor until it cracks and goes black.

"Walk up the stairs," John says and takes his bag. "Keep in front of me, and take me to another way out. An emergency exit, if there is one."

The receptionist begins to cry again. "There is. If I show you, can I go?"

"Yes," John says to calm her, but he knows that he will have to bring her along; the woman is too harried. No threat will stop her from breaking down and telling the police everything.

The receptionist nods, rises and walks slowly towards the stairs. After three steps, John tells her to stop.

Motionless, he stares at the entrance, oblivious to the risk of being seen. A sound on the border of his awareness has caught his attention. A remote, blaring song. Two distant notes of imprisonment and ruin.

Sirens.

They are coming closer; he can see flashes of blue in the windows across the street. He turns to the receptionist, who stands unmoving on the stairs, and she understands the look on John's face.

"No," she says, hysteria rising in her voice. "It wasn't me. I swear. You watched me all the time. I didn't call. You have to believe me."

John turns away. Even if the receptionist had managed to trip an alarm, it is irrelevant now. The police are coming, and he must escape. Only that matters. Fear is a concept left behind in Molly's flat.

"Lie down behind the desk," John says.

The receptionist turns around, stumbles to the floor, and crawls to her chair. Once she is out of sight behind the desk, John walks over to the entrance door, pulls it open, soaks the lock with the spray glue, and pushes the door shut. The sirens, now more than one, howl in the distance.

John leans close to the glass pane and looks down the street. A police car is speeding down the road. Behind it are a large van and more police cars. There are seconds left before they are outside the entrance, metres from John. If he runs now, they will be too close behind him.

"Stay there," he tells the receptionist.

John crosses the floor and fetches the fire extinguisher. As the police car skids to a stop outside and its blue lights flick across the marble walls, he rips off the safety seal, turns the muzzle towards the entrance, and squeezes the handle.

The fire extinguisher spews a torrential cascade of dry powder that instantly transforms the hall into a wintry landscape, filling the air and blocking all sight through the windows. The sirens screech as if raging at losing sight of him. John coughs, holds his breath, and continues to spray. When the hall is thoroughly clouded, he drops the fire extinguisher, returns behind the desk, and draws the gun again.

Someone bangs on the entrance and rattles the handle. "Police," a male voice barks over the sirens. "Open the door." More bangs follow. John hears the glass crack. A few more hits and it will break.

"Where is the fire alarm?" John asks the receptionist.

She points to a small red box near the staircase. John looks between the alarm button, the stairs, and the front door. The entrance is a faint rectangle of light behind the churning white powder.

"Go back to the stairs," John says.

"Why?" the receptionist stammers. "Where are we going?"

John does not answer. He stands up, turns to the entrance, and raises his gun.

The receptionist raises her hand to her mouth. "No, don't—"

The shots are much louder than John had anticipated, and the violent recoil almost wrenches the weapon out of his hands. He grips it firmly, squares his feet, and keeps firing.

Two of the bullets miss the window and bury themselves in the mortar behind the marble. The remaining six bullets tear through the white cloud and through the window. Next to the staircase, the receptionist screams and covers her face.

After all eight shots, the gun clicks. Screams and shouts sound over the sirens outside. A car alarm bleats manically near the entrance. John breaks the glass cover of the fire alarm with the butt of the gun and punches the button.

A piercing ringing joins the pandemonium. Outside, a voice shouts inaudible words in a megaphone. The receptionist looks at John through her fingers. Her eyes flicker to the gun. She does not know the magazine is empty.

"Show me the emergency exit," John shouts. "One far from this room. If you choose to stall, I will shoot you in your spine. You will die or be crippled for life. Understood?"

She shakes her head. "There are people up there. I can't help if someone sees—"

"That doesn't matter. If they stop us, I'll shoot them."

"Okay." Her breathing is rapid. "Oh, God. Okay."

She rises and walks up the stairs unsteadily. On the first floor, the receptionist opens a door and leads John into an office. John closes the door behind them and looks around.

A long corridor, five doors on either side. Wooden floor, white walls, framed art posters. At the far end of the corridor is another door; above it, an emergency exit sign.

Keeping the receptionist in front of him, John walks down the corridor and peers inside the rooms he passes. Broad desks, computer monitors, unplugged cables and coffee cups. The air smells of beer and Xerox machines. All lights are off. No people in sight. Outside, sirens howl, car doors slam, and people shout, all against the backdrop of the manic car alarm.

When they reach the door at the end of the corridor, John tells the receptionist to stop.

"Is this the way out?" he asks.

She nods and swallows. "The stairs behind the door lead to an exit to the plaza on the other side of the building."

"Step aside." John looks through the window in the door. Inside is a spiral staircase in matte metal. Below the stairs, he glimpses another windowed door, and beyond that, the streets outside. He sees no police officers.

He closes the door, looks around the corridor, and finds what he is looking for. Lowering his bag to the floor, he turns back to the receptionist.

"Close your eyes," John says.

*

CHAPTER 41

Lena

Frenetic shouts surround Lena while she peers through the car's shattered side window.

"Drop your weapon and come out—"

"There's too much blood. Get a bandage—"

"Watch his finger. It's going to—"

"I got it. Hold still—"

"Keep your head down—"

Her head rings from screams, car alarms, sirens, clanging alarm bells, radio calls and the metallic rustle of weapons. Breathing is difficult; her lungs feel as stiff as concrete.

"Fucking hell," a response team officer next to her growls. "He's armed."

"Really?" Lena lets out a shuddering breath. She grimaces and wipes fragments of the car's window from her clothes. Slivers of glass protrude up from the snow around her.

She turns away from the side window and slides down, her back pressed against the car door. Her hands are sweaty around the black metal of her gun. Tasting iron in her mouth, she spits blood on the ground. She must have bit her tongue when she took cover.

The tactical response team beat Lena and the other police officers to the scene by seconds. Their bulky blue and white van stopped right outside the entrance. Agnes parked right behind it, so close she had to reverse to let them open the back doors of the van. Three more police cars stopped at haphazard angles in the snow behind Lena and Agnes's car.

Lena spotted trouble straight away: the entrance to Tom's office looked like white glass, but the whiteness was moving, shifting and rolling like a pale cloud behind the windows.

Car doors opened and shut as police filled the street, equipment was readied, radios hissed and cracked, voices snapped commands. The noise cut Lena's eardrums; she sensed a tremendous headache building up. She tried to ask the response team leader if they had surrounded the building, but her questions went unheard in the cacophony.

Then someone had fired at them.

Bullets zipped out of the white cloud, cut clean through windows, and smashed into the brickwork around the police officers. One shot tore straight through the window of a police car. Another hit an officer's hand and left one finger dangling by threads. Shattered glass and pulverized mortar rained down.

The bangs were almost inaudible over the racket; Lena felt rather than heard the impacts. She threw herself on the ground and half-dragged Agnes down with her. There had been at least seven or eight shots, and there could easily be more. The ringing around her seems to have tripled in volume.

The tactical response team officer next to Lena curses again. "We didn't expect this. I was told the suspect was likely to run."

"Pity no one asked me," Lena says. John is unpredictability personified. She might be able to track him, but there is no knowing what he will do next.

"Did you know he has a gun?" The tactical response officer looks at her.

Lena does not reply. She is not even sure it was John who fired at them, but the timing and her gut feeling agree: This is no coincidence. Somewhere in the depth of the white cloud are John and a weapon. She does not know where he found it, what type it is, or how much ammunition he has.

One thing is clear: he is not afraid to use it. In a way, it is a good sign; perhaps they have him cornered.

Agnes crouches next to Lena and leans against the car, her gun in her hands. The strange white cloud still conceals the interior of the entrance. Calls for the shooter to stand down and come out have had no result. Huddled together behind their van, the tactical response team put on gas masks while two groups of police officers move to each side of the entrance, weapons drawn.

Lena overhears the response team leader as he gives orders: His team will fire tear gas into the entrance and enter through nearby windows in hope of cutting off the shooter's escape routes. A round of nods later, they dash away from behind the van.

One response team officer leans around the van and levels a tear gas rifle at the entrance. He squints and begins to pull the trigger, but the team leader jumps back, bats the tear gas rifle to the side, and points to the entrance.

Dozens of people are staggering out of the smoke, blinking, gaping, and coughing. Bewildered, they stop in the middle of the street and stare at the police. One of them raises his hands slowly.

"Hold your fire," the team leader screams. He points to the people who are leaving the building. "All of you, down on the ground, now. Drop *down*, for fuck's sake."

Slowly, the stunned group obeys. One man pauses to arrange his jacket on the snow before he gingerly sits down. The tactical response team leader sends his team in with a series of gestures, and the group of indignant, astonished people is dragged away from the street and into cover. Lena hears protests and raised voices demanding answers.

"What's going on?" one man shouts. "Where's the fire?"

Lena realizes that a fire alarm is blending with the din of sirens and the car alarm. She looks down the street and sees people exit from two other doors. Young women and men, smart clothes, precise haircuts. Several of them carry coffee cups. One woman holds a champagne glass. Fortunately, there are only a few dozen; had it been a weekday, the street would have been packed.

Other people crowd the street farther away, staring and pointing. An ambulance arrives, adding its wail to the cacophony as it parks well out of range of the entrance.

"We must go in," Lena says to Agnes.

"Without the response team?"

"Yes. No. Goddamn it, what's holding them back?"

"All the people coming out, I think. John's shots must have set off the alarm."

"Unless he set it off on purpose." Lena suspects that he did; if the street had not been filled with confused, hungover people, the police could have searched half the building by now.

"There's smoke inside the entrance," Lena says, "but I can't smell anything burning. And the smoke is too white. Do you think it's gas?"

"No idea," Agnes says. "Wait." She points to the entrance. "Look, the smoke is thinning."

Lena watches the entrance slowly emerge out of the white haze. There does not seem to be anyone inside. She turns to the response team leader, who is listening closely to his radio. "Is John among the people who just came out?" she asks, knowing he will not be.

The team leader shakes his head. "No one matches the suspect."

"What about Tom?" Lena asks. "He should be here." Unless John has found him, in which case Tom is in trouble. Or already beyond trouble.

"Who's Tom?"

"Another suspect. Sort of. His full name is Tom Lundberg. If you find him, detain him."

The response team leader nods. "I'll find out if he's around."

"We've got to find John before he does something worse," Lena says. "We don't know what happened in there before we got here. There could be people dying or dead. Any idea what that smoke is?"

"I'd guess a fire extinguisher," he says. "I have to go." He leaves and joins his team behind the large van.

Two police officers seal off the street with police tape to keep bystanders away from an eventual gunman's line of fire. Three other officers take statements from the people who left because of the fire alarm.

Precious minutes pass while Lena waits behind her car and listens to calls for the gunman to surrender. More people drift from other exits and are rounded up by the tactical response team. Still no sign of John.

When repeated calls for the shooter to give up have no result, the response team finally moves in. Their leader shouts a string of commands, and his team rushes into position next to the entrance. The tear gas rifle makes a hollow *chunk* as it fires a cartridge into the hall, where it detonates in a spinning whirl of smoke.

Waiting behind the car, Lena hears the sound of running boots and glass being smashed. She looks up and sees the last member of the response team vanish into the fading white mist. Distant calls echo as they search room after room. No gunshots or screams. The fire alarm keeps ringing.

This is a catastrophe in the making. If the response team blocks John's way or points their guns at him, John will do what he must to keep moving. People will die. John will die. She will fail.

She rises, runs to the back of the response team's van, and snatches a gas mask from a basket. Agnes calls out behind her, but her focus is engulfed by the idea of a stand-off between John and the response team. They do not know, cannot begin to anticipate what they are up against.

Pressing the mask against her face with one hand, she darts to the entrance, moves up to a wall, and edges towards the stairs. In here, the fire alarm is deafening. The entrance is partially filled with smoke again, though this time, it is tear gas. One lungful can bring her to her knees in a vomiting fit in an instant. Even though she presses the mask hard against her face, her eyes water as tendrils of the chemical inferno sneak under the rubber.

Holding her gun aimed down, she runs up to the landing of the first floor. The door is open. She leans in and sees part of the tactical response team working their way down the corridor, securing room after room.

She is about to walk in when she hears coughing from higher up in the stairwell.

A young man in a crisp shirt walks cautiously down the stairs, blinking hard and covering his mouth with his hands. He stops when he sees Lena. Behind him, more people crowd the stairwell.

"You," Lena shouts at the man over the alarm. "Have you seen a man heading up the stairs?" She describes John in a few words.

The man stares at her gun and shakes his head. "No…one." He coughs brutally and sways. "Just us," he wheezes.

"Run down, out and right. Do not breathe. Don't stop outside the entrance." Lena raises her voice. "All of you. Move it, get out."

She lets the parade of stunned and coughing people pass and walks into the corridor on the first floor. Not only is she worrying about John; she cannot get in the way of the response team. Not because she might distract them, but if they thought she caused a problem and reported that to Gren, she knows what will happen.

*

CHAPTER 42

John Andersson

The laughter is an amused chuckle, soft yet still sharp, worming its way through the din of the wind.

It's also familiar. He heard it a lifetime and a moment ago, just before he fell, shortly after he burst through Molly's open front door and found her dead.

It belongs to the thing that stole Molly's features.

The puppeteer who, through some macabre trick and his own stupid eagerness to do anything to channel his rage, cast him down here. It's close, within whispering distance. Perhaps near enough to reach him. He cranes his neck and squints up at the night above.

The being that wears Molly's face levitates just above him. Its mouth is stretched wide in what perhaps is meant to be a smile. It floats in the air, perfectly at home. Unbothered by cold, wind, and gravity.

It still wears one of Molly's dresses, the one with bold patterns in vivid red and bright yellow. John bought it as a gift for Molly soon after they got together. He'd chosen it because it went with her nature: sunny, striking, and daring. On this creature, however, it is a mockery. A dazzling reminder of what he's lost. Which he guesses is the point.

John tries to turn sideways, but he can't look away from the apparition. Even now, on the other side of all the lies, perhaps of life itself, Molly's features have him transfixed.

"This is most unusual," the creature says in feigned surprise. "But then, so was your arrival. Most come here on the tide of their final breath. You, on the other hand, couldn't wait to chase after your prey. That kind of desperation is a rare, beautiful thing."

John searches for a path between the pits, but the passages between them are slim and coated with frost. Walking is possible, but if he runs, he'll inevitably stumble and fall.

"You tricked me," John says.

He backs away until he balances on the edge between two of the pits. The creature laughs softly and floats closer.

"I could tell you how many times we've heard that particular excuse," it says. "But the number is so large it'd turn your brain to ash."

"What do you want from me?" John demands.

The creature holding his throat looks up at the bright aura inside the clouds. Its eyes are filled with the greed and hunger of a starved, feral beast.

For the briefest of moments, the illusion of Molly slips and reveals the entity underneath: a hard, visceral absence of warmth, like a sentient void glowing with malice. Shapeshifting, cunning, and insatiable.

"I told you," it hisses. "We want *her*. Soon, there'll be blood on her hands, and her resolve will fracture and break. Her precious principles will come crashing down like a burning tower. Then, at last, she'll be ours."

*

CHAPTER 43

Lena

Trailing behind the tactical response team, Lena watches them search the floor, opening every door, investigating every cupboard, eliminating all hiding spaces. No John. The team declares the area clear and extends the sweep to other floors.

Lena puts her hand on the arm of a hulking tactical response team officer as he jogs by. He stops and stares hard at her from behind his mask.

"What?" he asks.

Lena points to the emergency exit at the end of the corridor. "Couldn't the shooter have left that way?"

"That door's jammed. It won't budge. If we can't get it open, the shooter couldn't. We need to secure the rest of the floors before we force the door open."

"Jammed?"

"You should be outside."

Lena removes her hand, and the man runs out into the stairwell. She is alone. Her hands are shaking badly. John is gone, vanished again. The certainty troubles her in so many ways she feels sick. His absence is as palpable as lack of air, as clear as if she could reach out and touch the vacant space where he had been.

She can hear herself explain the idea to Gren. *Yes, I can sense him when he's close. I'm clairvoyant, obviously. Here's my idea for a costume and a cape. Or a straitjacket.*

Breathing slowly in her mask, she leans back against a wall and wonders if her deteriorating mental health is the root of all her recent thoughts. When the wall that separates a fragile mind from a broken one is breached, how will she know? Did it feel like an epiphany in reverse? A slight vertigo and then an endless fall?

The voice she heard in the bathroom haunts her. Perhaps that fateful raid had chased away Lena's sanity and left her behind like an empty shell, ready to be filled by something more sinister. The thought has crossed her mind more than once.

Shaking herself, she continues down the corridor towards the emergency exit. Her palms are soaked with sweat. Halfway down the corridor, papers and catalogues clutter the floor in the otherwise neat office. She kicks the papers to the side and advances on the door with her gun raised. Her fingers are away from the trigger; her nerves are electrified, and she flinches at every imagined hint of movement.

When she reaches the door, she peeks through its window down into the stairwell. Spiral stairs, alarm bell on the wall, a dull soft glow of daylight from the door below. No sign of John.

She lowers her gun and pulls the handle. As the tactical response team officer said, the door is stuck. She cannot find any locks or latches barring the door, but she cannot open it. The door feels as if it has been welded into its frame.

When her fingers brush against the wall near the lock, she pulls her hand back with a start. Crouching slowly, she leans closer, lifts her mask up, and sniffs.

Glue.

She rushes out of the office, down the stairs, and through the smoke. Once she is outside, she rips off her mask and stops in front of Agnes. When she opens her mouth to speak, all she manages is a bout of dry coughing.

"Back door," Lena eventually croaks, blinking and resting her hands on her knees. "John."

Agnes puts a hand on Lena's shoulder to keep her from keeling over. "John's at the back door?" she asks and glances down at Lena's hand.

"No, he's – *shit*." Lena coughs and grimaces. Her sluggish mind reminds her that she is still holding her gun, and she tries to holster it discreetly. "He's gone. Tell the tactical response team to go around the building."

"They already have." Agnes gestures at the far end of the block. "They sent a small team just after they hauled those people away. I don't think they saw the suspect."

Lena closes her eyes. Snow settles on her hair while she stands still. Her energy ebbs out of her. "Not again," she whispers. "We were so close. What about Tom?"

"Sorry," Agnes says. "He's not here. The response team checked everyone. I'll talk to them again."

"Call the headquarters and have them put up roadblocks," Lena says. "Get the underground trains not to stop at–" She tries to remember the name of the nearest station, but her memory fails her. Her body is starting to rebel against the prolonged push; she is tired, exhausted, and her headache sends splinters of light through her cranium. And she is hungry.

"I know what to do," Agnes assures Lena, then walks away and raises her phone.

Lena slumps against the car, crosses her arms on the roof, and rests her head. She tries to shut out the turmoil and plan. Tom is gone: A relief and a problem in one sentence. The man has not been found mutilated, which is a boon, but he is also missing. He could have left before Lena or John got to the office, but then John too would have left. Which, she realises, is precisely what he did.

She turns to look at the subdued and frozen group of people that ran out when the fire alarm went off. With luck, one of them knows where Tom is. Rubbing her cold hands, she walks over to the group.

"Who here works for Lundberg Invest?" she asks. "I know some of you do, so just raise your hands. Now, if you will."

A few seconds pass without anyone putting their hand up; then a dark woman in a grey office suit waves cautiously at Lena.

Lena jerks her head. "Come with me."

"Wait." The woman looks terrified. "I don't work for them."

"Then why the hell did you raise your hand?"

"I just – I know some of them, and they're not here."

"That's funny, because I know they are."

"They were," the woman says and points at the office. "I talked with – um, some of them earlier today, and they've gone to a conference."

Lena knows the woman does not want to say with whom she talked. Lundberg Invest will be worth looking into, but that will have to wait. "Where?" she asks.

"I don't know."

"Then who does?" Lena's patience hangs on a thread.

"Katarina. She'll know."

Lena stares at the woman until she goes on.

"Ah, she's the receptionist," the woman continues. She turns around and looks at the group around her. "Katarina? Are you here?"

A chorus of shrugs and turning heads tells Lena the receptionist is missing. "Was she in today?"

The woman nods. "Perhaps she left when the alarm went off."

"Have you got her number?"

The woman gives Lena a phone number. Lena calls, but there is no answer. She tries the number dialled from the phone booth. Voicemail. Raising her eyes to the sky, she breathes out slowly. There has to be a quick way to find out where they are.

"Agnes?" Lena shouts.

"I'm right here," Agnes calls and jogs over to Lena.

"Tell someone to get in touch with an employee at Lundberg Invest. We need to know where they are, and where the hell they're going."

"Got it."

Lena walks towards the entrance. The tear gas prickles her eyes and her sinuses, but it has dissipated enough for her to breathe freely. She studies the patterns of white powder in the broken glass that covers the floor. On the floor near the desk are two bullet cases. They are almost as thick as her thumb. A sweat breaks out on her neck.

Agnes appears by her side. "I've called," she says. "They're working on it. What's happening?"

"The receptionist knows where Tom is," Lena explains, "but she's disappeared. I'm going to have a look at her desk." She walks around the desk and sees the broken monitor. "Oh, bloody hell."

Agnes follows her gaze. "John did that?"

"It could be." Lena wonders if John has taken the receptionist with him, or if she is hiding somewhere in the office.

"That must be her handbag." Agnes points to a brown leather bag slung over the back of the office chair.

Lena upends the bag on the desk. Make-up, wallet, hair brush, tissue, pepper spray, and a mobile phone. Its screen is lit.

She picks it up and sees her own phone number. Unless the receptionist has fled, she is either with John or somewhere in the office. Or John has silenced her and hid her himself. The image of Niklas glued to a wardrobe door flashes through her mind.

Lena runs out with the phone in her hand and shouts for the tactical response team leader. Outside the police tape barricade, hundreds of people gawk at the scene. Almost everyone is clad in hues of black and grey, hands deep in pockets or holding mobile phones and cameras. Part funeral gathering, part voyeur convention. She wishes she could hijack the response team's van and run them all down.

The response team leader stands next to the officers who monitor the people who have left the building. He looks up at Lena with a shadow of annoyance on his face.

"The receptionist's gone," Lena says. "I think John's taken her."

The team leader makes a hushing gesture. Lena is about to tell him she can be as loud as she damn well pleases but then realizes her mistake: One of the spectators murmurs *hostage*, and the word races around the crowd. Thumbs work touch screens manically as the news is passed on. Half the city will know in minutes. The press will be here in no time. Pictures of the scene will already be descending on blogs and newspapers.

A crease forms on the team leader's forehead – the closest he comes to a scowl, Lena supposes – and he motions for Lena to follow him in behind the van. Out of earshot, he asks her to tell him more.

"The woman is gone," Lena says impatiently, "but her bag's still there. Her computer screen has been smashed." She stabs with her index finger at the building and speaks through her teeth. "John. Has. Her. Or at least he's the reason she's gone. Trust me on this one."

Glancing at the office, he nods. "We'll do another sweep." He barks a series of commands in his radio and turns to leave.

"Sweep?" Lena runs around him and stops in his path. "John's already gone. We need to start looking for him."

"Do you have any idea where he is?" The team leader locks eyes with Lena. His voice is hushed but strained. "Because if you haven't, I'm not going to waste time searching every bloody block. My priority is time and the safety of my team. We have called in the National Task Force, and they're mobilising as we speak. They'll go in as soon as the suspect is sighted again."

Lena's headache intensifies. With the National Task Force deployed, all bets were off, and John's chances to escape shrank to almost nil. He could get away with overwhelming and kidnapping unprepared individuals, but the task force was another beast entirely.

And they were not discreet. The press would chase them like dogs. Rumours would fly wild.

"Where exactly would they go in?" Lena demands. "John's gone, and the task force aren't searching for him. I am."

The tactical response team leader leans close to Lena's face. "Then I suggest you better start looking, Detective."

Lena opens and closes her mouth, then turns away. Everyone is losing their mind. Perhaps John is to blame: Molly's elusive avenger is turning into a void that will claim them all. A human black hole swallowing the unwary.

She stalks back to her car and finds Agnes sitting in the passenger seat and speaking on her phone.

Agnes looks up at Lena and shakes her head: No sign of John. Thirty minutes have passed since the shots were fired. John could be in Stockholm proper, and all Lena can do is wait for someone to spot him.

Looking at the entrance, a thought comes to her. She knocks on the car window to get Agnes's attention and motions for her to hang up.

After a few seconds, Agnes lowers the side window. "There's no sign of him so far," she says.

"You're good with computers." Lena has long since learned that her own temper disagrees with the tardiness of technology, while Agnes is happy to wait minutes for a computer to open a file.

Agnes frowns. "A little. Why?"

"Can you make the receptionist's computer work?"

"Maybe, if it's just the screen that's broken."

"You'd need a new screen?"

"That might do it. The computer itself didn't look broken, but I didn't look close—"

"I'll find one."

Lena waits while the tactical response team files into the office to search again and follows them up the stairs. One of them turns to look at her, but Lena waves apologetically and mumbles about double-checking a detail.

Once they are inside the vacated office, she ducks into a room, yanks the cables out of the smallest monitor she finds, and carries it downstairs, its cables trailing behind her. Hopefully, the forensic team has not arrived yet. If Gren hears of this, he will fire her on the spot.

Agnes waits for Lena behind the desk downstairs. The computer hums under the table; Agnes has managed to start it up. The crowd outside seems impossibly large. A news broadcast team moves among the people. Their camera's spotlight flashes over Lena, and she crouches behind the desk.

"It works," Agnes says and kneels down next to Lena. "It's not even logged out. Do you want me to check recent documents?"

"Anything that helps," Lena says quietly.

Agnes nods and turns to the computer. Lena's eyes stray to the spent bullet casings on the floor, left there by John when he released the salvo towards the police outside.

She wishes she knew what had gone through his head while the bullets crossed the distance between his hand and the police. Fury, hate, terror, confusion or glee. So many options. What she fears the most is that he felt nothing.

"Here," Agnes says and points to the screen. "These are the documents used today. The most recent one looks like a ticket – oh, look."

"What?" Lena can tell from Agnes's expression that she has found something. A camera flashes outside. Police officers order some overly curious spectators to move back.

"This was viewed just before we got here," Agnes says.

Lena looks at the screen. A mass of pink and blue boxes filled with text and data. "It's a flight ticket," she says and leans closer. "In Tom's name. From Arlanda, this afternoon. When was it last opened?"

Agnes scrolls down. "Not long before you tried calling the office."

They look at each other. Arlanda: Sweden's largest airport. Five terminals, hundreds of corridors and thousands of people. And soon John, armed and hunting.

"The car," Lena breathes. "Now."

*

CHAPTER 44

The other John

John drives towards the airport.

He follows the slow flow of the traffic past rolling fields dotted by barns, country cottages, radio masts and copses of pine and spruce worn by hard wind and rain. Heavy clouds create an artificial dusk over the landscape.

Gusts pummel and push at the car, threatening to force it off the highway and into the ditch, but he keeps it steady, overtaking other vehicles only when safe. At his current speed, a collision would at best cripple John, but it would give Tom time to escape. There will be no more escapes. Not for Tom, not for John.

"Where are we going?" asks the man cowering on the floor in the back of the car.

"I told you to be quiet," John says. "I'm in a hurry. If you distract me, I'll stop by the roadside and make sure you won't do it again."

"Please," the man begs. "I have kids."

"Then you have a good incentive to do as I say."

"Okay. I will be quiet. I promise."

A film of snow screens the meadows and groves that line the road. Soon, driving will be difficult and even slower. John competes with both time and climate.

He touches the handle of the knife in his bag to reassure himself the weapon is there. His arsenal is reduced: On his way out of the city, he parked by the roadside and tried to reload the gun, out of sight of his hostage, but he cannot understand how to open the weapon. It is a setback, but he has the knife and his hands. That will have to do.

Twenty minutes earlier, John exited Tom's office building, crossed the road, and walked down a long, narrow street between blocks of old and luxurious flats. Less than a minute after he closed the emergency exit door behind him, he passed a middle-aged man who was loading slalom skis into a Packline mounted on a white Volvo SUV. There was no one nearby.

John stopped and waited until the man reached for his gloves in the back seat, then walked and pressed his knife to the man's body.

To many, guns are things of fiction that do not belong in humdrum life. Their reaction to seeing one might be delayed. But a blade that pricks a soft part of your body is an immediate, physical threat that leaves no room for doubt or debate. John ordered the man to get in the car, and a minute later they were on their way out of Stockholm.

John passes the first of the many signposts for the different airport terminals. By the time he reaches the turn to the fifth terminal, the heavy snowfall cuts visibility to less than a hundred meters.

He overtakes a car and drives faster. Tom is an imaginary dot on the horizon, his personal, offensive North Star, the beacon of his journey.

Soon, he will extinguish it.

*

CHAPTER 45

Lena

Lena ignores the gawking onlookers as she runs to her car. All she sees are obstacles slowing her down: a crowd, slippery snow, the closed door, finding the car key. As soon as the engine roars to life, she slams into first gear. Agnes barely manages to get in the passenger seat before the car is in motion.

Ahead are more hindrances: parked cars, ambulances, mounds of snow, and a fire engine that has materialized without her noticing. She flicks the siren on, sounds the horn, and keeps going down the street. Screams and curses follow her as the car shoots past stunned people, brushing against legs and jackets.

She veers onto the busy plaza and almost slides sideways into a bus. Both lanes are full of cars. The fastest are moving at walking speed.

"Double back," Agnes says. "Then straight ahead. Past the intersection."

Lena circles the block, drives out onto a wider street, cuts off a taxi, and shoots past a local bus. She zigzags through the lanes, overtaking cars and trucks. The traffic is still light, but seems to move in slow motion.

She wills her car to go faster and magically close the gap between her and John. Fashion shops, restaurants, travel agencies and cafés form a glossy neon blur on her left and right. In the wake, a cascade of dirty snow sprays nearby pedestrians.

Agnes takes Lena's radio and rattles off reports to the central command, the tactical response team, and Gren, pausing every other sentence to give Lena directions. Lena tries to listen in, but in her mind she is already at the airport. John is heading into a net he cannot escape. If he enters any of the terminals, he will be caught; the exits are easily monitored, and there are CCTV camera/s everywhere. If he turns back, the roads will be cut off.

"Have you called the airport yet?" Lena asks Agnes.

"Gren's doing it now. He said he'll call you too."

"Why?"

"He didn't say."

They pass under a series of viaducts, and century-old buildings give way to scattered office blocks, lush parkland and small lakes. Lena enters the motorway and glances at the clock. Eight minutes since they left the scene. How fast would John drive? At what speed will someone without fear, doubt or self-preservation travel? She accelerates and grips the steering wheel harder.

Snowflakes whip off the windscreen and wash over the car. The sky ahead is a wall of deep blue clouds; before long, the road will be a stretch of darkness blurred by waves of snow. She feels as if she drives vertically, heading down a cliff.

She passes a lumbering coach and is about to change lanes when her phone rings. Knowing who the caller will be, she takes the call without looking at the display.

"Speak loudly," she shouts over the siren.

"It's Gren here. You know why I'm calling."

"You want to tell me not to go in alone?"

"Stay away from the terminals entirely. The National Task Force are on their way with a hostage negotiator. They will probably pass over you soon. The airport police have been notified."

"Tell them to be discreet. John will fire if threatened. He won't back down."

"Agnes told me what you found on the computer." Gren pauses. "Are you sure he's heading to the airport?"

"Completely."

"And that he's got a hostage?"

"I think John took the receptionist with him to keep her from telling anyone where he went." That was a best-case scenario; John had demonstrated that he knew other ways to silence those in his path. Her radio beeps, and she hands it to Agnes for her to answer.

211

"Have you stopped the airport trains?" Lena asks Gren.

"The trains and the coaches are informed. John won't get on them without us knowing. The airport's been notified, and they're calling for Tom over the PA. We tried to contact Tom directly, but his phone is switched off. We've left a message."

"His whole bloody company is there. Someone must have a working phone. Try to text him."

"We've tried that. We're looking up the others in his company. Don't worry. Soon we'll have a number; then we'll talk to Tom and make sure he's out of harm's way. We have a few questions for him."

"What about the task force?" Lena asks. "If John runs into them before they can disarm him or pick up Tom, it'll get ugly."

"No one's going to get hurt."

Lena does not reply; she is distracted by Agnes, who motions for Lena to take the radio. "I have to go," she tells Gren. She hangs up and takes the radio. "Who is it?" she whispers to Agnes.

"The tactical response team leader."

Lena grimaces and takes the radio. Most likely, he wants to reprimand her for interfering with their search. "Franke here," she says and braces herself.

"We have the receptionist."

Lena loses control of the car. The vehicle careens into the adjacent lane, but Agnes throws herself at the wheel and turns it the other way, narrowly avoiding an oncoming minibus. Agnes keeps hold of the steering wheel until she sees that Lena is in control of herself again.

"How?" Lena asks. Is she wrong? Is John still in the city while Lena races farther away on a ghost hunt? If so, she has directed all the search effort towards a blind spot.

"She was tied up and hidden in a storage space in the corridor. Some kind of built-in wardrobe. The suspect had glued a framed painting over the hinges."

"Bloody hell," Lena breathes.

"That's why we missed her during the first sweep. The glue's probably the same he used to jam the emergency exit. And on that other man. I heard about it."

Lena's numbness turns to a cold. "Did he–"

"He glued the painting to the wall, that's all. The woman's mouth was duct taped. She's okay. But she refuses to talk."

"Why?"

He clears his throat. "Shock, I think. We're trying to get information out of her, but she won't talk about the suspect. Just shakes her head. We've got an ambulance here to bring her in."

"Damn it, she's the last one who's seen John. Hasn't she said anything useful?"

"Just one thing." A pause. "She said Tom's dead."

The tornado of thoughts in Lena's head picks up speed. Had John killed Tom and hidden him too? That cannot be right; the woman outside the office said Tom had left by the time Lena and Agnes got there.

"Tom can't be dead," Lena says. "That doesn't fit."

"He's not. We've asked around, and we're positive Tom's at the airport."

"Make some goddamned sense, will you?"

"I'm guessing here." The response team leader's patient voice is laden with static. "But I think she meant that Tom is as good as dead."

Lena looks into the distance. "I understand."

A distant thudding growl on her left makes her look out the window. Two bulky military helicopters scythe through the low clouds, heading north parallel with the highway. The National Task Force, rushing towards the airport.

"Make sure she's looked after," Lena says. "Out."

She drops the radio on the floor and drives faster.

*

CHAPTER 46

The other John

John arrives at the airport.

On his right is terminal five, a vast complex of steel and glass. Across the street is a large circular parking garage. Buses and cars compete for space outside the sliding doors as travellers march between the buildings or wrestle their luggage into baggage compartments. Hard winds funnel snow between the buildings and into unzipped jackets, tax-free shopping bags and squinting eyes. A plane takes off, the flat thunder of its jet engines temporarily drowning out all other sounds.

John drives slowly between coaches and taxis while he studies the area. Near the middle entrance are three police cars. They are parked not immediately outside the doors, but close enough for the officers inside the cars to monitor the entrance. Inside the terminal are security guards eyeing everyone who passes through the doors. The alarm has been raised.

He considers the gun in his bag and the number of police officers he has seen. Once, he travelled to Spain for a week on the Canary Islands, leaving a balmy, sun-drenched Stockholm for six days of incessant rain and one day of blasting sunshine that burned his face lobster red.

The flight had left from Arlanda. He recalls the passport controls, security gates and locked doors, but his memories are old, separated from today by a decade of terrorism, paranoia and several airport extensions. He knows at which gate Tom is supposed to be, but not how many officers and barriers he would encounter if he tries to reach Tom by speed and force. When he last travelled, the passport control alone consisted of two doors of bulletproof glass. It would be even more secure today.

He needs a new plan.

Watching out for police cars, he drives past the terminal and parks the car a few minutes walking distance from the entrances.

"What are you doing?" the man in the back seat asks.

"I'm leaving the car," John says. "You will stay here. Keep in mind that I know your address. If I see you anywhere outside this car, I will go to your home, and I will use my knife on your family."

The man tenses, and John raises the gun a fraction. Mentioning the man's family was reckless; he has pushed the father too far. A fight in the car could draw attention and could ruin John's plan.

"I've changed my mind," John says. "Wait here for an hour; then do what you want. You won't see me again."

"All right," the man says after a moment. "I'll stay."

John takes the man's mobile phone and his wallet. He will have to move fast, so he puts the sheathed knife in a pocket and leaves his bag in the car.

He shuts the car door and walks towards the distant terminal, a blur of shadows and neon in the thick snowfall. His hand throbs fiercely, and his gait is unsteady. Those are bad signs, but he will last a little longer.

John passes rows of cars buried under snow, waits while a group of people pull their luggage across his path, and walks up to the parking garage opposite the terminal. Stopping in a shadow, he pretends to make a phone call while he looks around.

The police cars are still there. Two officers inside, middle-aged men. They talk and laugh, but their eyes are watchful, nervous. Above him, another jet roars and fades into a remote growl.

John takes out the phone he took from the man in the car and texts Tom.

Run. The cops are coming. I have a car outside. Niklas

While John waits for a reply, he hears far-off sirens slowly coming closer.

The phone rings. An anonymous caller. John kills the call and texts Tom again.

Can't speak, the cops are too close. Just run.

215

The reply comes quickly. *The cops just called and said there's trouble. Some fucker looking for me.*

It's a trap. Avoid the cops and the security points.

The sirens are a fraction closer when Tom replies.

Fuck it, I'll kill him. Where are you?

In the parking garage, John texts back. *Run, now. Don't let the cops see you.*

A new message from Tom. *Stay there. On my way.*

John walks into the parking garage and looks for a place to hide. Cars enter and leave in a steady stream, but there is an alcove in the back cloaked in deep shadow. He leans against the wall inside the entrance and waits.

Three minutes later, John sees Tom exit the terminal.

Tom resembles the passport photo, but he is taller than John expects. Grey suit, pink shirt, brown leather belt and matching shoes. His black hair is ruffled by stress and wind. He walks slowly but fidgets with his wristwatch and looks over his shoulder.

John knows Tom's face is flushed from more than anxiety: One moment Tom is heading for a day of drinks and negotiations, the next he is fleeing like a squirrel exposed on a field. When Tom sees a police car, he turns around, crosses the street behind a coach, and heads for the parking garage again.

John watches Tom come closer.

When Tom is a few moments away, John retreats into the parking garage and runs to the alcove. The small space is a bin storage with no door. It is sooty, cramped, and reeks of old garbage. Cars drive past up on the curved ramps that lead to the upper floors.

John presses himself to the wall inside and holds the knife behind his back. If he is right, he will look like a shadow when seen from the entrance, and Niklas would have all reason to hide. By the time Tom is close enough to see John's face, it will be too late.

Tom enters the parking garage. He pauses in the entrance, runs his hands through his hair, and looks around. John pulls himself deeper into the shadow and calls out, trying to sound coarse and discreet. When Tom does not notice, John calls again, louder.

Tom starts and peers at the shadow where John hides. "Niklas?" he calls. "Where are you? Stop fucking around."

"I'm here," John says. "Come, quickly."

Tom hesitates, curses, and runs over to the alcove.

John pulls back again. The knife is in his hand. In a moment, Tom will be inside the alcove; John hears the man's heavy breathing, the crush of gravel under his soles, the rustle of his suit.

Tom steps inside and sees John. "What the–"

No speech precedes John's attack. There is no elaboration on righteousness or scornful remark, no smirk or victorious gesture. He has a weapon, a target and a goal. Severing the chain that hurt him is the purpose of his existence; beyond that, nothing matters. A chase, a stab, and then peace.

But Tom twists to the side, and John's knife cuts through empty air. John follows with a sideways stab, but Tom blocks John's arm and drives his fist into John's abdomen.

John drops the knife, falls backwards into the wall, and slumps down on the grimy floor, coughing and retching.

*

CHAPTER 47

Tom

Tom picks up the knife and looks down at John, wondering who the chubby, ill-dressed pretender hit man is. He has plenty of enemies, ranging from wealthy competitors vying for his circle of sub-dealers to former friends who feel cheated or betrayed for whatever reason.

But whoever sent this would-be assassin does not know Tom. This man is a joke. Tom's body is trimmed to perfection by countless hours in VIP gyms and three kinds of illegal anabolic substances, whereas this man looks like a car sales rep on a bad diet. The attack had been beyond clumsy, too; Tom had taken down better fighters a decade ago when he roamed the suburbs as a teenager.

Nevertheless, the man at his feet is a sure sign of trouble. So are the police. While a constant presence at Arlanda, there are many more officers around now than a few minutes ago. Tom wonders if they are searching for him, the useless knifeman, or both of them.

He looks out of the alcove. No one close. Cars drive past only a few steps away; however the space is too dark for any driver to see what goes on inside.

Tom crouches next to John, grabs John's jacket, and hoists him off the ground. "Getting me out here was clever," Tom spits in John's face. "I should've known the texts were fake; Niklas's spelling is even worse than yours. Now pay attention." With a quick punch he breaks John's nose.

"You're going to tell me who sent you," Tom says. "You have three seconds before I write my autograph in your puffy face with your own knife." He waves the blade in front of John. "One. Two. Three. Your loss."

Tom cuts a deep gash in John's forehead. Blood wells up and runs back into John's hair, but John does not make a sound. A calm stare is his only response while he shifts slightly in Tom's grip. Tom frowns. Maybe the man is a professional after all, only a bad one.

"Let's try again," Tom says. "This time, I'll take one of your eyes. Let's see if you can stonewall that. One. Two. What was that?"

John mumbles a word and coughs blood; his broken nose has flooded his mouth. He shifts again and lies still.

"Speak louder," Tom barks and slaps John's face. Sirens blare in the distance. He has to move on soon. "Start talking. Who sent you?"

John mumbles again, but the sentence is lost in a wet gargle. "Who?" Tom demands and leans closer to John's mouth.

John speaks again, and this time his voice is clear and level. He says one word, close to Tom's ear.

"Molly."

John twists and runs a hand-sized shard of glass into Tom's face, through his cheek, and into his mouth.

*

CHAPTER 48

The other John

John rolls away while Tom rears up and screams, his howl coming out more like a long, thick sneeze.

The knife clatters to the ground. John tries to kick at Tom's legs, but Tom stumbles away, rips out the shard of smudged glass stuck in his cheek, and stares at it with an incredulous look on his face, as if he has discovered a childhood treasure. Blood pours from the gash and down his shirt.

"Fuck," Tom gurgles. "Oh my – *fuck.*" He stares at John with the eyes of a panicked animal.

John picks up the knife, rises slowly, and meets Tom's eyes.

Tom turns and runs.

John staggers to his feet and follows Tom. Had it not been for the piece of glass that his fingers had found among the filth on the floor, he would have been too wounded to go on, but the thought is no comfort. Tom is alive. The balance is still wrong.

His forehead throbs with pain, and blood trickles into his eyes, but he keeps running. Ahead, Tom zigzags between cars like a stricken rat. John is seconds behind. People stop and stare. The police officers in the cars frown and point. Sirens moan between the buildings. A helicopter thunders above.

Tom screams in panic, and John runs faster.

John expects Tom to flee into the terminal, but instead he sprints along parked buses and cars, away from the lights. From behind comes the crackle of a megaphone, followed by high-pitched commands to stand still.

Tom passes a line of taxi cars, barrels through people queuing outside a coach, turns into the street, and disappears from John's view. John shoves bewildered travellers out of his way and rounds the corner, giving it some berth in case Tom tries to ambush him.

When he catches sight of Tom again, Tom is dragging a man out of a car. John sprints towards the car, but before he reaches it, Tom hops in, slams the door, and speeds down the road in a spray of wet snow. The man whose car Tom stole stands next to John and mumbles incoherently.

More commands are shouted in the megaphone. The helicopter is coming closer. A few hundred metres away are flaring blue lights. Police cars, approaching fast.

John runs up to the last car in the taxi line and tries to open the driver's door, but it is locked. The driver inside shouts and waves. John ignores him, runs to the next car, and tests the door. This one too is locked. He runs to the third car, and the driver's door swings open.

The driver, a young, red-haired man, shouts in surprise and looks up at John. A large newspaper is spread over the dashboard. The stereo plays heavy metal on low volume.

John shoves his knife under the man's jaw and tells him to leave the keys and get out. The man blinks, nods, undoes the safety belt, and crawls out of the vehicle.

John starts the car, does a U-turn, and races after Tom.

*

CHAPTER 49

John Andersson

John takes another step back, wobbles for a moment, and finds his balance.

He's growing acutely aware of the hungry nothingness that lurks beneath Molly's features. There are more of them too, hiding farther out in the darkness, filling the night like a vast cloud of flies. It's a matter of time before they descend on him.

"Did you climb in hope to escape?" The creature tilts its head and studies John. "Only a handful have managed to crawl and squirm their way here. So much ambition, but so little wits. We send everyone back down to where they belong. We'll do the same to you. And then, you'll sink."

"Sink where?" John asks, hoping to stall. "Down into the ice?"

The creature nods. "*Through* the ice. It takes an eternity, sometimes two. Enough time to consider your mistakes. All the could've-beens and if-onlys. At some point, however, you drop into our arms. That's when the genuine fun begins. We'll be waiting for you, below the lake, teeth and tools at the ready."

The creature pauses.

"You do know who we are, yes?" it asks.

John nods. He's known since the moment he heard its laughter. Perhaps he understood what he faced already back in Molly's bedroom. All he needed to wrap the impossibility in words was more experience, more time to witness the madness from the inside. He has that now.

"Demon," John says quietly. "That is your name."

"Bravo." The creature's smile is too wide for its stolen face. "Then you understand your predicament. Some of you cretins cling to denial, no matter what games we play. There's a certain kind of thickness no whip or scalpel can carve away. Fascinating, but often tedious."

"Leave me alone." John dares another step away. The edge of the nearest pit is just behind him.

"Oh, but we can't. Not even if we wanted to, and we most certainly don't. We are your wardens, John. Your personal playmates in a house of endless entertainment. Believe us, you've seen nothing yet. There's so, so much more to discover."

"You sadistic bastard," John spits. "You fooled me before. I don't know why, but I'm not letting it happen—"

The creature lashes out and grips John by his jugular, forcing him closer to its face.

"Manners," the creature whispers. "Remember that you're a guest. A permanent one, but still."

"Let me go," John croaks.

"Never." The creature pulls John closer. "Enough of your insolence. It is time to play. We have countless games waiting for you."

John wilts under the creature's radiant malice. Slack and trembling, he tethers on the brink of absolute submission. Fighting is as useless as denial. Even if he were strong enough to wrench out of the creature's iron grip, there's nowhere to run, and fewer places to hide. In an act of stubborn defiance, he looks up to face his nemesis.

John's slide towards defeat comes to a halt.

The creature must've chosen to resemble Molly in order to torment John. For a time, it worked, but the deceit is losing its effect. Perhaps he's become attuned to the beast behind the mask.

Instead of despair, Molly's face triggers an avalanche of memories: tender moments, exchanged thoughts and insights, hours spent together in cafés, on the streets, or in the soft gloom of her bedroom.

He relives, if only for a moment, the electric, exhilarating joy of having found someone who can quicken him, long after he'd given up on finding happiness outside of the edges of his canvases.

Like a net, the memories snare him in his fall towards abandon, and catapults him back. The woman he loved is gone, but some of her essence, a faint but precious outline, remains in the scrapbook of his mind.

A mind he's on the verge of losing, perhaps literally. Unless he gets out.

The light.

*

CHAPTER 50

Lena

When Lena arrives at Arlanda Airport, her mood matches the blizzard.

She drives up the ramp that leads up to terminal five to the chorus of sirens and the thudding snarl of the helicopter. Her plan is to make sure John is inside the building and then seal off every window and vent until no one and nothing can escape. After that, they will turn the terminal upside down until they find John.

She hates airports. Not because she dislikes flying, although being stuck inside an airborne canister with hundreds of complaining drunks is not her idea of a good time. The reason she loathes airports is they are big labyrinths located too far from everything else. She is always late getting to them, and when she arrives, she inevitably gets lost.

Now this nightmarish chase will come to a conclusion either in the airport's maze of corridors or in the snow outside. She hopes for the latter.

Both Lena and Agnes have been silent for the past ten minutes. Lena has fought to control the tumult of fear, anger and priorities in her head. Agnes looks out the window as if in a trance. The woman's face could be made from marble.

On a different day, Lena would have been worried, but only John matters now. She feels the tug of the imagined string stronger than ever. If the name-callers back at the office found out, they would have a field day. Lena the mind-reading cop. The psychic psycho.

A string of police cars caught up with her on her way to the airport, including the tactical response team's van. The airport's own security staff and police force have moved into positions to make sure John or Tom cannot leave or enter the airport unnoticed. Extra personnel monitor the CCTV for hints of either of the two.

A helicopter with an infrared scanner circles the airport, waiting for instructions, and a military helicopter with the National Task Force on board is minutes from landing inside the compound. A small army against one injured ordinary man. And still she worries.

Lena pokes Agnes. "Are you awake?" she asks, expecting to start Agnes out of her reverie.

Unruffled and calm, Agnes turns and looks at Lena.

"Right," Lena says. "I'll park just outside. Get on the radio and find the one who's in charge of the terminal's security; what's his name?"

"Circovic."

"Tell him we're here, and ask if there's been any sign of John or Tom. Or anything else."

"Sure."

Lena continues up the ramp, then brakes hard to avoid colliding with a coach parked at an angle across the road.

"What the hell?" she says, staring at the standstill.

Horns blare incessantly. She does not have to leave the car to know that something is wrong; the wide road is the arterial to the terminal. Stopping for longer than a minute means vicious parking tickets. Were it not for the weather, she would have driven around the mess.

She peers down the street. The blizzard turns everything more than fifty metres away into a grainy haze. Given the security checks, she was prepared for queues outside the terminal, but this is bizarre. The airport is a clockwork built to cope with hard wind, heavy snow and rotten weather in general.

This is no ordinary traffic jam.

"No sign of the suspects," Agnes says and puts down the radio.

Lena shakes her head. "John's here. This is his fault. No, I don't know for sure, but I trust my gut feeling. Wherever he goes, chaos follows."

"They've got the entrances tightly monitored."

"Do you really believe that helps?" Lena asks.

She knows how this is planned: the police, the tactical response team and the task force will work alongside each other. The police and the airport security will try to locate John while the response remains outside, going in as soon as John has been spotted. The task force will deploy at a central location and rush in behind the response team. Too many officers will raise concern and tip John off. If anyone asks, it is a drill.

Lena listens to the chatter over the radio and reads between the lines of taut exchanges between officers. Even the tactical response team are nervous. To an outsider, the huge number of officers involved would look ridiculous, but the rumour of John's actions has reached the farthest capillaries of the force. The term *rabid dog* is used more than once in the communications. Voices brim with adrenaline.

"To hell with it," Lena mumbles and cuts the engine. Snapping commands over her radio, she orders the officers under her command to spread out in teams of two. When her instructions have been acknowledged, she steps out of the car.

As soon as she leaves the vehicle, the wind rams her and pushes her into the side window. The road is a horizontal tornado of furious travellers, motionless cars and whirling snow. She tries to slam the door shut, fails, leaves it open, and stalks towards the terminal.

Terminal five is a flat, rectangular building a few hundred metres long and with several wide entrances facing the street. She walks up to the nearest entrance and shows her card to the security staff and the police officer stationed at the doorway. The men are tense but professional; there is no such thing as lax airport security this side of the millennium. She hopes they have the wits to look out for Tom as well as John. Behind her are eight other police officers. The response team still wait in their van.

"Where's Tom?" Lena asks.

"He hasn't shown up," the police officer says just as his radio beeps. "One moment," he says and turns away.

Lena runs her hand through her hair. "Agnes, we'll do a sweep down the hall, starting at gate one. What?"

The police who spoke on his radio points to the street. "There's been an incident at the taxi line."

Lena's skin grows cold. "What kind of incident?"

"A fight. And car thefts, I think."

Lena catches her breath. It is John. It must be. But it makes no sense; he would not leave the airport without finding Tom. John would run if he had to, although only if he had good reason. The police's presence would make him cautious, not scared. He would stay close to Tom.

The police officer's choice of words sinks in: he said cars, not car.

Lena steps closer to the officer. "How many cars were stolen?"

"Two. One taxi, one private."

The pieces fall into place. She is right. John is hunting Tom.

"I don't believe this," Lena says. "What the hell is Tom doing outside the airport? Where did they go? What type of cars did they steal?"

"I'm not sure, but I can a–"

"Where's the taxi line?"

The officer points. "At the other end of the terminal."

Lena backs away. "I want to know what kind of cars they took," she shouts. "The makes and colours. *Now.*"

She turns to the other officers who wait behind her. "Back to the cars. Agnes, make sure every single road from the airport is blocked. And tell the others to follow me."

Lena runs to her car and fumbles with the keys. Agnes gets in the passenger seat just as Lena revs the engine and turns the siren back on.

"The helicopter too?" Agnes asks as she fastens her safety belt.

"All of them," Lena barks.

She wrestles the car into gear and rips past the other police cars. John is not getting away. She will reel him in, whatever the cost.

*

CHAPTER 51

Lena

Lena overtakes a truck, cuts across a junction, and swerves as her car loses traction. Wrenching the steering wheel to avoid sliding into the ditch, she floors the gas and drives onto a smaller road.

Leafless bushes scrape the sides of the car. On her right is a flight control tower, a pillar of black and white rising out of the white landscape.

If she is right, the shortcut will take her to the road on which John and Tom drove away. A helicopter swoops over her car and turns in the direction of where she is heading.

"Can you see who that is?" Lena asks Agnes and points to the air. "I want to talk to them."

Agnes leans forward and glances up. "It's too small to be the task force. It must be one of ours."

"Open a channel and put the radio on loudspeaker," Lena says.

Agnes works the radio's control panel, puts the radio between the car seats and pushes a button. "Calling helicopter Caesar twelve."

A loud rasping noise is followed by a man's voice. "Helicopter Caesar twelve here," he shouts over the sound of the rotor blades. "Come in?"

"This is Detective Franke," Lena says just as the car rattles over a metal grille. A yellow gate appears out of the blizzard. "Oh, for fuck's sake – hold on, Agnes."

Lena lowers her head and grits her teeth as the car smacks into the gate. A gunshot-like bang later, the car rushes on and leaves the shattered gate behind. Agnes's side window is smashed into a matrix of fine lines where the gate struck the glass.

A small roundabout takes them on to the road that leads away from the terminal. The helicopter is a shadow above. Behind her, more police cars and the tactical response team's van clear the roundabout. Sirens start up again. Blue flashing lights fill her rear-view mirrors like stroboscopes.

"Hello?" the radio sounds. "Are you there? Over."

Lena breathes and shifts gears. "Tell me you know where the cars went," she shouts.

"We're looking for them right now. We received the descriptions a moment ago."

"Screw the descriptions," Lena snaps. "Look for two speeding cars. It'll be them."

Agnes taps on the control panel of the car's communication unit. "They've blocked the road south," she says to Lena. "The queues are going to build up fast."

"Wait," the man in the helicopter says.

"I can't bloody wait," Lena shouts.

"They're just ahead. I almost missed them. They are not on the highway."

Lena brakes hard, remembers the other cars behind her, and floors the gas pedal. Agnes holds on to her seat and looks at Lena in alarm.

"Where are they?" Lena asks. "I need directions, fast."

"They're on a road parallel to the highway. In the forest, on your right. I think they're heading back to the airport."

"Don't let them out of your sight," Lena says. "We're going back to cut them off. Out."

She slows down and looks for a good spot to turn around. Tom and John are returning into the tightening net. For once, things are going her way.

"If you go back," the man in the helicopter above says, "you'll miss them."

"You said they're heading back?" Lena asks.

"Yes, but not to the terminal. The cars are driving towards a gate."

"A gate to what?"

"The airfield."

"Where's the turn?" Lena asks.

"Just ahead of where you are."

Lena sees the sign. Hoping the drivers behind her are paying attention, she slows down, turns right onto the narrow road, and stops. On their sides are sparse woods draped in a pale gloom by the blizzard.

"You drive," Lena tells Agnes. "If they crash and run, I'll go after them."

Shielding her eyes, Lena leaves the car and runs around to the passenger door while Agnes scoots over to the driver's seat. As soon as Lena is back inside, Agnes accelerates hard, forcing Lena to cling to the door handle.

Lena peers into the distance and curses the weather. Were it not for the helicopter above, they would never have found the fleeing cars. At least she cannot be far behind them; Agnes, who usually makes a point of obeying every traffic law in existence, guns the car like a racing driver on a crusade. The other police cars are somewhere behind them, but Agnes has outrun them in seconds.

Lena's phone rings. An unknown number. Going this fast, she does not want to take her hands off the handle, but the call might be important. As quickly as she can, she accepts it and switches on the loudspeaker.

"Franke here – *Jesus*, mind that tree – who's this?"

"This is Jan Bjurman," a man says. "I'm head of security at Arlanda. I've been appointed crisis coordinator, but I'm not sure – are you in pursuit of the car thief?"

"We're heading towards the airfield just south of Arlanda," Lena shouts, holding on to her seat.

"I see," he says. "That's good."

"In what way?" Lena demands.

"The airfield is surrounded by a fence six metres high," he explains. "We've got patrols with IR sensors nearby, and the gates are reinforced. You need a code and swipe cards to get through."

"Is this road in use?" Lena asks, noting that there is less snow here than she expected.

"It's used by trucks and maintenance vehicles, so we keep it ploughed. It's also a dead end."

Lena holds on as the car drifts through a curve and accelerates again. Agnes leans forward and stares at the road as if challenging it to fight.

"I can't see the task force," Lena says. "Are they close?"

"They should be."

"Tell them to stay back."

"But my directives are – why?"

"John's got a fucking gun is why. He'll shoot at them."

"I don't have the authority to tell them what to do. But they know the suspect is armed."

Lena almost laughs. She considers telling him that the problem here is not the gun, but the man wielding it. "Try anyway."

"I'll talk to them. No promises."

"And make sure no one is close."

"The security on the other side has been told to give you room."

"What about planes?"

"We have to let inbound flights land. They can't circle in this storm. All outbound flights are grounded, but passengers are restless. People whisper about terrorists."

"There," Agnes says and points ahead.

Lena hangs up on the manager and squints into the whiteout. A few hundred metres ahead, red tail lights appear and vanish again, so quickly she almost thinks she imagines them. On cue, the radio beeps.

"Helicopter Caesar twelve here. You're close to the cars."

"Are we gaining on them?" Lena asks.

"Slowly. The leading car swerves a lot, but it's going fast. It's less than a kilometre to the gates."

"How far apart are the cars?"

"It's hard to tell. I'd say a hundred meters. Maybe less."

Lena strains her eyes for another glimpse of the lights. A thousand metres left to the end. She tries to picture the closure: A dash through the snow, John giving up, a stand-off, or John committing suicide. A whirlwind whisking her away to a dull Kansas, where she can sleep and toilets are not haunted.

The car rocks from side to side as the forest rushes past. In front of them, the lights creep closer and are soon in constant view. Two dual smears of red in the white. Reluctantly, she pulls her pistol, checks the clip, and puts the weapon back in its holster. Its grip is even colder than her hand.

"You're closing the gap," the man in the helicopter reports.

Lena wheezes as the car drifts sideways through another curve and rockets onto a straight stretch. They have to be near the gates.

"Damn it," Agnes whispers.

"What?"

"They're going faster." Agnes flinches as they zip past a tree so close it touches the side of the car.

"You can still catch up with them, can't you?" Lena asks. "The helicopter says we're gaining."

"That's not the problem. The gates are just ahead."

"The cars are right up at the gate," the officer in the helicopter says. "Christ, they're going really fast. I think the first car's going to try to—"

"Hold on," Agnes says and goes faster.

Lena and Agnes burn through the blizzard. The wind tries to shunt their vehicle into the forest, but to Lena's amazement, Agnes keeps the car on the road. Metre after metre, they gain on John and Tom.

"I see the bastards," Lena says. "You're right. They aren't slowing down." She pauses. "He's going to try to break through."

The fence bleeds into view like a horizontal dark line beyond the cars. There is no way John or Tom can stop in time. Tom will crash, and John will not hesitate to run his car straight into Tom's.

At the last moment, Tom's car veers right and smashes into the fence next to the gate.

"Oh no," Lena says. "No, no, *no*."

Had Tom hit the gate, the thick metal bars would have reduced him to a sticky paste, but the fence is more brittle. Made to withstand frost and wire cutters, the mesh is tough enough to keep out animals and trespassers; however a car travelling at breakneck speed is a different matter.

For a moment, Lena thinks Tom has run clean through, but one of the car's wheels stays tangled in the frayed metal strands and sends the car spinning. It turns violently, slams into a metal railing on the airfield, and stops.

Lena jumps in surprise as klaxons awake like a choir of banshees: Tom has set off the intruder alarm. Red warning lights flare up and cast the twisted fence in a fiery glow. The volume sends splinters through her head. It is the last thing she needs.

John brakes hard in front of the hole made by Tom's car, and Agnes turns sharply to avoid colliding. Lena and Agnes's car lurches into the forest, slides between trees and boulders, crosses a mound with a grating hiss, and comes to a spine-juddering halt less than thirty metres from John's car.

"Mother of a—" Lena takes a deep breath and swallows hard. She cannot believe she is still alive.

Shaking herself into action, she flings her safety belt away and shoves her door open. John is on the far side; Lena and Agnes's car will provide cover if John shoots at them.

"Brief the coordinator," Lena says and climbs out. "Make sure his people inside the fence pinch Tom."

John's car is next to the hole. She cannot see through its windows, but the doors look closed. John is inside. The helicopter climbs, seeking an altitude safe from gunfire. Snow cascades from trees from the noise and the wind. Competing with the klaxons are more sirens. The other police cars, closing in.

John cannot run or shoot them all. Whatever he chooses to do, his flight ends here.

*

CHAPTER 52

Lena

Lena pulls her gun, points it at the ground, and looks over the car. At the shooting range, the weapon is usually a dead weight, but now it is a near-weightless trinket of metal and plastic.

She imagines the chain of reactions that will originate in her mind and end with bullets digging into another body. The trigger is a nerve, alert and ready, even keen. A shiver is enough. A sigh. An idea.

"Damn it," Lena says and presses her fist to her temple. She must focus. This is the home stretch. She will keep together a little longer.

Agnes looks up from the radio inside the car. "Sorry?"

"Nothing." Lena covers her eyes from the snow. "There's no one moving in John's car. I think he's knocked out."

"He's still in the car," Agnes says. "I see his shadow."

"Really." Lena squints and tilts her head. "I can't see a thing."

"He's there," Agnes says calmly. "Trust me."

"I do," Lena pulls out a small megaphone from inside the car.

"John," she calls, hoping her amplified voice will cut through the noise. "It's over. You're surrounded. Come out with your hands on your head."

Lena has shouted the same words before, but the line has never felt so weak. The command is meant to be imposing, instilling a sense of inevitable defeat, and the police's advantage in numbers is supposed to overwhelm the fugitive.

In John's case, it is like pointing a gun at a wolf: The threat is real, but there will not be any recognition or fear. Not this time.

Agnes finishes briefing the coordinator, crawls over Lena's seat, and climbs out. She looks at John's car. "He's not going to come."

Lena cannot tell if Agnes means it as a question or a statement. "He'll leave that car one way or the other," Lena says. "But we have to talk him through this, or he'll do something stupid."

The sirens are closer. Out on the airfield, deep in the blizzard, are the orange and blue flashes of the airport security homing in on Tom. The helicopter circles overhead. Farther away, the task force's helicopter is nearing; she can hear the rumble of its giant engine.

"You still want to help John," Agnes says softly. "After all he has done."

"I want to make sure no one gets hurt."

"John has already hurt many others."

"He's desperate," Lena says, trying to see the shadow Agnes claims is in the car.

"He could be a murderer," Agnes insists.

Lena looks at Agnes from the corner of her eyes. "So?"

"Yet you want to save him."

"What the hell, Agnes?" Lena turns and stares at her colleague. "Don't give me this devil's advocate bullshit. John is going to prison, but he's going there alive. Understood?" The past twenty-four hours have hardened Agnes so much Lena hardly recognizes her. John's broken mind seems to rub off on those close to him.

Agnes is silent. Her eyes are still on John's car. "He's leaving."

"What?" Lena snaps her head back. She can barely make out the form of John's car, but there is no mistaking the shadow that emerges from a side door. She raises the megaphone.

"John, hold it," she calls. "Do not move."

The coordinator calls over the radio inside the car. "Franke, the suspect inside the airport is on the move."

Lena lunges into the car and snatches up the radio. "Repeat?"

"The other suspect is running. My team is in pursuit. Have you apprehended the other man?"

"No, he's–"

The shadow that left John's car slips through the fence and darts towards Tom's car. One moment John had been next to invisible, the next he is fading away in the storm again.

"John's inside the fence," Lena screams into the radio and runs towards John's car. "I repeat, John is on the airfield. He's armed. I'm following him."

"My team will—"

"Your team will stay the fuck back," Lena barks. "He will engage you. I have to talk to him." She reaches John's car and scrambles over the hood to get to the hole. Agnes is close behind her. The other police cars come into view, engines roaring, lights blazing, sirens calling. John is a disappearing speck of grey. Tom is nowhere in sight.

"I have different orders," the coordinator shouts back. "My team or the task force will seize him. You are to keep out of their way."

"Says who?"

"Your commander."

Lena edges through the hole in the fence and stumbles onto the airfield. "I can't hear you," she says. "Too much interference. Out." She throws the radio away, shifts her gun to her right hand, and runs after John.

On her far right, the task force spill out of their helicopter and set off at a sprint, towards John. The airport security team have left their cars and follow the task force on foot. She has a head start, but only by seconds.

Her legs are on fire as she dashes across the tarmac. She is not a natural runner; the police force's yearly tests always leave her nauseated, but she refuses to lose sight of John. Soon, she can see him a few steps behind the skidding and flailing shape of Tom.

Running on her right, Agnes veers away and dashes diagonally, picking up speed. Perhaps she plans to cut John and Tom off in case they change direction. Lena is too focused on breathing and staying on her feet to be concerned.

Behind Lena are the National Task Force, the other officers and the airport security team, all following her like a comet's tail. Getting in the way of the task force could cost Lena her job, but their tactics will fail against John. Making someone give up takes fear, or at least some scrap of self-preservation.

John has neither. They cannot intimidate him or coax him into surrendering. When they surround John, he will do something unexpected, and mayhem will follow. Under his haggard appearance hides a callous machine. If he gets hold of one of the task force's machine guns, no one in the airport is safe.

Some thirty metres ahead, John stops, fades and emerges again but smaller, his shape wrong. At first, Lena cannot make sense of what happened, but then she understands: John has caught up with Tom and brought him to the ground.

She closes on the men as they wrestle and strike each other with frenetic but feeble punches. The task force fans out and forms a semicircle around the two men. The airport security team takes up positions behind them. Everyone is wary of John's supposed gun.

The police helicopter thunders overhead. John and Tom are a flurry of arms and legs. Shrill orders and counter-orders echo around the airfield. The task force edges closer, tightening their noose, and bark commands over raised sub-machine guns.

Tom screams in pain, and the task force stops, hovering between rushing in and looking for a clear shot. John is only a few seconds away.

Lena runs towards the two men and finds John sitting on Tom's chest. His hands are around Tom's throat. Tom claws at John's clothes, but his face is reddened and bulbous. He is burning through the last oxygen in his lungs. The fight is leaving him.

Both men's faces are smeared with blood. Neither of them looks at Lena. There are no guns or knives in sight. Only fists, panic and fury.

Lena goes from running to a sliding tackle and slams her right shoulder into John, shoving him off Tom. John lands on his back but springs back up, crouching like an animal. He looks at Lena, who lies sideways over Tom's twisting body. His eyes are lifeless and flat and more chilling than anything Lena has ever seen.

She tries to stand back up, slips on the icy tarmac, and falls back onto Tom. When John tenses, Lena aims her pistol at his face.

"Don't," she says.

For the first time, Lena is so close to John she can reach out and touch him, but a deep instinct makes her want to recoil. While his expression is confused, his features are contorted and feral, lips peeled back and eyes wider than seems possible. Lena is an obstacle between a hunter and his kill. A barrier that must be breached.

Still, she is mesmerized, knowing she balances at a crossroads. One bad decision, a moment's hesitation, and John will die one way or another. Others are at risk: Agnes, Tom, the task force. The weight of lives hanging in the balance presses down on her as she gazes at John over her gun.

Tom touches his throat, makes a croaked sound, and tries to move away from underneath Lena. Keeping her eyes on John, Lena motions for Tom to keep still. She knows John is looking for an opening to rush past her or to snatch her weapon.

Tom lashes out and closes his hand around Lena's gun.

"What the—" Lena tries to pull her weapon away from Tom's hand, but he holds on.

"Give me," Tom mutters. "I'll kill him, I swear. Give it to me."

"Let go, you idiot." Lena stares at Tom in disbelief. "Have you lost your fucking mind?"

"*Give it to me,*" Tom screams.

John tenses again. Tom holds on. The task force's commands are a deafening cacophony. Lena curses, rises to her knees, and throws herself down onto Tom's face, putting all her weight behind her elbow as she rams it across his jaw. Tom's head lolls sideways, and he lets go of Lena's gun.

John moves.

Lena twists and aims, but John slaps the gun from her frozen hands and sends the weapon disappearing into the snow. She kicks John's legs out from underneath him. John pushes himself up and tackles Lena, driving her down into the snow. His face is stiff and his eyes are blank like mirrors.

It is, she knows, the expression of a resolute executioner.

*

CHAPTER 53

John Andersson

Free from the shackles of the creature's gaze, John turns to the brightness above.

This close, the light is different, more complex and alive with motion. Swift shadows are followed by flashes of bright light. The shapes grow more distinct: curled fingers and bared teeth, dark eyes and brown hair, offset by a backdrop of pure white. A woman, her face twisted with pain or rage. Her eyes are locked on his. A line of sight spanning a whole sky. As if she were in fact –

The insight hits him as if he were run through by a spear.

He fell down, away from everything he knew, and into a place he's rejected out of hand throughout his life. But this prison is buried in the dungeons of his mind. Or, maybe, everyone's mind.

What matters is that it's part of him. Its bars might be forged by rules beyond his understanding, although rules can be bent with trickery or tools.

Or, he hopes, with resolution.

"I understand," John whispers.

"You know nothing," the creature hisses. "But we'll take turns to teach you. We'll educate you with imagination, vigour, and at length. There are seven kinds of agony, combinable in fascinating ways. We will turn your hide into a map that charts them all."

John keeps his eyes fixed on the sky. *Let this work. For Molly's sake.*

"You made a mistake," John whispers.

The creature laughs. "We guide the plotting of masterminds. We dictated the original betrayal. We make no mistakes, but you did. You should've stayed down on the ice instead of wasting our time."

"And you," John says, "should've stolen another face."

John wrenches away from the creature's grip. It lashes out at him, but surprise or outrage makes it pause. It's all the time he needs. He turns his face to the sky and pictures it as an ocean, then closes his eyes.

And pushes *away*.

*

John rises through incoherent words and fragments of sentences echoing around him, fading in and out of his head like splinters of someone else's dream.

Without warning, his ascent turns into a fall. An unyielding surface slams into his back and dazes him to the edge of unconsciousness.

His eyes spring open.

Once again, he's freezing and on his back, but this time he's not on an iced-over lake. The cliffs are gone. Above is the brilliant, furious smear of a daytime blizzard. Snow peppers his eyes. His clothes are torn and stained, and countless cuts and bruises scream in chorus. Around are people, living and moving around, shouting commands he's much too dazed to understand.

Impressions flood his senses so fast he's close to vomiting. Still, one cast-iron certainty stands out in the storm of impressions.

He is home again.

*

CHAPTER 54

Lena

Lena feels the fight go out of John. He stops moving and goes limp, the change as sudden as when he attacked her.

She rolls away and rises to a crouch. Her gun is gone. Around her, the task force closes in, edging nearer, tense and robot-like. They still think John is armed. The red dots of laser targeting aids dance on John's and Lena's bodies.

"Stop," Lena shouts. "Keep back." She spits blood and coughs; screaming feels like drinking acid.

The task force hesitates. Lena turns back to John.

"John Andersson," she rasps, "you're under arrest."

She takes a deep breath and recites the legal phrases, pausing to suck air in her lungs. As she speaks, she wonders if the words mean anything to someone so far beyond human behaviour.

John says nothing. He lies perfectly still, breathing heavily, sprawled on his back and staring at the sky. The wild look on his face is gone.

"I'm here," he mumbles. "At last."

Lena frowns. The sudden change in behaviour could be a deceit; she if anyone knows what he is capable of doing. Still, she cannot rule out shock or trauma.

"John," Lena says, "I got here in time. You didn't kill him. Don't screw this up now. Put your hands on your head, slowly."

John does not move or answer. Tom mumbles incoherently behind Lena.

"Damn it," Lena says, louder. "No more bloody games. You've got everyone on edge. I'm trying to save you. You'll get help and whatever support you need."

"I had support." John rises to his hands and knees. "I had Molly.

He took her away." His eyes move to Tom.

"It wasn't him." Lena holds up her hands. If John loses his temper again, he's finished.

John shakes his head. "He helped."

"Perhaps," Lena says, grasping for words that will soothe John. "But he's going to prison for a long time."

"Prison isn't enough."

"He's not the murderer. You've done enough."

"What are you talking about?"

"Torture." Lena stabs her finger at John. "Armed assault. Theft. Break and enter." She stops when John's eyes grow wide.

John's voice is weak. "Torture?"

"You're telling me you don't remember."

"I would never torture anyone."

The task force moves closer, but Lena holds them back with a warning hand. She wonders why they obey; perhaps they think she and John are in a stand-off. John is lying or suffering from memory loss. Either way, things can go downhill fast.

"You tried to kill Tom a minute ago," Lena says, emphasizing every word. "You don't want that. I've been where you are, and I know what's happening to you. It'll destroy you."

"You're the one they want." John's eyes focus on Lena, as if seeing her clearly for the first time.

"What?"

"The ones who want to destroy us. It's you they're after."

"Now listen to me–"

"I saw you," John insists, "up in the clouds, and it spoke of you. But there are more than one. I can still see them, like shadows, around us. They want you to suffer for something you've done. Your past sins, something like that. Please."

John's words make her loosen her hold on him. *Her past sins.* She must've misheard, although she knows she didn't. He must be talking about the raid. But he can't know. Only a handful are aware of the event and its catastrophic fallout, and she's told no one about the horrific compulsion that made her taunt the man she gunned down.

Yet John knows.

"You make no sense." Lena's throat is choked, causing her to wheeze. "Do as I say, and put your–"

"*Look out.*" John points at something behind Lena.

Before she can turn around, a shove in her back throws her forward and down onto her stomach, next to John's feet. Someone kicks her hard in her side, but she cannot see who it is. Another kick cracks one of her ribs while John scrambles backwards.

The impact rolls her over on her back and lets her see her attacker: Tom, standing next to her, pulling his foot back to kick her again. His savaged face is distorted into the visage of a demon.

"Cunt," Tom rasps. "You thought you'd take me, did you? I'll teach you." He pulls back to kick her again.

Lena turns on her side and brings her fists up to protect herself. Her body screams with pain.

Tom's shoe connects with her right arm, and she cries out as red lightning crackles in her mind. The task force shift their laser sights onto Tom, but Tom either ignores them or does not notice. Some of the dots dance on Lena. She knows that the task force wants to rush in, but the snowfall blocks their view; she can hear calls for them not to shoot.

She can barely move her arms as Tom pulls his foot back for another kick. If he hits her head or her side again, she might faint.

If she passes out, Tom will turn on John sitting hapless and open-mouthed a few steps away. Someone will be shot. Hopefully Tom, but maybe John. That cannot happen.

When Tom kicks again, Lena sacrifices her guard and reaches for Tom's legs. The kick slams into Lena's thigh, but she shuts out the pain, grabs one leg of Tom's trousers, and pulls down. Tom sways and tries to regain his balance. She pulls again, and Tom crashes down on top of her, cursing and screaming.

For a moment, her vision blackens when the last air is forced from her lungs. She had hoped to bring him down on the ground next to her; instead Tom holds her down, spins on his side, and straddles her, oblivious to the clusters of glowing red points on his body.

Looking down at her, Tom balls his fist and lands a glancing blow on her temple.

Lena screams and bucks to get Tom off her, but he weighs too much. When he leans back, she almost catches his head with a wild kick, but he ducks and drives his fist hard into her chest.

The punch sends splinters of raw hurt throughout her body. For a moment, she drifts off, sinking into a dark quietness.

Then, just as quickly, rage pulls her back, and she resurfaces to see him leering down at her.

Meat, she thinks, or hears herself think; the voice does not quite seem to be her own. The words slip into her consciousness like stage whispers, impossible to ignore.

Grinning, useless flesh. Unworthy to breathe. Unfit to be.
I will shut you down.

The swarm of red shimmering dots crosses Tom's face, and he pauses with his fist in the air. He looks up at the officers and troops around him as if seeing them for the first time. His furious expression changes into resigned surprise, and he sags.

"Fuck it," he wheezes. "You win. Don't shoot."

The task force shouts at him to put his hands on his head and stand up. Tom obliges and shifts his legs to rise.

"I got it," Tom calls. "All right? I'm doing it."

Lena's right hand touches cold metal buried in the snow. Her gun. She closes her hand around the grip, whisks up the weapon, and trains it on Tom's face. Her vision narrows down to his face. One small movement is all it takes to silence him.

Tom stares down at Lena. "I said I give up," he shouts. "Put your fucking gun down, will you?"

When Lena doesn't obey, Tom reaches for her hand, in fear or out of hope to snatch her gun. Lena smiles and tightens her finger around the trigger.

A shot rings out, and Tom's throat explodes in a red cloud.

For an endless second, Tom remains sitting up, then slumps forward over Lena. He convulses once and grows still, his forehead resting on Lena's shoulder.

After another long moment, the task force closes in.

Lena pushes Tom's body off her and rolls away, leaving Tom sprawled on his chest, arms wide. His ruined chin is raised, as if waiting for a wind to lift him. Agitated voices call for ambulances and hands prod at her, but she is too numb to respond. The world, so capricious a moment ago, has solidified into cold air and distant voices.

She looks towards the shapes in the blizzard and sees Agnes, her gun raised. Her face is pale but serene.

Agnes?

Lena tries to curse, but blood trickles into her mouth and turns the profanity into a gurgle.

She had wanted to shoot Tom. As she aimed, she pictured the wound erupting in his face. She transformed a human being into a stain that needed to be erased, just as she had done on that wretched raid so many years ago.

She had thought herself in control and chased John until the rope's end to stop him from becoming a monster, only to once again lose control to the demon she already had become. The door had been open, and she had nearly fallen through.

But she had also glimpsed the beast that hid inside. It had come close to possessing her; however now she understood its form, how it moved behind her frenzy. She sensed the subtle shift in her temper that had unlocked the gates of her mind and let the monster in.

The temptation to hurt lingers, and with it a voice. *Rid the world of them all,* it murmurs. *Carve them out, pick them off, shed them like used skin. Let them suffer, teach them pain. Bare your heart, and show them no mercy.*

Then, reluctantly, the voice fades.

The wind around her is liquid ice. Her veins are tapped of blood and filled with soreness. All sounds blur to a dull hum. Around her, shapes move in, lift her up, and carry her away. Looking up at the blizzard, she wonders about the voice she heard and if she ever will hear it again. If she does, she has her answer ready.

Never, she will say. *I have seen you. I know your voice. Next time, I will see you coming. And I will slam the door in your face.*

Although ignoring the voice will be hard. The speaker, who or whatever it is, knows her too well. And she knows she'll hear it again.

*

CHAPTER 55

One week later

Five minutes after the café opens, Lena has claimed a corner table, where she cradles her coffee cup and watches the sunrise.

She winces and shifts in her seat: sudden moves still hurt her ribs. So does walking, yawning, and laughing. Her bruised cheeks make even sipping coffee a challenge. But she can sip it, because despite all that transpired a week ago, she's still alive. So is John Andersson. Not that he will enjoy the luxury of coffee for some time.

One day, probably soon, she'll check up on what happened to the devastated man. The words he whispered at the landing strip refuse to leave her. So does the impression that he has something to share. However, the moment that hit her the hardest was when their eyes met, just as he stopped fighting her. It'd been like staring at a mirror.

His gaze spoke of someone who had been to a bad place, a domain in which no level of brutality was unjust. Someone who is determined not to end up there again. In that constant fight, they are united. It's a connection she can't and won't attempt to explain to anyone else.

She squints at the sun. Shafts of light the colour of bleached copper climb over rooftops, shoot between blocks of flats, and glitter in frost-coated brickwork. While the blizzard has abated and the skies are clear, hard winds still pummel the city, howling and whining as they rip through tunnels and alleyways. The café's window budges and creaks with every gust that thumps against the glass. As if an invisible hand were pressing against it, hoping to break through.

The café is one of her favourites: a small pearl on Stockholm's vanishing string of classic caffeine haunts, with friendly staff, few guests, strong coffee and no advertising. Her seat provides her with a view of the strait outside Old Town. In summer, cruisers and ferries fill the quayside. This time of the year, the waters are frozen almost completely solid, hiding the bottom from view.

The ambient music is muted down to a soothing whisper. More than one case has moved forward at a brisk pace after withdrawing here to ponder this or that detail. Today, she wants only its calm ambience, as well as the peculiar flavour of privacy found only in half-empty public spaces.

She checks her phone. Almost quarter past eight in the morning. She looks up just as Superintendent Gren, punctual as ever, enters the café, bringing with him a small cloud of snow. He nods at her, shrugs off his coat, and takes the opposite seat.

"The bakery here better be worth the slog," Gren says and brushes snowflakes out of his hair. "What's wrong with the office canteen?"

"Would you like an alphabetical rundown?" Lena asks. "You'll need to take notes."

Gren snorts and orders a hot chocolate. Lena watches her boss while his back is turned. The banter is an old, tried-and-tested way to establish common ground before moving on to more serious topics. She smiles, then stops when her jaw hurts.

Gren turns back and studies Lena.

"How are you feeling?" he asks after a moment.

"I'm recovering," Lena says. "Another week or so, and I'll be back to normal."

"I'm glad to hear that, even if I don't quite believe you. Are you getting enough sleep?"

"Do I seem exhausted?" Lena wonders.

In fact, she's slept better than she has done in years. Her dreams are still unpleasant and tend to wake her up, but sheer physical strain dragged her back down under just as quickly as she surfaced. The several evenings she's spent in the basement gym have helped, too.

"Actually," Gren says, "you don't. But I know you've been struggling to rest. It's clear from how you look."

"Don't worry. I'm dealing only with cuts and scrapes."

"In difference to the victim." Gren raises his eyebrows. "That's what you're thinking, isn't it?"

"Maybe." Lena shrugs. "To be honest, it'll take a while to put this case behind me."

She can't raise how concerned she is with John Andersson and the things he said at the point of his arrest. Gren is humane, but also a full-fledged pragmatic. In his view, John is a psychotic criminal, in need of care but also dangerous.

"That's normal." Gren sips from his mug. "Take a few days off, travel somewhere, put your feet up. It'll make you feel better."

"I can't," Lena says. "There's work that needs doing."

"And there are dozens of others who can do it. But I won't argue, because I don't like losing."

"Why did you want to meet outside of the office?" Catching up before work had been Gren's suggestion, although he hadn't provided a reason.

"To see how you're coping," Gren says. "And give you a chance to vent, if you want. I'm aware that this case was difficult. There are so many reports I haven't yet had time to read through them all. What's the final word on the shooting that started all of this?"

"In short, it was a botched robbery. We got a testimony from the dealer who John clubbed in the flat. He has lost vision in one eye and will slur for the rest of his life, but once he grew lucid, he was happy to talk. Said he'll do anything to stay in the hospital, away from John."

"Can't blame him," Gren murmurs.

"It was his friend who shot the woman," Lena continues. "That's the man John glued to the door. He'd been trying doors around the suburb."

Thieves chasing from block to block in search of open doors is a common offence in Stockholm, as well as many other cities. Typically, the perpetrator is desperate in the extreme, or just high as a runaway kite.

"What about the one John used the glue on?" Gren wonders.

"He's alive, but only with the aid of a room full of machines. The doctors give him a one-in-ten chance. If he makes it, he will be bed-bound for the rest of his miserable life."

Gren's face is hard as he looks out the window. "An unpleasant mess," he notes. "It was just about money, then?"

"Just money." Lena pauses. "I have a couple of small questions."

"Of course." Gren composes himself and turns back to Lena.

"How come I still have my job?" she asks. "I got an unofficial warning from our department's board, but I expected worse. And you've been worryingly calm. Even I know I was out of line, at least on a few occasions."

"You were," Gren agrees. "But I spoke with a consultant who said that you, and I quote, *acted inexpertly but possibly prevented the loss of further lives.* In short, it's another way of saying you screwed up, but possibly saved people from getting shot. That counted in your favour."

Lena nods slowly. Gren had probably pulled more than one string to keep her on the force. She owes him one.

"What's the other question?" Gren asks.

Lena takes a deep breath. "Where's Agnes?" Despite all the violence and stress, this is the issue that bothers her the most.

"She left," Gren says.

"I know that much. Please, level with me. She was my partner. I thought she'd been put on mandatory leave, which would've made sense after all she went through. Then I hear she disappeared. After that, just rumours."

Lena had been ushered to the airport's medical bay almost immediately after John Andersson was arrested. Agnes travelled in the same car, but remained quiet during the short trip, staring out the side window while Lena was on the phone with the airport security.

She'd been even paler than normal. A shadow hung over her eyes as she searched the sky, as if looking for answers.

That was the last time Lena saw her.

The following morning, Lena read Agnes's statement over and over, each time with a greater sense of disbelief. According to Agnes, Tom had reached for his inner pocket, and Agnes thought he was trying to pull a concealed weapon. Being closer than the task force and having a clear shot, she made a call and opened fire.

In truth, there had been no concealed weapon. Sure enough, Tom had reached for Lena's hand, but that didn't warrant the use of lethal force. What *had* happened was that Lena succumbed to that gleeful, homicidal persona that hid in her head. She wanted an excuse to shoot Tom. She would have, too. Agnes just beat her to it.

Maybe Agnes misread Tom's actions. Brawls are always confusing in the extreme, and the weather didn't help. It's possible that she aimed high in order to avoid shooting Lena, and accidentally hit Tom in his neck.

Yet Agnes is calmness personified. Always analytical, careful and strategic, even when she drove at lethal speeds through the blizzard outside Arlanda Airport. She's also a terrific marksman. Lena recalls seeing mentions of hunting in the summary of her background, back when she lived in Northern Sweden.

So many questions that need answers. Most of all, Lena simply wants to talk to Agnes. She wants to hear her calm, analytical take on why John had come to his senses, why he said what he did when he gave up. Why the world is becoming darker, more unpredictable, and more hostile. It seems that conversation won't happen. Agnes is gone.

"I haven't got the full story," Gren says. "What I do know is that during the night after John's arrest, Agnes made her way back to the headquarters and left around an hour later, long before I came in. All her documents were sorted, gun and ID card in a drawer, the rest of her equipment in her open locker. She'd filed the mandatory reports related to using one's weapon."

"Did anyone check her place?" Lena asks.

"A patrol went to her flat, but no one answered the door. I called the property managers, who told me someone had dropped the keys into their mailbox, along with the remaining rent and a cancellation of the tenancy. Apparently, the flat was spotless, the fridge was clean and switched off, the bed was made, and all sinks were dry."

"That sounds like Agnes."

"The following day," Gren continues, "I received Agnes's signed resignation form in the post."

"Have you approved it?" Lena asks.

"Not officially. Did you read the memo I sent around?"

Lena nods. "You said that pressure got the best of her, and that she's expected to return. I was hoping that you could give me a bit more."

"Do you think I'm holding back?"

"I think I haven't got the full story."

Gren sighs and scratches his neck. "Truth be told, I don't know much more. Agnes has probably gone to ground because of stress. She wouldn't be the first one. If my memory serves me right, she's from the countryside. Maybe duty in the city was what she expected. Quite a few officers who come from outside of Stockholm relocate back to smaller, calmer towns after serving here."

Lena tries to picture Agnes overwhelmed by working in the capital, or broken by the manic chase a week ago. It doesn't fit. Agnes is too level-headed. The search for John had only intensified the woman's focus. In hindsight, Agnes had seemed equally preoccupied with Lena's well-being. One more mystery to join the other ones.

"Or," Gren continues, "perhaps the hunt for John Andersson got to her. After all, she killed a man. That can be traumatic." He pauses. "You know all about that," he adds gently.

"She should see a counsellor," Lena argues.

"And she will," Gren assures her, "as soon as she's back."

"You sound very sure that she'll return."

"She struck me as the diligent kind. Most likely, she's staying with a relative or a friend. There'll be a reprimand for unapproved absence, and that'll be that. Please don't get me wrong. I too would like to know where she is and why she bolted, but I'm simply too busy. I've circulated a request to all stations to let me know if they spot her. That's all I can do for now."

Lena nods and looks out the window, mostly to avoid meeting Gren's gaze. She hasn't told anyone of the Post-it note Agnes slipped into Lena's calendar the morning she took off. Revealing its existence would be wrong. It was meant for her alone. Besides, the four words were as cryptic as the woman who penned them.

Don't worry.

Yours,
Agnes.

Lena has fallen asleep staring at the note every night since finding it, always failing to make sense of its meaning. One day, she will find Agnes and ask her what made her go into hiding. Or maybe Agnes will find her.

Gren eyes the pastries and makes a rueful grimace.

"I should get to the office," he says, "before I cave in and order that cake for breakfast. Want to walk with me?"

"I'll stay for a little while," Lena says. "But thanks."

Gren nods and opens the door, letting another burst of powdery snow inside the café, and drags it shut behind him.

Lena turns back to the window. The winds show no sign of calming down. According to a distant digital noticeboard, the temperature is murderous, even for this time of year. Trekking to the police headquarters will be a dreary, time-consuming challenge. But the cold will wake her up. Hopefully, it'll distract her, too.

She rises and winces as she puts on her jacket. Her desk waits. Tasks are filling up her agenda. Injustices are being committed and traces are being left. She will manage the issues one at a time.

Just like she'll deal with the problems she keeps shackled in her mind.

*

CHAPTER 56

Epilogue

Emma Nyland sits down across from John Andersson, opens her folder, and clears her throat.

She's deep inside Lindhaga Hospital, a bastion of mortar and barred windows tucked away in a hilly, forest-clad area an hour's drive north of Stockholm. From a distance, the hospital looks like a nineteenth-century mansion overlooking a tranquil archipelago. Its proud front faces the sea and a scattering of small distant islands, while open grassy fields stretch away from the building's sides and rear. Beyond the fields are dense and deep spruce forests where the gloom hangs heavy even in daylight.

Twenty-six years ago, the building was converted from a private rehabilitation centre into a joint facility run by the government's correctional department and a university psychology faculty. Bars, pool tables and gyms were replaced by a small number of Sweden's most difficult criminals. The staff is trained and numerous; security top-notch and constantly maintained.

The hospital's only sign is mounted next to the only gate in the brick wall that encircles the building. There are no signposts at the nearby highway, and the turn looks like any other private lane that crisscrosses the forests.

The message wasn't lost on Emma: if you cannot find the hospital, you have no business there.

"Good morning," Emma says to John. "How are you feeling?"

John's gaze is steady but unfocused. Or rather, he seems to be studying a point in the air behind her. After a long moment, he meets her eyes.

"Worn and bruised," John says. "No great wonder, given what happened yesterday. But you're not here to examine my wounds."

"You're quite right, John." Emma smiles. "I've talked to the resident doctors, as well as the nurses. They told me that you're seeing things. Distressing visions of some sort. Is that correct?"

John Andersson is silent. His arms and legs are secured by metal wires that force him to hobble rather than walk, and the table is large enough to put him at a safe distance. As an extra precaution, the staff searched him for sharp objects prior to the meeting. Two male nurses have taken up position on his left and right, ready to restrain the patient if need be. More security measures than usual. Given what John Andersson has done, it's understandable that the staff isn't taking any chances, but Emma can't ignore the impression that they're a trifle more tense than she's seen them before.

Just over a week has passed since the police caught him. Outside Lindhaga Hospital, the late afternoon is shrouded in a light snowfall. Grey skies stretch out in every direction. Emma expected the call since the minute she heard about the arrest of John Andersson: as one of the city's leading psychiatric consultants, and specialized in violent criminals, her insights will be important when deciding how to treat the patient.

According to the hospital's record, the patient first claimed to remember nothing about what happened during the two frenzied days the police searched for him. Other reports detail how he has broken down into hysterics when confronted with his actions. Gradually, his memories returned, bringing with them more trauma, troubled sleep and disturbing visions. At least that's what the staff says; the patient has made no complaints.

If only she could get a bearing on the man. Typically, she can draw a rough outline of her interviewees and their personas after a few minutes in their presence. Probable backgrounds, psychological conditions, and other rudimentary aspects of their psychology. Those summaries may not be medically accurate, but they're helpful for directing topics and teasing out profound answers.

Not so with John Andersson. His face is calm and composed, although not in a detached or callous manner. If anything, he looks resigned and frustrated, as if he's aware of his situation. He's also eager to confirm that he committed all the felonies he's charged with. His remorsefulness appears, at a glance, genuine.

Yet his gaze sets her on edge. There's a cool, unflinching depth to his eyes, like a classic thousand-mile stare, but wholly alert and focussed. It disturbs her in a way that never has happened before.

A pearl of sweat crosses Emma's forehead. She pulls her legs in under her chair in a reflexive, irrational way. If she had a choice, she would postpone the interview for another day. Preferably one when she has a tighter grip on her emotions. Not even the worst breed of psychotic butcherers she's confronted has fazed her this badly.

Only one thing can unnerve her like this, and she's quite certain none of *those* are present in this room.

"You're right about the visions," John says. "I see them all the time. Whenever I look out the window, close my eyes and drift off, or merely zone out. As soon as I lose focus, they bleed into view."

"Who is it that you see?" Emma asks. "The men you tortured?"

John shakes his head. "Them, I only dream about. I'm talking about the ones right here. Those who move among us as we speak."

"In this room?"

John nods. "And outside, too. They're everywhere."

"Although I can't see them?" Emma asks. "Is that so?"

"A week ago, I couldn't see them either." John shakes his head as if chasing unwanted thoughts away. "It's different now. You haven't wandered where I have. You don't know what to look for."

"You have some sort of special talent?"

"It's a curse." John looks down. "I glimpsed something I can't unsee. You know how it's hard to turn away from a nasty accident or a disfigured face?"

"Go on," Emma says.

"It's like that, in a way. I was lost for a while, and part of me still is. It left me aware of them. I know how they try to snare us. They'll take any shape, use any voice, put on whatever mask that does the job."

"I see." Emma makes a note of John's comments and taps her pen against her pad. This paranoia needs to be explored. Perhaps it's the key to the patient's ongoing delusions, as well as his capacity for hideous actions.

"Do you believe you're unsafe here?" Emma asks.

"It's not me I'm worried about." John smiles thinly. "As I said before, I can see them for what they are. It's too late for them to slither inside my armour. I'm an anomaly. There might be others like me, though. I can't be the only one."

"Please tell me more about these people you think want to harm you," she says.

"Beings," John corrects. "Not people."

"Creatures?" Emma wonders. "Monsters, maybe?"

"You can call them monsters, I suppose. Although they're different to what you think. These ones roam free, unfettered, curious, and dangerous. We attract them, you see. Just like warm bodies at night pull in things that bite and drain. We're their livestock, as well as their playthings."

"That's a rather macabre picture," Emma says.

She jots down a summary of John's ideas and circles a few of the words. This will be a long and fascinating study. Most likely, the patient's psyche is distorting a strong fear of repercussions, feeding his brain with images of monstrosities that seek revenge. That would be a classic scenario. Yet the idea doesn't sit right with her; John Andersson swings between apparent lucidity and blatant confusion faster than any other patient she's interviewed.

It might be useful to let him elaborate on his fantasies, and see where his reasoning takes him. Chances are he'll become too agitated and grow dangerously hysterical. Should that happen, the nurses will know what to do. From what she's read, the staff at this particular hospital is hand-picked and professional. They deal with the worst of the worst.

"Can you explain more about these monsters?" Emma asks. "Describe them in detail if you can. What they look like, how they behave. Any powers they might possess."

"They move fast," John says softly, his eyes darting around the room. "Quick as silverfish, easy as smoke, chasing through the conduits between us and-and their place." He shakes his head and breathes faster. "Their home is a dark, endless playground filled with sadistic children, and we're the only sparks in their permanent midnight. We are gloves they long to fill, and reach out, and clasp, and *twist* and *rip* and *tear* and—"

"Easy," one of the nurses orders John in a deep voice. "Stay calm. Remember the rules."

John closes his eyes and struggles to control his breathing. After a short moment, he calms and looks up.

"Listen closely," John says, his voice steady again. "They are inside all of us, waiting for a moment to take control. We're just mouthpieces and marionettes to them. Toys to be shook and tortured for fun, then thrown away."

"Do these monsters have a name?" Emma wonders.

"I wouldn't know," John says. "But I think they have many. Just as *they* are many. A legion of purpose, old as life itself. Perhaps even older."

Emma sighs and takes off her glasses. This interview will be a challenge; the patient is more complex than she anticipated. John's face is drawn, but his eyes are clear and his voice is filled with both wonder and conviction. Whatever wild horrors galloped through his mind clearly linger in some corner of his mind. He will have to remain under lock, key and supervision indefinitely.

After a moment, she realises that John is studying her.

"You're staring," Emma notes.

"I've learned to make out their shapes," John says. "Or rather, the forms they use as camouflage when hiding inside others. They're very cunning, able to slip through the smallest weak moment without us noticing. Sometimes they claim us completely. That's what happened to me. But most of the time, they're waiting, watching, taunting us. Most of us don't even realize they're there."

"How intriguing." Emma raises her eyebrows. This mental condition is proving increasingly surprising the more she delves into it.

John watches her. "The shapes of your demons are quite clear."

Emma stops with her pen hovering above the pad. A chill seems to waft through the room.

"The shape of my what, exactly?" Emma asks.

"Of the ones that want you," John says. "They're after you, too. Not as desperately as they wish to destroy the detective, but make no mistake, you're on their list."

"Are you suggesting that I'm in danger?"

"Not just you." John grimaces. "We're prey, all of us. No one walks safe. They're behind every pair of eyes you meet, scheming and pushing, nudging and cajoling, doing all they can to pull us down. Don't you see?"

"Just keep talking, please. I know it's difficult, but sharing your burden will help." Emma pauses. "You said 'pull us down'," she notes. "To where?"

"Their home," John insists. "Where they dwell. I think it's just one place, but hidden inside everyone. Do you follow me?"

"Like some form of collective idea shared between several individuals?" Emma suggests.

"Exactly." John nods. "But it's real, not a fantasy. And we're the conduits that lead there. I've been giving this a lot of thought over the past days."

"It does indeed sound as if you have. Please, continue."

"Before they get you," John says, "you have to break or be close to falling apart. I suspect that's how they get inside your head. That's why they wear the face or the shape of something that hurts you. Or something you fear. Your worst nightmare taken physical form."

Emma raises her eyebrows and jots down more notes. The scope of the patient's delusion is certainly impressive. This will be a memorable case, that's for sure.

"Would you say," Emma wonders, "that you're describing Hell?"

John nods. "I can't think of any other name."

"Fascinating." Emma adds another note.

John pauses. "You don't believe me."

"I trust you, John." Emma looks at John over the rim of her glasses. "And I'm listening to every word you say. That's a promise."

"But you think I'm talking gibberish."

"I'm not judging—"

"Everything I've told you will be broken down to simple words, discussed in meetings and papers, while you hope to understand what's wrong with me."

"Look," Emma says gently. "I believe you're in pain."

John nods, but looks resigned.

"Like I said," John says after a moment, "I can glimpse the ones that crawl around you. The ones nestled inside thoughts."

"I'm sure you can. It's time for you to rest. We've made progress today, and—"

"Tell me this," John says, speaking softly but not unkindly. "How do you feel about spiders?"

Emma's head snaps up. She's never mentioned her dread of spiders to anyone else. Merely seeing one makes her want to turn inside out in horror.

Her wild, uncontrollable fear of the intolerable critters is why she became a psychologist, in the hope that she could overcome her phobia. Dedicating her life to understanding the horrors of others seemed a reasonable way to deal with her own irrational fear. It didn't work.

On the contrary, her horror has grown worse over the years. She still loathes walking through dense undergrowth, rock-strewn beaches and tangles of roots, any place where the horrific, nightmarish animals tend to hide. It remains her secret Achilles heel.

Only it's no longer a secret.

Emma shrinks back in her chair. A cold fingernail claws its way down her spine while the room seems to contract and spin. The disorientation stems from shock, but she must still lean against the table to stop from toppling over.

"This meeting is over," Emma croaks and slams her pad shut. "We – we will continue the – interview at a later point."

Her words come out as incoherent mumbling. She stands and holds on to the table for support. The nurses frown and reach out to help her, but she shakes her head.

Spiders. He said he sees spiders. Where are they? And how does he know?

"You see?" John says. "I'm not insane. Not the way you think. I'll tell you what worries me the most."

"I have to go." Emma darts out of the room, knocking her chair over in the process. She can't stand being in the same building as John another moment. Her head is a wasp's nest of thoughts burning to escape. Gasping for breath, she stumbles down the corridor, towards the stairs and the fresh air outside. She won't come back. Someone else must deal with this patient. Part of her wants him to be locked away forever, out of sight and mind. Especially her mind.

"It's the detective." John's voice echoes in the corridor behind her as he keeps shouting. "She almost gave in, then fought back, and got away."

Emma clamps her hands over her ears and runs on, but she can't keep John's words out.

"They don't accept that," John screams until his voice cracks. "Resistance is the ultimate insult. They want revenge. They want her sanity, and they won't stop. They will *never, ever stop.*"

*

THE END

ACKNOWLEDGEMENTS

This story originated from several different ideas that orbited me for some time before they, as ideas do, decided to dance, collide, and bounce off in unexpected directions.

All locations in Stockholm are real. As for Hell, impressions may vary.

THANK YOU

Tove Jorgensen: explorer in arms, charter of stars, midnight muse.

Also

Class of '11, who taught me not to pull any punches.
Marti Leimbach, who told me to run with this story.
Pauline Nolet, proofreader extraordinaire.
All members of XP regn (past, present and future), for evenings and nights spent elsewhere.

STORIES BY ERIK BOMAN

The Detective Lena Franke series

Siren Song
Book 1

Summer Nights
Book 2

Into the Woods
Book 3

Other books

Southbound
A dystopian thriller set in Sweden and the UK

Short Cuts
Collected short stories

Short Cuts 2: Stories from the Brink of Dusk
Collected short stories

Manufactured by Amazon.ca
Bolton, ON